# RAVENWOOD
## Stepson of Mystery

# Return of the Dugpa

AIRSHIP 27 PRODUCTIONS

Ravenwood Stepson of Mystery
"Return of the Dugpa" © 2015 Micah S. Harris

An Airship 27 Production
www.airship27.com
www.airship27hangar.com

Interior and cover illustrations © 2015 Bret Blevins

Editor: Ron Fortier
Associate Editor: Jerry Edwards
Production and design by Rob Davis
Marketing and promotion: Michael Vance

ISBN-13: 978-0692470800 (Airship 27)
ISBN-10: 0692470808

Printed in the United States of America

10 9 8 7 6 5 4 3 2 1

# RAVENWOOD

## Stepson of Mystery

# Return
of the
Dugpa

### by Micah S. Harris

# PROLOGUE:
## Alvarado Court, Los Angeles, February, 1922

To his acquaintances present, some of whom had last seen him alive only a few hours earlier, the corpse's arrangement made him seem not so much dead as indifferent.

Stretched on his back on the floor of his Hollywood home, arms at his sides, William Desmond Taylor appeared in a therapeutic repose from which he could not be disturbed to acknowledge the rifling through his property by friend and stranger alike. When those friends looked away from the drawers or cabinets they were searching to where the deceased director lay, they struggled to understand how, still meticulously attired as he was in life, he could be so apathetic about that unseemly dried ribbon of blood at the corner of his mouth.

The chief inspector had his men stand by as anything with the remotest chance of provoking yet another Hollywood scandal was boxed up and carried off. Proliferating stories of drug rings and orgies were threatening to transform the young film capital back forever into a small town of orange groves and rutted dirt roads.

A set of envelopes, postmarked from all over the Middle East, were tossed in one box piled with papers from Taylor's career, among them the single scenario for *The Ordeal*. This was the film he had been discussing the previous afternoon with studio head Jesse Lasky as Taylor's next Famous Players project. The intertitles and continuity under the scenario's title page, however, told a story radically different from the society melodrama that the trades had described.

Police officer Horatio Stagg curled his upper lip as he watched people all but step over the corpse in their plundering. Why couldn't the stiff have gotten shot a week later? When Stagg would be back on the East Coast? Back to mom's clam chowder and the dance marathons with Babs Ostopczech? Back to where some *normal* people lived? And where the rule of law still held sway?

As far as his outlook was concerned, this was still the Wild West and the studio heads no better than robber barons. And these Alvarado Court people, they all were in show business, too. They had to be: the way they acted like they could just do however they wanted with no respect for his authority. In the process, they had compromised this crime scene six ways to Sunday almost exactly from the moment the body was discovered. Stagg knew. He was the second man on the scene.

At 7:30 A.M., he had been on the round of his beat that brought him by Alvarado Court when he heard a man scream. A black man in a white valet's uniform flew out of the front door of a far corner bungalow; the third in a row on the courtyard's left side. Stagg intercepted the man as he passed the courtyard's gazebo, grabbed him by his upper arms and shook him hard.

"He's dead!" the man shrieked.

"Get a hold of yerself! Who's dead?"

"Mr. Taylor…lemme go! Gotta tell Mr. Jersserun …"

"Who?"

"The landlord! Lemme go, *lemme go!*"

"I'm a cop! You don't go to the landlord when you find someone dead; you come to me! Now, hands over your head."

The man complied as Stagg patted him down. "Who are you exactly?" he asked.

"Henry Peavey; Mr. Taylor's house boy."

"All right then," Stagg said, satisfied that Peavey was unarmed. "Suppose you tell me what you saw in there?"

"Mr. Taylor…dead!"

"Tell me what you *saw!*" Stagg snapped, ready to rattle Peavey's bones again.

"He's on his back. There's blood on his mouth. He wasn't breathing and his skin's like chalk. His face was a…a *blank*. Mr. Taylor's gone!"

"Was there a weapon near the body? Like he was defending himself?" Before entering the bungalow, Stagg wanted to be sure that if Taylor *wasn't* as dead as Peavey was convinced, he would be in no danger if the victim confused him with his assailant.

"No, sir."

"Did you see anybody else inside? Or hear something that might indicate another person in there?"

"No, sir."

"All right then," Stagg said, drawing his gun. "Show me to the door."

Peavey had just begun to lead Stagg back to the bungalow when another man's voice sounded from behind them in the early morning stillness: "Hey! What's the problem?"

Stagg looked back across the courtyard to see a man in a bathrobe and pajamas addressing him from his open front door.

"Police matter!" Stagg said. "That the landlord?" he asked Peavey, who nodded.

"Okay, Peavey, you go inform him what goes on, have him call the police, and the two of you stay put until you hear otherwise from me. Get me?"

"Yes sir," the valet said and quickly joined the landlord.

Stagg ran up the steps, quickly crossed the bungalow's porch, and pressed his back against the wall next to the open front door. He peered inside while also listening for any indication that there was someone there other than the man on the floor. Gun at the ready, he shouted, "Police! Come out with your hands up!"

When no one responded, he entered cautiously, ascertained that Taylor indeed was dead, then began searching room to room. Satisfied there was no one other than himself who was still alive in the house, Stagg returned to observe the corpse again.

"I called the police."

Stagg looked up to see the landlord in the open doorway.

"I told you to stay put," Stagg said.

The landlord did not heed him but approached the body tentatively, incredulity distorting his face. "Bill?" he addressed the corpse. "How could this have happened? Who would have ever wanted to...?"

Stagg noticed several other denizens of Alvarado Court had appeared in the doorway, and, emboldened by their landlord's presence in the house, they now began entering to get a look at the body.

"Hey, you people," Stagg said. "You need to back out!"

No one acknowledged him. By the time the officer from the Central Detective Bureau had arrived, people were wandering about all over the bottom floor of the house. At the detective's request, the small crowd reluctantly shifted toward the door. Then one of their number, a gray haired man already suited up for the day at this early hour, suddenly announced, as though he had just recalled it himself, that he was a doctor.

The detective did not ask for credentials or attempt to stop him as he hovered over the body, palpating the torso at certain spots. Looking up, the stranger pronounced, "This man died from either a heart attack or a stomach hemorrhage."

"And who are *you*?" Stagg demanded. "Does anybody know this guy?"

"Officer!" the detective said. "The man *said* he was a doctor."

After that, the detective began allowing Taylor's close friends, and the studio representatives who had arrived by now, to rifle through his possessions. Peavey, apparently over his initial shock, had recovered enough to wash dishes in the kitchen. One of the men carrying a box of studio related papers out the door bumped into Stagg.

"Watch where yer goin'!" Stagg snapped. The man just stared up at him, eyes tearing and lips stammering. He looked as though he wanted Stagg to explain it all. Stagg just snorted and pushed by him.

And then he saw the self-proclaimed doctor bent over one of the boxes Jesse Lasky's representative had ordered filled with Famous Players materials. An envelope dropped from his hand into the box.

"What are you looking for, 'doc'?" Stagg thought. "A prescription?" Noticing Stagg's stare, the stranger slid something inside his coat and began to jostle his way toward the door.

Stagg, certain he'd be called down again by the detective "in charge" if he shouted "halt," chose to follow. The stranger was able to clear the door while Stagg was still wedging himself through the crowd.

Thrusting aside the last few people in his way, Stagg stepped out onto Taylor's porch. He could hear the rapid clack of shoes echoing down the walkway between Taylor's house and his garage.

Stagg rounded the corner of the bungalow just in time to see "the doctor" at the other end of the walkway, descending the steps that led onto Maryland Street.

Stagg sprinted the length of the walkway and down the steps, catching sight of his quarry taking long strides up Maryland.

"Hey! You! Stop in the name of the law!" Stagg shouted. The man looked over his shoulder and ran.

A soon huffing Stagg pursued. *Starting to get a stomach,* he thought. *What will Babs think if I can't keep up with her on the dance floor? Time to lay off the roasted peanuts.*

But his waist line was already burgeoning enough to allow the self-proclaimed doctor to outdistance him. Stagg blew his policeman's whistle just as the stranger rounded a corner and disappeared from sight.

When Stagg made the corner, the object of his pursuit was nowhere to be seen. The shrilling of his whistle again pierced the early morning air. He continued to blow, alerting the cops on the adjacent beats to be on the lookout for anyone acting out of the ordinary; such as a dignified man in a suit running to beat the devil for no apparent reason.

While pausing to catch his breath, Stagg studied the entrance to a dead end alley ahead that he knew from his beat. He had no doubt his quarry was already far away; the natural instinct of even the most stupid thug who was outdistancing a cop was to keep running. Still, he was responsible to check every possible place of refuge which a fleeing miscreant might avail himself of along the way.

Walking softly as he could, Stagg approached the alley's opening. When he peered inside, his brow furrowed and his lower jaw dropped at what he saw:

A heavily perspiring man in the exact style of suit and shoes as the fleeing "doctor" stood there, quickly combing his hair. But this person was taller, his hair color different, and his *face*...

The shock from seeing that face discombobulated Stagg so much that he was still grappling to remove his gun from its holster as he stepped into the alley and shouted "Police! Hands up!"

"I will most happily acquiesce, officer," the man said as Stagg aimed his gun at him. The *voice* was clearly the same that had pronounced William Desmond Taylor dead of natural causes. But not the mouth. The man calmly tucked his comb into his coat's breast pocket and raised both hands over his head.

Then with his left fingers he immediately began tracing signs in the air, mumbling something indiscernible. The lower part of his coat lifted as though blown from beneath. Within moments, he was spinning in a mini-cyclone that lifted him a full foot off the ground. Scattered bits of litter and dead leaves rose and swirled in the canyon of the alley. Stagg dared not fire his gun: blown dirt worried his eyes, and he could only squint through tears at the spinning man. A shot intended to wound might kill instead, and the stranger or Stagg himself catching a fatal ricochet in the enclosed space was too much of a possibility.

The wind now caught Stagg and slung him into an alley wall, the sharp crack of his head against the bricks sending him to his knees. As he blacked out, something rushed by him with the heaving breathing of a horse that had been run wet. He fully expected to be trampled.

By the time he had regained his senses, and the alley its mid-winter's morning stillness, the "doctor" was gone. Then Stagg sighted something odd among the alley's debris: a very old piece of paper, a card, depicting a man sporting long chin hair and a conical crown with a large feather on each side. He was half-risen from a couch, and in hands raised over his head, he held what looked like two crosses looped at the top.

*Just a piece of trash*, he thought. *A fortune telling card so worn out it's been tossed by one of the gypsies I've seen around LA with the carnies this winter.*

Yet, could he simply leave the card on the ground? Because there was another possibility: what if this was what the "doctor" had stolen from that box in Taylor's bungalow but lost in his escape?

Stagg knew exactly "what": if the card proved to be part of a deck that connected Taylor with the occult, it would be boxed up and carried off with everything else that might put the late director, and by extension Hollywood, in a negative light.

Further, Stagg knew any details in his report that included his recollection of a man levitating in a whirlwind, a man with *that* face of all people, would be attributed to the knock he took to his head. He could end up discharged as mentally unstable from the police force he had wanted to be part of ever since he was a kid. In fact, he *had* to believe that blow had deluded his memories of his encounter...

...or accept as a fact that the man he had momentarily apprehended in the alley was the same person still lying dead on William Desmond Taylor's bungalow floor.

# CHAPTER ONE:
## The Fellowship
## of the
## Laughing Basilisk

Ravenwood looked up from his library desk at the tall man in the tailored suit and crisp Arrow collar who stood before him, Stetson hat in hand. The Stepson of Mystery almost winced at how much their broad shouldered and nattily attired physiques matched. He did not wish to be a reflection of this person.

Again he cast his chameleon eyes over the talisman the man had placed on his desk, picked it up and held it close, hoping for a sign of forgery. He sighed, knowing beforehand there would be none. The icon of the Laughing Basilisk itself was esoteric enough, but under his fingers he could feel the flaw from the mold from which the fourteen such basilisks in the world were cast before the mold was melted.

Ravenwood set the Laughing Basilisk down on his desk and slid it toward the man who took it and casually slipped the icon into his pocket as though it were a watch on a fob. Ravenwood frowned, eyes turning gray.

"I don't doubt that you came by that honestly," Ravenwood said, "but I dare say you aren't worthy of it. I acknowledge that we are part of a society, but that only requires a fraternal consideration of hearing your request. I've considered: the answer's 'no.'"

*My son, you should receive this man's message; I sense it is of far more importance than he suspects himself...*

Ravenwood sighed. *And 1931 had been going so well*, he thought. He closed his eyes, seeking his center. When he opened them again, they were blue. "My master bids me receive you, Hank Arneau."

Arneau brightened. "I may be seated, then?" he asked.

Ravenwood nodded and pointed at the chair before his desk.

"And might I inquire what your problem is with me?" Arneau asked as, having seated himself, he tugged his coat back into its proper sartorial drape over his fit torso, then adjusted a cuff link.

"You're a dilettante, Mr. Arneau," Ravenwood said, running a hand through his dark hair. "You're a magnate of textiles and steel who's decided that now he wants to produce movies..."

"And Louis B. Mayer was a junk man and Carl Laemmle a bookkeeper for Oshkosh," Hank said and smiled. "So?"

"*So*...it's the same attitude with which you took up occult studies and then squandered them, having taken the place where a more fit man would have learned and applied the secret wisdom in the pursuit of righteousness and judgment. Instead, you elected to pursue mammon."

Arneau made a conspicuous survey of Ravenwood's penthouse library. "And just how exclusive *are* the Sussex Towers, Ravenwood?"

Ravenwood felt the hot pinpoint prickling of his cheeks. "My possessions are but tools toward a greater end."

"Yeah, and it's a pip reaching that end in your coupe, I bet."

"You came here with a problem, Hank Arneau," Ravenwood huffed, eyes again gray. "Before I lose my center, would you please tell it to me? *Now?*"

"Very well: it appears the movie I'm making is cursed."

Ravenwood leaned back, tucked his chin, and steepled his fingers. "I'm listening."

"You remember the murder of William Desmond Taylor?"

"Of course. It's an enigma to this day. A blond hair on the body matched that of that ingenue who was mad for him...what was her name?"

"Mary Miles Minter."

"...but her family swore she was with them the entire night of the murder. Even the entry and exit path of the bullet through his vest and coat was inconclusive. He either could have been writing at his desk or had both hands raised over his head when shot. Then someone took time to arrange the body; obviously, he didn't land as though lying in state."

"Even a dilettante knows that stuff, Ravenwood. What *isn't* public knowledge is the movie he was planning at the time of his murder. Officially it was leaked out to be a society melodrama. But the real project was secret."

"And you know this secret how?"

"A few months ago, word got out that someone had been secretly plundering Famous Players' archives, and this included boxes taken from Taylor's bungalow the day of his death. They were to be part of an underground auction.

"Most of the people there were interested in scandal. You know, hoping for a pair of panties or a nude photo of a starlet tucked in a book. But I was interested in Lot 249 because it had the scenario for the movie he never lived to make. I was looking for promotional properties for Astoria Studios, and this one had nine years of publicity behind it in the form of an unsolved murder."

"Taste is truly timeless, Hank. Go on," Ravenwood said.

"Hey, don't be so quick to judge. You didn't see what else was at that auction. I could have had Valentino's testicles in a jar if I had wanted. Anyway, there were odd things in Lot 249 along with the scenario: envelopes postmarked Cairo, Istanbul, Damascus and other exotic spots, each containing a card, sometimes two or three, that made it look like Taylor was assembling the most antique tarot deck in the world. The handwriting on the envelopes was someone's other than Taylor's, though.

"He'd collected a complete Major Arcana except for the twelfth card, 'the Hanged Man.' I've never been sure if the cards were just thrown in that lot randomly to even it out or if there was some connection with the movie scenario.

"Anyway, *The Ordeal* is an operatic tale set in the days of King Arthur. Taylor had big plans for the major city venues: full orchestra accompaniment and singers, in German, on stage, in synch with the action on screen.

"Me, I'm thinking more lowbrow: this could be a swell swashbuckler. And there's a supernatural element, too; so, hoping he'd agree to adapt the continuity and intertitles into a script, I sent a copy of *The Ordeal* to Murphy Fort. He's a writer at Universal who I heard was also their unofficial occult authority.

"Fort's too busy doing revisions on this vampire script to write mine, but he informs me that what I've got, what Taylor's final movie was going to be, is based on a Wagner fragment that, as it turns out, was posthumously scored by other hands for one incomplete performance. And only the occult society called the Order of the Golden Dawn saw that much.

"Librettos for it are rarer than archaeopteryx teeth, the Golden Dawn only numbered around three hundred, and all the copies that are accounted for have the last page in German cut out. The ending wasn't even allowed to play out on the stage. Like I said: 'one *incomplete* performance.' There was a shout from someone and the curtains and lights dropped. The stage lights never came up, but the house lights did and everyone was cleared out and the librettos collected.

"According to Fort, a man named Joseph Wright, a member of the Golden Dawn's inner circle and a brilliant young composer, bought Wagner's fragment from the estate of someone who had won it at an auction when Wagner was raising money to build his opera house at Bayreuth. All that Wagner had written of *The Ordeal* before he abandoned it was a prose-poem version. Wright wrote the music and took the libretto from the prose-poem."

"So," Ravenwood said. "Lyrics by Wagner; music by Wright. Not destined to be the Rodgers and Hart of The Golden Dawn. Proceed."

"Now, the libretto has German on the left page with the English translation on the right. So, although the ending in German has been cut, it can be translated back from the English on the facing page that remains. But that's not necessarily the same thing as *Wagner's* German. You're translating a translation. The word choices the translator makes may or may not accurately convey what Wagner actually wrote. And apparently whatever is so egregious doesn't translate *back* from English into German or the English version would have been cut out, too. Those Germans, you know, have words for concepts we never verbalize in English.

"So if the offending element can't be verbalized, why bother to curse any further productions?" Ravenwood asked.

"Because there's still a chance it *will* be spoken. According to Fort, the Golden Dawn failed to mutilate *every* copy of the libretto. There's at least one unexpurgated one out there with the German ending, and Wagner's prose-poem remains unaccounted for, too.

"Fort said the Golden Dawn took the possibility of *The Ordeal's* perpetuation seriously enough that they summoned a 'hostile current' in retaliation against Wright, and shortly thereafter, Wright was found floating in the Thames. Then twenty-three years later, William Desmond Taylor, although making every effort to keep the project secret, takes a bullet before he can revive *The Ordeal* for the cinema.

"Not that I believe in curses, Ravenwood. I was just trying to get your attention before. My opinion is that Wright was bumped off by more mundane means just as Taylor was to abort *his* production."

"Is there any evidence Taylor's scenario was indeed based on the unexpurgated version?"

"No libretto was among the auction items, so there's no way to compare his source with the scenario I have. The ending there struck me as Grand Guignol, but if there was any occult significance in the action or dialogue, I wouldn't know. Fort can fill you in on the details if you decide to take the case. Maybe the two of you putting your heads together can figure it out."

"Assuming the killer took the libretto," Ravenwood said, "why would he have left Taylor's scenario behind?"

"Probably whoever left that blond hair on Taylor's body frightened him away before he could confiscate it. Anyway, we're betting my announced revived production will draw out who was responsible for Taylor's murder. That, for the Master, is the main reason that this movie must proceed. Time for some long overdue justice."

"Wait … 'we?' 'The Master?'"

"You mean I didn't tell you about him? Oh, well, you didn't think you're the *only* rich kid on the block who gets a master, did you, Ravenwood?" Arneau said. "And let me tell you, not every one of them is all sweetness and light like yours. This guy shows up, calls himself 'the Dark Eminence,' the pompous ass, and announces my life is on loan from now on. He *knows* things."

"What kind of things?"

"According to him, things Wall Street never learned about stagflation, indemnity and usury; see what I mean? Pompous! Turns out, I've been going gangbusters since the crash because *he's* made my business a 'fiscal phoenix from the ashes of the stock market,' and he can turn it back any old time into the grubby little worm that the phoenix was before self-immolation. 'Phoenix;' 'Self-immolation'… *his* words. See?"

"Pompous?"

"And *how*, brother."

"You didn't report any of this to the police?"

"Are you kidding? You think I don't *want* him to 'do that voodoo that he do so well?' This is tops! Plus, my blood pressure is down, I can take time to hit the gym; I'm in the best shape of my life! But, from time to time, I have to work for him, helping him out on his crusades in the name of truth and justice, but that's jake with me, too. So, today, I'm a movie producer and largest stock holder in Astoria Studios.

"But what I *can't* be is a detective 'conversant with the milieu of the occult' … his words, who can recognize those type of arcane connections in the Taylor case that went by all the other investigators nine years ago.

"And I'm not just 'playing' the new head of Astoria Studios, by the way. The studio has felt this Depression, too, and needs to go forward with this film. It means work for a *lot* of people: I've decided to upscale it to a prestige production. On the West Coast, on the Pathe lot, there's this giant wall left over from DeMille's *King of Kings* that was part of the temple set. That's already been turned into the gateway to Monsalvant, where our finale takes place, and that's just the beginning of the construction we're going to be doing out there.

"So, Ravenwood, are you game? To smoke out a killer? To see to it that my movie gets made and some honest Astoria workers stay out of the bread lines?"

"This has never been a game, Arneau," Ravenwood said.

"Then are you ready for *war*, Ravenwood? Maybe an *occult* war?"

Ravenwood arched a brow at Hank. "Yes," he said, "but only by my rules under the guidance of *my* master. Is that understood by you and *yours*?"

Hank beamed, caught up his Stetson hat from his lap, placed it on his head and with two hands put a quick, stylish twist to the brim as he rose to his feet. "Swell," he said. "I'll be in touch. Right now, I have to scoot over to the Astoria Studio, look at some screen tests. I have to find the girl who'll be my Lita Clerval; that's the lead role."

Ravenwood frowned up at Arneau. "A girl is the star?"

"What? Do I stutter?"

"No, but do you intend to let her know the potentially lethal history of the movie, considering she might be targeted?"

"If the guy who murdered William Desmond Taylor comes gunning for anyone, it's going to be me. And I'm not worried. Dark Eminence has me covered. Oh, and here's my card. Has both my home and Astoria office numbers. I'll show myself out."

No sooner had Arneau closed the door behind him, than the voice of Ravenwood's master, the Nameless One, again spoke to him telepathically.

*Join me my son. We must speak. William Desmond Taylor is known to me.*

# CHAPTER TWO:
## Known to the Nameless One

F ragrance of spice and resin. Aromas of attars of sandalwood and flower petals distilled in water. As soon as he stepped over the threshold of his master's room, these scents haunted Ravenwood's olfactory nerve, yet no incense burned in the chamber of the Nameless One despite the haze in the air that partially veiled the wise man. He wore only a loin cloth from which wizened yet supple legs were folded in the lotus position. His head was bowed so that his long white hair draped down over his taut, brown torso.

His master's chamber always seemed to exist a world apart from that of the blowing car horns and rushing pedestrians of Manhattan below. But never more so than now. Through the windowless room, a breeze fresh with the scent of rain wafted by him. Pink flower petals materialized and eddied on the air, one tickling the end of his nose. He realized that a stream trickled at his feet, and the Nameless One was now sitting between two cherry trees. Ravenwood felt as though he had stepped into the oriental snow globe with non-soluable flakes of pink soap for cherry blossoms which his long dead parents once gave him as a child. The thin lips of the Nameless One curved in a slight smile as he looked up at his unofficial stepson.

"As a boy, I played in an orchard with these trees, chased that swarm of blossoms, placed my young feet in this icy stream until I could stand it no more."

"You...brought *this*...from *that* orchard...here? As it *was*?"

"My son: time can be seen to exist without distinction of past, present, and future. Thus, all can be made manifest, all can be...shifted. Or, as one of your own poets of the West has said, 'Here, my son, time turns into space.'"

Ravenwood took a half-step back. He understood the interconnection of all things, accepted telepathy and prognostication which he practiced himself, but this...this was beyond his ken and should be beyond that of *any* man. The Nameless One, whom he loved and trusted as a father, was actually beginning to frighten him.

"You summoned me, my master," Ravenwood managed.

"Yes my son. I hoped that today we might walk together through the orchards of my boyhood, but with the arrival of this Hank Arneau, I sensed a pressing danger, one that may soon arc over the world. That he came to you to enlist your aid in solving William Desmond Taylor's murder must be related to this threat."

"You said Taylor was known to you."

"At the turn of the present century, there were many initiates of India's Ascended Chieftains operating occult societies in London. Greatest of these was the Order of the Golden Dawn. These acolytes tended to be artistic, including some of the theatrical community. William Desmond Taylor, an actor in London's West End, became a courier between the Ascended Chieftains and the Order of the Golden Dawn."

"Then, that association is how he knew about *The Ordeal*."

"True. But as a mere courier and not an actual member of the Golden Dawn, it is unlikely he would have attended the opera's performance. His hopes, though, *were* for induction, and the position of courier was an honorable one, trusted only to candidates with the most potential. But when his career did not progress as quickly as he believed he deserved, he became insolent and forfeited his chance of ever entering the Inner Circle of the Golden Dawn."

"Then Taylor must have turned his back completely on occult pursuits for other pastures. From what I read in the papers at the time of his murder, he had spent years in Hollywood working his way up from actor to major director. He created an entirely new life for himself ..."

"What is it my son?"

"Based on what you've just told me, his Hollywood career was at least his *third* life. After his death, it came out that previous to his film career, he had been an antique dealer in New York who was married under another name, and that he had, without explanation, disappeared—abandoning his business and deserting his wife and young daughter. The next time either of them saw him was on a movie screen."

"This man displayed a protean propensity in life," the Nameless One said. "But such a scheme as you have just described is ultimately but mundane. There is an occult power that is the source of the threat looming above us all, and Hank Arneau's revival of Taylor's movie is somehow involved.

"Thus, you must discover exactly what led to Taylor's death and why he sought to revive this opera as a film."

"It's an extremely cold case, my master and one, no doubt, that was covered up immediately. Hollywood was going through a major public relations crisis at the time: comedian Fatty Arbuckle was accused of rape, and America's greatest beauty Olive Thomas and her 'boy next door' husband Jack Pickford had earned a reputation for decadent living. Taylor's studio would have scrambled immediately to bury anything unsavory or potentially scandalous about his murder. That would certainly include anything allegedly occult. No doubt the police were paid well to keep mum."

"But there *is* one. Long known to you. Ready to talk."

Ravenwood was suddenly aware of the ringing of his library phone. After the third ring, he could faintly hear the voice of Sterling, his gentleman's gentleman, answering the call. He looked at the Nameless One whose chin now was tucked to his chest, eyes closed. The brook and the cherry blossom trees had vanished, and Ravenwood realized that his beloved master, though physically present, had departed with them.

Exiting the Nameless One's chamber, Ravenwood saw his butler already on his way to meet him, white gloves tugging at his waist coat to smooth out some unevenness he sensed in his otherwise crisp attire.

"It was Inspector Stagg for you, sir," Sterling said. "I informed him that you were indisposed. He was much insistent. But for once his tone did not suggest he believed you could account for the whereabouts of Justice Joseph Crater, or that you should come prepared to provide a handwriting sample of the word 'Croatan.' You are to meet him this evening promptly at six at..."

Ravenwood suddenly turned his face slightly away from Sterling's and stared into space with a knit of his brow. "He wishes for me to meet him at...the *Club Samedi*?"

Sterling looked at Ravenwood sidelong with an expression somewhere in between sardonic and incredulous. "I was not aware that Inspector Staggs shared your passion for jazz. Nor do I understand why he should expect *you* to share his apparent passion for...."

Ravenwood smiled and clasped Sterling's shoulder. "I'm fully aware the *Club Samedi* is a house of ill repute...by ill reputation only, of course. But they *do* maintain the tradition of purest jazz in the restaurant front of the establishment. After all, 'the houses of ill repute' in New Orleans was where it all began."

"I prefer opera, myself, sir."

"Opera? When did that happen?"

"It's an acquired taste, sir."

"Oh. You mean Rosie decided the two of you needed more cultural exposure than a Busby Berkeley leg show at the *RKO Mayfair*, eh?"

"Your psychic acumen is as honed as ever, Master Ravenwood."

Ravenwood smiled. "I know. It's starting to get monotonous. Tell me, man of the world, who said, 'Here, my son, time turns into space?'"

"That would be from Wagner's *Parsifal*, sir."

"*Wagner?*"

Ravenwood quickly looked back down the hall toward the Nameless One's room. Then he looked at where Hank Arneau had stood. "This is no coincidence," he said aloud to himself.

"I'm sure I don't know what you're talking about, sir."

"Well, *I'm* sure any business Inspector Stagg and I conduct at the *Club Samedi* will be held in a booth up front with nothing hotter than a sax solo for company. Thanks for your concern for my virtue, though, Sterling, old boy. Oh, and I'll need my umbrella tonight."

"Weather report or premonition, sir?"

"Radio says clear skies through Thursday. Get me my umbrella, will you?"

Sterling sighed. "Of course, sir."

"And, by the way, Sterling," Ravenwood said as he tugged on his leather driving gloves. "I'd like to know how *you* know about the *Club Samedi*."

"A man of the world inevitably hears of such places, sir," Sterling said.

"Indubitably," Ravewood said, grinned, and reached out and pulled one of Sterling's suddenly crimson ear lobes.

# CHAPTER THREE:
## "*Yttle Elumi Shall Not Rise!*"

The saxophone brayed with so powerful a bellowing from the musician's lungs that it seemed his instrument might violently shiver into metal shards in his hands. Then the high flung cries suddenly dropped to throaty rumbles. The saxophonist swayed, at times carried along by his music and then, just as suddenly, the musician was again the master.

Ravenwood tapped his foot and peered through the blue haze of cigar smoke until he saw Inspector Stagg's squat bulk squeezed into a booth against the wall. He began pushing through the press of bodies, both black and white; the latter the society swells taking a fashionable dip into Harlem.

*"This is no coincidence."*

"Inspector Stagg," Ravenwood said, smiling as he slid into the booth. "I presume you called me here on business and not the pleasure of a jazz set and a rack of ribs?"

"If you're so psychic, why do you need to presume anything?" Stagg asked, cocking his head with a slight drop of the jaw as he pinned Ravenwood with his stare.

"Oh," Ravenwood said as he raised his hand to summon a waiter, "it comes; it goes."

Stagg reached out, grabbed Ravenwood's wrist and brought his hand down onto the table. "There'll be none of that. I called you here for back up."

"Instead of to vilify me? That's not your modus operandi at all."

"Shut up," Stagg said. "You don't think it galls me to do this? You know I don't buy for one minute all your inscrutable orient mumbo jumbo..."

Ravenwood raised a forefinger. "Get it straight: Mumbo Jumbo is from Africa."

"Shut up. You know what I mean. Still, your occult knowledge has come in useful in cases that, you have to admit, usually have a rational explanation."

"Agreed."

"Okay. There's something that's been eating at me off and on for going on ten years. Mostly, I've ignored it, but just lately, it's gotten worst. When it doesn't have me tossing and turning, it's in my dreams. The William Desmond Taylor case."

Ravenwood leaned forward on his umbrella. "*You* were on that case?"

"Back when I was a street cop, there was an East Coast / West Coast exchange program. A couple months in sunny California in the middle of a New York winter? I went for it and got a beat in Los Angeles. And, unfortunately, William Desmond Taylor's bungalow was on that beat. I happened to be walking by when his valet came running out in the courtyard screaming."

"You were first on the scene after the valet?"

"Yeah, but that honor was given to Taylor's landlord. My role was conveniently erased from the record. I guess I was a little too loud about how I didn't like the way things were mishandled. Right after that, my superiors told me I might be much happier if I returned east a little earlier than planned, and I wholeheartedly agreed."

"What happened that morning, Inspector Stagg?"

"It was more like a rummage sale than a crime scene. People everywhere taking things while the detective just stood by. Then some guy came out of the crowd and pronounced Taylor dead from natural causes. Claimed he was a doctor but was never required to offer any proof. I asked around later; he was a complete stranger to Alvarado Court. After 'examining' the body, he joined in the pillaging, and I saw him pinch something from the premises. I chased him down to an alley. What I saw then..."

Stagg was staring into space, his jaw slightly slack. This unexpected show of vulnerability on the brusque bully's part actually touched Ravenwood. Inspector Stagg had lost his certainty. The needle that had always obstinately refused to point any way but north now oscillated on the compass' face.

"Saw *what*, Inspector Stagg?"

"He, uhm, raised his hands...and...started to spin...whipped up...a whirlwind..."

"He *what*?"

"No!" Stagg snapped, and set his jaw. His eyes narrowed. "The world works a certain way. There are *laws*, Ravenwood, men's laws and nature's laws, and if they're not fixed, then...

"Bottom line, he got away, but he *might* have dropped something what looked to me like one of them fortune telling cards."

"A tarot card? *That's* what he took from the Taylor crime scene?" Ravenwood asked, remembering the Major Arcana cards from Hank Arneau's auction lot were short the twelfth.

"Maybe. I mean, if you're the typical person snatching souvenirs from the death scene of a famous movie director, you're going for something like an autographed picture of Taylor with Mary Pickford, right? So why would he want this? And why would Taylor have it, if he did? I mean, this 'doctor' was definitely covering up something: he acted guilty as hell. Were he and Taylor part of some occult society that should have at least been questioned about Taylor's murder?

"On the other hand, I didn't know this card was what he took. It was so old and worn...maybe it was just trash from one of the carny gypsies who winter in LA. But there was something about it, this feeling in my gut that wouldn't let me just leave it in the alley. I guess it was because I could never be sure if it had any significance to the case or not, so I've held on to it all these years."

"*You* withheld potential evidence? Inspector Stagg, I am appalled."

"Quit grinnin' with those feathers stickin' out of the corner of your mouth. It ain't becomin'. The authorities just wanted Taylor's crime scene sanitized and nobody puttin' any flies in their ointment, get me? Sure, I could have shown it around, seen if any other cards like it had turned up in Taylor's stuff, but if that was the case, I knew they'd just box it up with the others. I felt like I would've been contributing to the cover-up.

"Now, look: I haven't ever asked any fortune teller before what this card means 'cause they're professional liars. And while I'm highly dubious of you, Ravenwood, I'm fairly certain you had nothing to do with William Desmond Taylor's murder, so you got nothing to gain by not giving me the straight skinny. I don't know if this is going to be outside your sphere of expertise, but you're the best I got: your occult studies might make you wise to if I'm being fed a load of baloney or not. So I want you with me."

"With you where?"

A red curtain to the side of the stage parted abruptly. There appeared a woman who seemed sculpted in ebony. Resplendent in yellow silk, Madame Thothmes stood in stiletto heels with ivory and jade dangling from long, bare limbs. Beneath a Nefertiti coif, her expression was as set and as indifferent as that of the Sphinx. With the flick of a red fingernail, she beckoned the two men.

Stagg nodded toward her. "Looks like we're up," he said to Ravenwood. "C'mon. Eyes and ears wide open."

Madame Thothmes held the curtain back for Ravenwood and the plain clothes inspector to enter. They both paused to bow.

"Which of you requested the reading?" she said, looking Ravenwood up and down.

"I did," Stagg said, "but it's an issue that involves us both."

She paused, looked at Stagg, then back at Ravenwood. "Very well," she said. "Enter and be seated."

The curtain swept closed behind them and Stagg and Ravenwood found themselves enveloped in a cell of cinnamon hue. On the wall behind her reading table, two Egyptian shields hung symmetrically with a short sword mounted horizontally under each. On an ebony bench that ran the length of the far wall was a row of twelve-inch effigies of coiled cobras with jaws yawning. On the end of the bench closest to the table was a small gong with a corresponding baton.

Madame Thothmes' smooth black marble table was in the shape of a crescent moon. Her high back chair, "throne" would not be inaccurate, was carved from the same polished stone and set within the table's curve. At the ends of both armrests were sculpted cat's skulls, and it was these skulls which each of her hands grasped when she was seated. Ravenwood noted how the chair's back was tapered at each top corner to suggest feline ears. The woman herself, once seated, suddenly appeared to be less flesh and blood and more one with the stone of the chair and table. Madame Thothmes' transformation into an Egyptian sphinx was complete.

Ravenwood and Stagg each sat on a black marble stool before the table. Thothmes regarded the men silently. Then, one hand moved from its clasped cat's skull and in the same motion conjured a stack of tarot cards out of the air. She dropped them in a perfectly squared pile onto the table. Arched hand moved over the cards, her long fingers in a flutter, like a spider creeping over the deck, fanning it.

"Draw," she said.

"Actually," Stagg said, reaching into his vest pocket and withdrawing his tarot card in the protective plastic bag in which he had kept it over the years, "I brought my own. I was hoping you might read it for me."

Stagg lightly tossed it on the crescent table and Ravenwood, even in the monochrome red of the room, could tell it was browning and wrinkled.

Madame Thothmes' eyes flared. She sprang upright as though Stagg had tossed an asp before her and pointed at them with the dagger tip of a nail.

"Defilers! Yttle Elumi will not rise!" she shouted. Ravenwood and Stagg leapt to their feet as she rounded the table and went to the bench with the row of cobra sculptures. First she struck the gong, its tone a warped warble rarely heard in the modern world. Then she went from snake effigy to snake effigy, knocking with the baton each one to the floor then crushing it under her left stiletto heel. With each strike, she repeated: "Yttle Elumi will not rise!"

"Lady," Stagg said, snatching the card back up from the table. "I don't know what your problem is. If you'd just calm down…"

Now a secret door in the wall behind the crescent table opened and two tall, muscular black men appeared in suits tailored to their powerful physiques. They drew the short swords and shields from the wall.

"Defilers!" Madame Thothmes shouted and pointed again at Ravenwood and Stagg. "These men are servants of Yttle Elumi; that great serpent Apep who would open the gate of the underworld so that his darkness is all in all!"

"Hey!" Stagg shouted and flashed his badge. "Officer of the law!"

The men's expressions changed from dour to sadistic.

"Wrong choice of words, Inspector Stagg," Ravenwood mumbled.

The man closest to the wall next to the stage slid open a small door from which orders were covertly taken when this club was a speakeasy. He shouted something to the band. Then the man slid the door back with the finality of dropping a lid on a coffin as the music on the stage grew even louder.

"They're raising the volume to cover the sounds of our execution, Inspector Stagg," Ravenwood said. "If anything could put me off jazz, I'm thinking this would be it."

"Hew them to pieces as our forefathers did theirs in the days of the Pharaohs!" Thothmes shouted. "We who have worshipped against Yttle Elumi across the millennia for this very hour will not fail now!"

# CHAPTER FOUR:
## Melee at the Club Samedi

Ravenwood popped open his umbrella in the face of the man charging him while at the same time unsheathing his rapier blade from the umbrella shaft. His assailant saw only the fabric spread on its frame and with a swipe of his short sword knocked it aside only to comprehend wide-eyed the tip of Ravenwood's blade just before it thrust through the momentarily exposed bicep of his sword arm.

The blade's point exited the back of the limb, and Ravenwood, with a twist of the wrist, turned the steel blade inside his opponent's muscle. The man bellowed in agony and, as Ravenwood withdrew his blade, went to his knees, his shield falling uselessly to the floor beside him. Stepping forward, Ravenwood brought the fist that still gripped his rapier into the man's temple, knocking him unconscious.

At the same moment Ravenwood had unsheathed his sword, Stagg had drawn his pistol from the shoulder holster under his coat. He fired but his sword-bearing antagonist easily deflected the bullet with his shield. It ricocheted into the far wall, nearly striking Madame Thothmes who screeched and darted for the safety of the passageway that had opened to admit the men.

Before Stagg could fire again, his assailant was on top of him, knocking his gun from his hand with his shield, and then driving the point of his sword at Stagg's eye. Simultaneously, Ravenwood dropped his rapier as he swooped up the shield of the fallen man, and, throwing the strength of his broad shoulders behind it, both intercepted the thrust and shoved Stagg's attacker backwards on staggering heels to the room's far side.

"Out you go, Inspector!" Ravenwood said, dropping the shield and snatching of his rapier. "I'll be right behind you."

As Stagg parted the curtain, the recovered swordsman charged Ravenwood. Ravenwood slipped through the opening Stagg left in his wake. Once on the other side, he raised his blade and sliced the cords that connected the heavy fabric to the rings running along the rod. His opponent rushed right into the falling curtains and was enveloped.

Ravenwood held his rapier down and close to him to keep from cutting anyone as he shouldered his way through the dance floor, pushing partners apart.

By the time their enemy had cut himself free and the curtain lay in piles of shreds at his feet, Ravenwood and Stagg were indistinguishable in the crowd of bodies gyrating to the "The Charlestonette." The sudden apparition of the angry giant with the drawn sword began a mad rush of those closest to the stage who were soon pushing along a screaming trampling mob; none of whom had any idea what had begun the rush for the doors.

As the crowd was erupting out of the *Club Samedi*, Ravenwood and Stagg were already speeding down the road in the former's coupe.

"What kind of tarot card did you show her, Inspector Stagg?" Ravenwood asked. "Because that was *not* a typical reaction to the standard issue Rider-Waite deck, I assure you."

"Get me to a telephone pole with a call box first and you can gander at it all you want!"

Ravenwood brought his auto up onto the curb and to a jarring stop at the first police box he saw. Stagg hefted his bulk over to it and reported a riot was in progress at the *Club Samedi*. Returning to the coupe, he reached inside his vest pocket and tossed the plastic-covered card onto the auto's seat. Ravenwood picked it up.

He immediately recognized on the extremely aged paper what was apparently the image of Osiris rising from the dead with an ankh in each hand held triumphantly over his head. But in the proper iconography, his arms would be crossed over his breast.

Ravenwood also noticed in the upper left corner what looked like a wicket with two parallel lines beneath it. Were the marks meant to represent an archway? Or...perhaps the Egyptian numeral for twelve?

*Hank Arneau,* Ravenwood thought, *Thanks to my stocky nemesis, I think I have just recovered your missing tarot card.*

But all he said was: "Rather queer something for a doctor to covet."

"Yeah, I hadn't thought about that," Stagg said, cocking his head at

Ravenwood. "I want someone to tell me something I *don't* know. What this means occult wise and also, now, why those three back there were after our hides when they saw it."

He looked off in the distance at the sound of trilling sirens. "Well, they'll be answering that question soon enough."

"Something tells me, Inspector," Ravenwood said, "that those three will not be part of any police round up you make tonight. However, if you will trust me with this card, I may be able to learn its significance *without* risking being hacked to bits."

Stagg tucked his head and massaged the back of his thick neck. "I guess I sort of got you in a jam back there, huh?" He shoved both hands into his pockets. "Sorry about that, Ravenwood. Look, I got a police car coming to take me back to the *Club Samedi* for the mop up. But what say at your earliest convenience you lemme buy you that rack of ribs, at a spot where they *don't* practice voodoo, say, the *Cobalt Club*? And then we're square, right? Everything will be jake, and I won't have cause to feel any remorse when I finally pin the dirty deed on you. Deal?"

Spreading his hands, Ravenwood said, "You, sir, are the very soul of equitability."

# CHAPTER FIVE:
## *Anne D'Arromanches.*

Claire Taverel stood backed to the edge of a precipice. Encroaching upon Claire was her mortal enemy, a phantom known until now only as "the Jaundiced Claw." A four -foot gap yawned between where she hovered and the top of a column of rock which possessed little more than enough dimension to stand on and matched the flat terrain of the cliff.

The Jaundiced Claw, emboldened by the certainty that this time he would succeed in killing her, detached and let drop the false bushy eyebrows and prosthetic hook of a nose, then tossed aside the fright wig that had made up the rest of his disguise along with some soluble body paint

"Carlton the valet!" Claire gasped. "*You* are the Jaundiced Claw?"

"I *warned* you about strolling too close to the edge of Cornwall's cliffs," he snarled and lunged.

Claire turned and leapt for the monolith, clearing the gap and landing on her feet.

"Very well," Carlton said, backing up. From inside his coat pocket he produced a hollowed bamboo reed into which he loaded a poisoned dart and blew.

Claire successfully dodged it.

"Your reflexes are impeccable, my dear," the Claw said. "But you have little room to maneuver, and you will eventually tire, while I have a copious supply of poisoned darts, and can afford to take my time."

Claire screamed loud and long.

"Please *do* shriek," the Claw said as he loaded up another blow dart. "The sounds of your fear are as arias to me."

Hank Arneau watched this play out from his upholstered chair in the projection room where he had spent the rest of the afternoon following his meeting with Ravenwood. Her scream *did* translate well over the recent medium of the optical soundtrack: a clear soprano that ended each shriek with the signature of wild yet melodious notes.

Artie the film editor was impressed, and, from two rows back, was urging Arneau to put that scream under contract even if he had already decided to fire the actress doing the yelling. But Arneau was no longer listening, neither to the girl's piteously imploring wails nor his editor's pleading.

What impressed *him* was that she was doing her own stunts atop the Hudson River palisades filling in for the Cornwall coast.

"What's the actress' name again?" Arneau asked Nate Tannen, the director slated for *The Ordeal*, who sat beside him.

"Anne D'Arromanches," Artie answered before Tannen could. Tannen ran his fingers through his sandy greased hair and rolled his eyes from under his tufts of brows at Arneau who grinned at the director's annoyance, then turned his attention back to the screen.

There was a sensuous quality to the pivot of her hips that made it clear this was no stunt man under a wig of long, blond hair. In life, as opposed to black and white, that hair was a reddish-gold froth and foam that, unpinned, spilled to the small of her back. She remained as sure-footed as a mountain hart as she almost went over backwards, and then found purchase at the last moment before throwing herself forward. Her frantic performance had been meticulously, if melodramatically, choreographed.

Hank Arneau clinched his fist and smiled. "What a brick that girl is!"

"Didn't I tell you as much?" Nate said. "Anne D'Arromanches *is* our Lita Clerval."

"I mean, she has as much guts as Harold Lloyd up in the air hanging from clock hands," Arneau said. "What a *brick!*"

"So you're firing her 'why'?" Artie asked Arneau. "I mean, the girl's a real sweetheart, too. Everybody's fallen in love with her. You might, too, if you'd just go talk to her."

"Now, Artie," Arneau said, "this is purely business. I have to jettison every unnecessary expense. A chapter play can run as long as four hours. We already have enough footage for a feature." He scratched his jaw. "Her arrival in Cornwall and the final scene in which she becomes the lady of the manor were the first things shot, right?"

"Right," Nate Tannen said. "Plenty of complications and reversals already in the can, including six of the planned eleven cliff hangers."

"There you go," Arneau said. "Exposition, conflict, resolution. We have a story, gentlemen, with a running time of, say, an hour, maybe an hour five minutes. That satisfies the exhibitors because they can get in an extra matinee or two for their rental. And we produced it on the cheap, which means Astoria will likely turn a profit. And that, my friends, is show biz."

As Arneau rose, his eyes locked on Nate Tannen's inquiring stare. He nodded his head. Tannen smiled, crossed his legs, and, taking a pen from his coat's breast pocket, began scribbling on his copy of *The Ordeal*'s script.

Arneau made his way from the Astoria screening room to the set where the former serial turned program-filler feature was filming the final scene. He arrived just in time to see Anne huddling over a small figure as she charged out of a burning stable atop a steed. The "baby" in swaddling blanket and bonnet was midget actor Harry Earles, who was currently appearing with the *Ringling Brothers and Barnum and Bailey Circus* at Madison Square Garden.

Anne was flushed as she slowed the horse and tugged the reins to bring him to a halt. Harry produced a baby bottle from the folds of his blanket and took a long, hard draw on the rubber nipple.

"Any rum left in that bottle, Harry?" Anne asked with a smile. "That last take was a little too close. Guess that's why the powers that be waited to film this scene last, huh?"

"*Mit* pleasure, *fräulein*," Harry said and passed her the bottle. Anne pried off the bottle's nipple and took a drink as stage hands hosed the stable's blaze.

Arneau smiled at the sight of the petite, fair skinned young beauty, so magnificent in her riding jodhpurs atop her steed, taking an undignified sip off a baby's bottle. "Bet she doesn't make a fuss about getting her hair wet in the rain, either," he thought. "Just the girl I'm looking for."

Anne quickly passed the bottle back to little Harry. "That'll do. Moderation in all things, you know. For the life of me, Harry," she said, "I can't understand why on your day off from Ringling Brothers, you'd put yourself through the indignity of dressing like a baby; let alone risking injury."

"Ah, *fräulein*," Harry said, extending his tiny arms around her neck and squeezing, "Who else? My last movie credit was 'midget in waste basket.' Such few opportunities in the flickers for one of my size that when I get a chance to cuddle with a beautiful leading lady, how could I possibly say *nein*?"

Anne blushed as Harry dangled for a moment by his hands from the saddle horn, dropped to the ground, then hiked his baby's petticoats to his knees and plodded to his dressing room.

Anne patted "Prodigious Paint the Wonder Horse" on the jaw and slipped him a sugar cube. "Bye, sweetie," she said as she dismounted. She began slowly walking off the set, eyes tearing, shoulders slightly slumped, as she tapped her riding crop against her jodhpurs.

"Excuse me, Miss D'Arromanches?" Hank said, producing an envelope. "I wanted to deliver your check personally. I'm Hank Arneau. I'm the…"

"The man who is shutting us down," she said, straightening her shoulders and curtly taking the envelope. "I *know* who you are, Mr. Arneau. Thank you. Now, if you'll excuse me, I have to go nickel hopping."

"You have to go what?"

"'Nickel hopping,' Mr. Arneau. I'm a nickel-a-dance girl, every Friday night, down at *O' Grady's Dance Hall.* So, if you'll excuse me, you *will* understand why I have to make very nickel count."

She moved to pass him but he cut her off. Anne slightly stomped her little foot, and Hank grinned at how dainty she was, even when angry. "*What*?" she asked.

"Miss D'Arromanches, I believe you are being unfair to me."

Anne's cheeks and ears burned red. "I have never witnessed such unmitigated self-centeredness! 'Unfair to you?' Do you know how many people you've just placed a check away from the bread lines?"

Hank scratched his jaw. "I dunno…the midget's doing pretty well for himself. And I've kept all my personal staff on pay role."

Anne put her hands on her hips. "Oh, your entire 'personal' staff? Would that be a blonde, a brunette, and a redhead? Grand total of three?"

"Uh, well, Artie's bald, and the rest of the hundred or so, I don't keep up with those fellows' coifs. Jenny, my secretary, she's getting a little gray so I pretend not to notice *her* hair."

Anne locked eyes with him. "You're feeding me a load of baloney, aren't you?"

"I would love to feed you caviar..."

Anne sighed as her shoulders again slumped slightly. "That's what I thought. No thank you, Mr. Arneau."

"...but I think everything should remain strictly business between us. You have an option in your contract, Miss D'Arromanches. I've chosen to exercise my option."

"You...what? You mean another serial?"

"No. An 'A' picture with all the classic romance and adventure and color. Swords crossing; maidenly bosoms heaving. You're my star."

"Do you mean like *The Sheik*? Or *Scaramouche*?"

"Something like Joan of Arc but in the days of King Arthur. Look, I saw you come flying out of that flaming barn; I've been watching your dailies, too. You can obviously handle the perils this role requires."

"I grew up in a Midwest orphanage; a self-supporting farm. I guess you'd say I'm pioneer hardy. Never occurred to me to scream at a mouse or a spider."

"But you *do* scream very well."

She smiled and lightly tapped his arm with her riding crop. "That's called *acting*, Mr. Arneau."

"Then let's talk about your acting some more for me, Miss D'Arromanches. Care to join me at the commissary?"

Anne held up her envelope. "I'll buy the bologna sandwiches," she said.

# CHAPTER SIX:
## *The Twelfth Hexagram*

Ravenwood entered the Nameless One's chamber, this time finding neither cherry trees nor rushing stream. Once again the room was little more than an ascetic's cell.

"Speak, my son."

"My master," Ravenwood said. "Among the possessions William Desmond Taylor left behind was the Major Arcana of an ancient Egyptian tarot deck. At an underground auction, they were part of the lot that included the scenario for *The Ordeal*. Hank Arneau won all of those cards except this one, the twelfth."

He presented this card to his master. "Osiris is an odd substitute for the twelfth card's traditional Hanged Man, and this isn't even the correct iconography of Osiris rising at that, but my volume on Egyptian numerology confirms that's a 'twelve' in the corner. None other than our friend Inspector Stagg  recovered this card from a stranger claiming to be a doctor who took it from the Taylor crime scene. The reason it wasn't in the lot Hank won is because it's been in Stagg's possession ever since... or did you know that already, too, just as you knew he was ready to talk about it?"

The Nameless One smiled. "Continue my son, and we shall learn from each other."

Ravenwood then related his and Inspector Stagg's adventure.

"Why did they react as they did, master? And who is this 'Yttle Elumi' whose harbingers Madame Thothmes thought we were?"

"Yttle Elumi," the Nameless One repeated. "I believed that title to have passed from the memory of the world when its owner was bound beneath the sea. Even I have forgotten the threat of his rising. Thankfully, the cult of Osiris, though with imperfect understanding, has not, and Madame Thothmes and her people yet watch, ready to strike at the first sign of his return."

"Pardon me, my father, if I do not share your gratitude and I find it hard to understand *yours*, considering they were intent on chopping your stepson into little pieces just an hour ago!"

"An unfortunate misunderstanding. You might have been allies except for Inspector Stagg's ignorant blundering through the occult world. His indiscretion was responsible for this near fatal altercation. Please do not mistake me, my beloved son; I rejoice that you escaped death. But you must understand: this altered image is a perversion of Osiris. By depicting him with raised hands, it becomes a representation of his and his cult's ancient enemy."

"This Yttle Elumi."

"The Osiris cult identified him with Apep, the Egyptian serpent god of death and darkness. The raised arms on this tarot card, a symbology retained by the Golden Dawn in the Lesser Ritual of the Hexagram, signifies Apep and his cohort Typhon rejoicing in triumph over Osiris' death.

"From Madame Thothmes point of view, then, who but Yttle Elumi's servants would so brazenly enter her domain and toss this card in her face? That was nothing less than a declaration of war, and I assure you, she saw you and Inspector Stagg as the aggressors."

"Who is this other entity linked with Apep?"

"Typhon. He was a chaotic water entity of the Indian Ocean, also identified with Yttle Elumi. As on this tarot card, the raised hands and the head together represent Typhon's symbol, the trident."

Ravenwood's chameleon eyes suddenly flashed, one a brilliant blue, the other green. "So that's 'Typhon' as in *typhoon*. Apparently, invoking him can generate a wind storm over land as well as water."

"Explain, please."

"Father, Stagg had to pursue a stranger who claimed to be a doctor to recover this card. When Stagg cornered him, the man raised his hands and a *whirlwind* immediately whipped up. Stagg would never admit it, but I'm sure that's how he escaped.

"And what was a 'doctor' no one in Alvarado Court had ever seen before doing at the crime scene first thing in the morning before Taylor's murder was news? How many people outside of Alvarado Court and the police knew he was lying dead on his floor at that hour of the day? Only one person, and that's the killer. His seeking out this tarot card meant he knew about Taylor's Major Arcana, which was *not* public knowledge. Perhaps he and Taylor were fellow occultists."

"But, my son, if this man was the killer, did he not have all of the previous night alone in the house to locate what he wished and take it?" the Nameless One said.

"There was a long blond hair on Taylor's body," Ravenwood said. "It's possible the woman who left it frightened off the killer before he had a chance to get what he wanted. So he *had* to return to the scene of the crime for the card."

Ravenwood pointed at the corrupted image of Osiris. "My master, the bullet holes in William Desmond Taylor's clothing showed that he may have died with *his* hands raised like the figure on this card. Given his association with the Order of the Golden Dawn, Taylor would have understood this as the sign of Apep-Typhon, too. Which could mean he was calling upon Yttle Elumi when he was murdered."

"Shot, then, by a fellow member of the cult who coveted his Major Arcana? My son, what you say makes sense of such facts as we have, but do not presume that as yet we possess *all* the facts," the Nameless One said.

"So far, though, everything focuses on Taylor's Major Arcana and this tarot card in particular," Ravenwood said. "In which case, Taylor's death had nothing to do with his planning to revive an Arthurian romance by Wagner. At least it looks like Hank Arneau and Astoria Studios have nothing to worry about on that score, though it's certain to disappoint Hank's 'Dark Eminence' who was hoping the production would draw the killer out."

"No one is safe, my son, while the threat of Yttle Elumi's return remains. Do not forget William Desmond Taylor's murder is but one piece of a larger whole, as all our lives and deaths are connected with a past that is not simply done and a future that already is.

"Hear me: in one form or another Yttle Elumi has been feared in the East for millennia. In Egypt, he was known as Apep, and in India he is known as Vitra in his serpent form. There is a variant in which Vitra was a pious Brahma who denounced the good of service to others and sought power for himself, challenging the deva themselves. This variant I feel to be closer to the truth of his story, yet nothing is certain and even his true name is lost to us.

"But this I do know: the myths of Apep and Typhon and Vitra are from men's distorted receptions of a powerful, sending mind, one confined in a sarcophagus under the waves. His followers prophesied Yttle Elumi would rise in the Indian Ocean, which is what the Arabs feared they were witnessing when a typhoon appeared, and thus the name Typhon was given to him."

"Yttle Elumi will not rise," Ravenwood repeated, putting his hand to his chin. "Rise from the sea, then? But the rising on the tarot card is like Osiris' from the dead. So, was Madame Thothmes declaring Yttle Elumi will not rise from the water or the dead or both? How long could he have survived down there? These myths from his 'sending mind' are ancient. When exactly was the last time anyone heard from him?"

"It may be that in rising from the sea he returns to physical life," the Nameless One said. "Perhaps he can achieve this because before he was submerged, he was already lord of the dead, for his origins are in the utter north, the top of the earth which some hold as the entrance to the underworld."

The Nameless One tucked his chin to his chest and closed his eyes. "For the conflict ahead, I must withdraw myself from communion with you for a time. Though my body remains upon this plane, I will send my mind to the Seven Unseen by Men, priest-kings and queens of Aslem-Beth who stand as giants at the rim of Elyon, the utter, upper abyss. From their vantage point, the full history of Yttle Elumi will be…"

The Nameless One's eyes flew open.

"My son! I am taken! To your father I vowed, 'Always the Nameless One will guard the flesh of your flesh.' But there is a prior covenant which binds me, one which I never foresaw I would be called to honor during your earthly life. Now the hour of trial nears; yes, even my own! You must turn the twelfth hexagram back to the eleventh! Forgive me...!"

And Ravenwood looked on slack-jawed as his master faded away. Then, clutching the tarot card, he ran to his library to his copy of the *I Ching*. The Nameless One had warned him against its use as divination, always encouraging him to develop his own intuitive and psychic powers. But the Nameless One allowed that in pre-history, *some* of the hexagrams had their origins in sigils and were not wrongly used in that time. Perhaps that ancient context had modern relevance yet. He began thumbing through the book from the back. Thus he came first to the hexagram for twelve:

Beneath three parallel horizontal lines were two columns of three shorter horizontal lines. The shorter lines appeared to be supporting the longer ones above, recalling the formation of the large standing stones at Stonehenge.

He then read the hexagram's significance: *Heaven draws away from earth. The self-willed will rule and the arrogant shall stand. Beware love and its appearing. Know no fear. Hold fast to your integrity in the hour of trial.*

This echoed the Nameless One's warning of "the hour of trial," but he had also told him to turn the twelfth hexagram *back* to the eleventh. Flipping the page, Ravenwood was surprised to see its formation was the inverse of that for the twelfth. Its meaning: *Heaven descends. The Great Ones return. The Arrogant is made to pass in flame. Peace, now, and good fortune.*

These hexagrams, then, would appear to have originally served as invocations of opposing powers or entities in a conflict of another age...a conflict that they, in the present day, remained appropriate in aiding to resolve: the defeat of Yttle Elumi.

Ravenwood closed the *I Ching* volume, then sighed and picked up the phone to call Hank Arneau. But Arneau was away from both the studio and his home. Ravenwood left a message with the butler that he needed to meet his boss tomorrow morning, at Astoria studios would be fine, and for Arneau to bring Taylor's entire Major Arcana. He had new information on its relation to the murder.

*"My son! I am taken!"*

# CHAPTER SEVEN:
## *Death Haunts Astoria*

When the sirens began encroaching on the Astoria Studio, Anne D'Arromanches was taking Prodigious Paint for an early morning ride on the other end of the lot. She had been enjoying the solitary romp when Hank Arneau had suddenly come alongside her on a chestnut mare.

"Mr. Arneau," she said her face pink from the sting of the cold air. "Wherever did you come from?"

"It's this power I have to become invisible always in the presence of beautiful women it seems. I was hoping I might actually be starting to lose it where you're concerned. I've been shadowing you for a while now," he said. "Wanted to see how you handled yourself on a horse when the cameras aren't rolling. Anne, you're splendid. May I call you Anne? Anne, I just happen to be on the lookout for a polo partner. Pays well, whether we win or not."

"Mr. Arneau," she began, "it's not that I didn't enjoy our bologna sandwich yesterday. Or our commissary chat. But it's only the next morning and you're *following* me? And, no, you may *not* call me 'Anne.' Giving me the lead in your picture, trying to cajole me into becoming your polo partner.... Mr. Arneau, it's the Depression and I *do* need the work, but it's as though you're wishing for a paid companion to whom you're joined at the hip. Quite frankly, you're starting to make me feel uncomfor..."

Suddenly Arneau's head rose as though he had caught a scent, and Anne was struck by the hawk-like profile he made. His head did not move, but his eyes oscillated rapidly.

She leaned forward over her saddle. "I said you're starting to make me feel uncomfortable."

"Trouble," he said, reared his horse and bounded for the other side of the lot. Anne paused for a moment, then spurred Prodigious Paint after him.

Only then did she hear the sirens. Following Arneau, she took her horse through the back lot's gate and onto the streets of Queens to reach the front entrance of the studio. Its stately façade of four stone columns seemed more appropriate for a museum than a building where "flickers" were produced. Arneau had already dismounted and was headed for the door when she arrived. Anne saw him hailed by a dark haired young man in a tailored suit. He was carrying an umbrella though there wasn't a cloud in the sky.

"Ravenwood," Arneau said. "Any idea what's going on?"

"I just got here, Arneau. You brought the cards?"

"Yes. But I have to see what this is all about before we head over to my office."

"Of course."

Anne dismounted Prodigious Paint, planning to stay out of the way. Then she saw an ambulance rounding the corner and realized whoever had left his coupe parked in front of the studio had unwittingly set up an obstacle for the hospital vehicle.

She ran to the auto, put it out of gear and began pushing it out of the way. She was succeeding only in shifting its bulk slowly, when suddenly another pair of hands was added to her own and the coupe was now rushing along. She looked over to see that the nattily dressed man with the umbrella, now tucked under his arm, was assisting her.

He smiled and nodded at her as the ambulance moved into the spot they had just left vacant. "Quick thinking, Miss. Thank you. I hope you'll forgive my ill choice of parking place. If anyone could have foreseen it would be a problem, it should have been me, Miss...?"

"D'Arromanches. Anne D'Arromanches."

"I am Ravenwood."

Two men in white coats stepped from the ambulance, its siren light gyring over the studio's museum-like pillars. As the men approached the entrance with a stretcher held flat against their sides, Arneau intercepted them.

"Gentlemen, I'm Hank Arneau, head of Astoria pictures. I just got here. Has someone been hurt?"

"No," the ambulance driver said. "At least, not recently. We got a report that there are human remains in your prop storage room, Mr. Arneau. Remains that have apparently been here a while."

"I'm sure I have no idea what you're talking about. Who reported these alleged human remains?"

"Prop boy looking for the mask of Genghis Khan. Opened a stage sarcophagus you have in storage, and, wouldn't you know, it had a real human skeleton in it."

"No, I *wouldn't* know. I don't know how a prop boy would recognize it for real, either."

"Said he'd been in medical school before the crash made him have to drop out. He knows real bones when he sees 'em."

Now a police car drove up to the curb, and the officer in the passenger's side hefted himself out.

"Inspector Stagg," Ravenwood said with a sigh. "Who else?"

"Well, well, Ravenwood," Stagg said. "Why am I not surprised?"

"Do I need to remind you, Inspector, there is still the matter of a rack of ribs which remains as yet unresolved?"

Meanwhile, the men from the ambulance had noticed the arrival of the police and took it as their cue to get back to business.

"Look, Mr. Arneau," the ambulance driver said. "With all due respect, we have to go inside and get that skeleton. Court order. So, if you'll point us to the storage room?"

Arneau, now focused on Ravenwood and Anne with a heavy set officer, jabbed his thumb over his shoulder.

"Security can get you there," he said. He then briskly walked over to join the trio.

"Hello, again, Ravenwood, old man," Arneau said with a brief hug of Ravenwood's shoulders. Then to Stagg: "I'm Hank Arneau, current head of Astoria Studios, Inspector...?"

Stagg pointed at Ravenwood. "You two know each other?"

"I'm proud to say Detective Ravenwood and I have recently become associates, yes."

"Then I don't like you already," Stagg said.

Anne couldn't suppress a snort of laughter at Stagg's pronouncement and tucked her head when Arneau looked at her.

"Word is that there's a skeleton in your studio's closet," Stagg said, squinting one eye at Arneau.

Ravenwood clapped. "Keep turning those phrases Inspector Stagg. Next stop: 'A rose is a rose is a rose.'"

"What else *would* it be?"

The men from the ambulance were now returning, bearing the stretcher between them. What was on it was covered with a sheet. As they moved past Arneau, he signaled for them to stop, then flipped back the covering.

There, indeed, were the browning bones of a man, and, however long ago he had died, he had had a rough go of it: the niches in the rib cage indicated multiple stabbings.

Anne wrinkled her nose and frowned; apparently at the indignity of such a display in public. Yet, though she tried to turn her head out of respect for the dead, she wasn't able to look away completely. In a few moments, she was tentatively craning her neck for a closer inspection.

"I...I think I know him," she said.

All looked at her, startled at her announcement, but hardly as startled as Anne herself, to judge by her expression.

"Oh, ho," Inspector Stagg said. "*You*, I like. Okay, little lady. Who are you and what do you do around here?"

"My name is Anne D'Arromanches, officer," she said. "I've been an extra here for some time."

"And who do you think this is? Someone you worked with here? You recall anyone disappearing?"

"Disappearing *when*?" Arneau asked, nodding down at the bones. "Back when George Méliès was filming the traffic? Those bones have been nothing *but* bones for a lot longer than Miss D'Arromanches has worked here." He flipped the sheet back over the skeleton. Anne's hand went to her stomach, and she took a deep breath at the removal of the remains from sight.

"What do I know bones from?" Stagg asked. "Maybe that's make-up or varnish to make 'em look old. We're taking them to have some lab work done..."

"I'm sorry, officer, but you are *not*."

All looked to see the *The Ordeal*'s director, Nate Tannen, standing there. No one had noticed his arrival, but apparently he had been there long enough to hear Anne's claim.

"There's no way Miss D'Arromanches could have known this man. This skeleton is on loan from Professor Hierynomous Cobb, whose find it is, and he dates it circa the fourteenth century. Authenticity is paramount in a crucial scene in an upcoming production, so I opted for a museum piece instead of resorting to grave robbing."

"You have documentation?" Stagg said.

"I certainly do. If you'll follow me to my office, then this studio can get back to making movies. Time is money. Correct, Mr. Arneau?"

"Correct, Nate," Arneau said. "I just wish you had informed me about 'Boney' here."

"I'm sorry, sir. But you did give me carte blanche because..."

"Because you are the former set designer, and I'm just a wannabe Thalberg. You're right, Nate. No apology needed."

"You men," Stagg addressed the stretcher-bearers. "Put that thing in the ambulance, and keep it there until this is sorted out."

"You'll have no argument from me there, Inspector," Nate said. "Please step this way."

"Mr. Arneau," Anne said, "please understand I wasn't trying to make trouble. But I really thought I recognized him. Somehow."

"Have you ever been tested for psychic aptitude, Miss D'Arromanches?" Ravenwood asked. "Certain people can get a sense of presence when in proximity to the dead, and there are cases in which this sense has led them to the remains of people whose fates have been a total mystery."

"Nothing like that...until today. Assuming it *was* psychic. I do have a recurring dream, though..."

"Of me, I hope?" Arneau interjected with a smile.

"...of a horrifying, large black shadow pursuing me," she said, looking him in the eye. Ravenwood laughed as the corners of Arneau's mouth sagged.

"Well, Arneau, it appears you're the shadow."

Arneau grinned. "Your psychic acumen is indeed as acute as advertised, Ravenwood," he said.

"Who needs to be psychic? It's painfully obvious that you're smitten."

Anne turned a lovely coral pink and deciding to ignore Ravewood's remark, interlocked her fingers and said to Hank: "Mr. Arneau, I apologize again. And that other gentleman who overheard me? Assuming you still wish me to be part of it, please say he's not the director of our film...."

"Yes I do, and yes he is."

"Ohhhh..."

"Not to worry, sweetheart. He's a big fan of yours. He was the one pushing me to get a look at you in *The Jaundiced Claw* and consider you for the lead in *The Ordeal*."

"I feel like I'm going through one right now."

"I'm certain he's already forgiven you. Besides, officially, you don't owe anything to him. I'm burying that you were discovered in a serial. I don't want that in *my* star's resume."

"I'm hardly anyone's 'star,' Mr. Arneau."

"Stars are *made*, Miss D'Arromanches. And you need a proper back story. I like this one better: 'she was in a crinoline dress, waving a lacy hanky with all the other Southern Belles giving their brothers and sweethearts a send-off to Gettysburg, when she was plucked out of the crowd to star in *The Ordeal*."

"*That's* a better back story?" Ravenwood asked.

"What can I say? There was just something about the way she waved that hanky."

"Might I borrow it? Because that was rather sad," Ravenwood said.

"Miss D'Arromanches, have you formally been introduced to the studio wag, Ravenwood?" Arneau asked.

"We've met."

"How do you do," Ravenwood said as he and Anne shook hands.

"Fine, Mr. Ravenwood. And what do you really do for Mr. Arneau?"

"Like I said, he amuses me," Arneau said. "Now, Miss D'Arromanches, might you do me the honor of joining me for breakfast in the commissary? This producer has much to discuss with his leading lady."

She nodded toward Prodigious Paint, who had come alongside Arneau's horse. "After Paint's had his morning oats. And a brushing. Could we meet in an hour? I'd like to get out of these riding clothes and cleaned up."

"Swell," Arneau said and nodded at Ravenwood. "The man of infinite jest here and I have some business to discuss in the interim."

"I think you've mixed me up with a guy called Yorick," Ravenwood said, raised his umbrella and pointed its tip at the ambulance. "He's in there, last I saw."

"Alas. Poor guy," Arneau said. "Miss D'Arromanches, how do you like your eggs?"

"Scrambled," she said as she mounted Prodigious Paint.

"Bacon?"

"Limp."

Arneau checked his watch. "Scrambled and limp and steaming on a plate when you get there at eight thirty. My *personal* table in the Astoria Room."

One of Anne's eyebrows, already arched by a fashionable plucking, arched higher on her forehead as she looked down on him Then she turned the horse and broke into a gallop back to the studio stables.

"Now, that's a woman, Arneau," Ravenwood said looking after her. "The kind that won't let you get away with anything."

"She is rather magnificent, isn't she?" Arneau said, and Ravenwood noted the appraisal in his eyes was not that of the love-struck, but a frank admiration totally divorced from anything romantic. Then it was gone, and Arneau had his elbow and was steering him up the Astoria's steps and inside the studio.

# CHAPTER EIGHT:
## Dead Man's Tarot

"Here's the Major Arcana," Arneau said, laying a steel briefcase on his office desk and opening it. "I use this as a strong box in which to store them."

Looking inside, Ravenwood saw an ancient deck.

"May I?" Ravenwood asked.

"Feel free."

Ravenwood took out the cards. Like the standard tarot, the deck began at zero with the image of a strolling man with a walking stick; except in this case the man was in Egyptian attire. This card was commonly called "the Fool." The number one card presented another Egyptian wearing a headdress and brandishing his staff at the viewer. Ravenwood took this staff as the equivalent of a magic wand, since card one in the common deck was "the Magician."

He noticed something written in tiny, faded pencil on the card's bottom border. He pulled it close to his eyes.

" 'James?'" he said, looking at Arneau. "Name ring a bell?"

Arneau shrugged. "Must be the name of some guy who once owned the card."

Ravenwood placed the card on the table and took up the next. He immediately noticed something penciled on its bottom border as well. The image was of a woman, which was typical since the Tarot's second card pictured 'the Empress.' Everything else, however, was *more* atypical than the previous cards: she sported a headdress of feathers, bore a scroll in one hand, and a nimbus behind her head highlighted her un-Egyptian blond locks. Ravenwood drew the card closer to read what was penciled there.

" 'Angel,'" he said. "But Egyptians did not have Angels and that halo behind her head is more Byzantine."

"Both are written in the same hand. Maybe an 'a' faded off and this is James' friend 'Angela,'" Arneau suggested. "Perhaps they were identifying themselves with these tarot characters for some occult purpose."

"No, no," Ravenwood said. "I have it. 'Angel' means 'messenger' and that was the role of the Egyptians' god Thoth; the bird-headed one. That's why she's wearing a feather headdress, has a scroll in her hand, and that 'nimbus' behind her head is the moon, which was Thoth's symbol."

Arneau nodded as Ravenwood resumed his count. He found no other pencil notations on cards three through eleven. Then he withdrew from his inner coat pocket Stagg's card and placed it on top of the eleventh.

"There's your missing card, Arneau. I checked it out: the underlined wicket is the Egyptian numeral for twelve."

The texture, the aging...the card certainly appeared of a piece with the others. Arneau looked up at Ravenwood, jaw slack at first, and then smiled. "Where did you...?"

"Believe it or not," Ravenwood said, "it was in the possession of Inspector Stagg, currently investigating charges of you having illegal body parts on the premises."

"*That* guy?"

"He was on the William Desmond Taylor crime scene. He told me how people were being allowed to go through Taylor's things while the law looked on. One rifler in particular stood out: a man who had walked in on the crime scene, proclaimed himself a doctor and gave a phony cause of death.

"This man made a point to pinch this card, and Inspector Stagg gave pursuit. He eluded Stagg, but lost this card. Although it is completely out of character, Inspector Stagg has held on to it all these years. Perhaps..."

Here Ravenwood looked Arneau in the eye "... perhaps he was meant to. Just as you were meant to bring the remainder of the deck from the West Coast to the East..."

"To rejoin Stagg's card, waiting for them here for nine years," Arneau said.

"I have to say, for a guy who doesn't believe in curses, it sounds like you're amazingly open to the possibility of occult influences," Ravenwood said.

"Belief in synchronicity and the sensationalism that sells papers when the Tut expedition starts dropping like flies is not the same thing, Ravenwood," Arneau said. "You know that."

"Believe me, I'm not here to try and convince you that a curse is indeed your problem. Neither hostile current *nor* hit man took out William Desmond Taylor because he was going to make *The Ordeal*."

"Why so sure?"

"Listen: Stagg and I were nearly killed last night when he showed his card to a fortune teller at the *Club Samedi*...I know, it's a house of ill-repute; wipe that dung eating grin off your face. It also happens to be one of the best jazz clubs in Harlem, and it comes with its own tarot reader.

When she saw this, she began shouting, 'Yttle Elumi will not rise!' and summoned two big men who proceeded to come at me and Stagg with swords."

" Swords?"

"They just happen to have some hanging on the wall. You know: the kind of décor that gives a joint atmosphere, when you're not using it to chop up the clientele. We escaped without injury, thanks for asking, and I conferred with my master. He said this Yttle Elumi was an ancient being whom the Egyptians associated with Apep, the serpent god of the underworld. Stagg and I encountered members of a secret society actively opposing the cult of Apep or Yttle Elumi, if you will.

"Though the image on this card depicts Osiris rising, his arms should be crossed over his chest. The raising of the arms is the sign of Apep's ally Typhon who is also syncretized with Yttle Elumi. Remember at the time of Taylor's death, there were only two possible positions of his arms, and one was with them raised over his head."

"But that's a typical pose to strike with a gun pointed at you," Arneau said, "Just because he possessed this card..."

"An extremely esoteric card, Hank. Part of an equally esoteric Major Arcana he searched the Middle East for. And there's more...

"Turns out Taylor had a previous association with none other than the Order of the Golden Dawn whose Lesser Ritual of the Hexagram included the raising of both hands to represent Apep and Typhon triumphant. And the man Stagg encountered was *not* concerned with removing the scenario for *The Ordeal* from circulation. He wanted this tarot card. I believe he was Taylor's fellow cult member who murdered him while Taylor was attempting to invoke Yttle Elumi for aid through the sign of Typhon. Didn't have time to get through, it seems. Anyway, if your master wants to find Taylor's murderer, he can narrow his list of suspects down by uncovering who's in the Yttle Elumi cult."

Arneau put his hand to his jaw and scratched. "Hmmm...well, the Dark Eminence has dealt with murderous cults before. Can't be any worse than the Bombay stranglers."

At this point, Ravenwood noticed a drawing resembling Stonehenge that was partially under a thick, hardback book on Arneau's desk. Ravenwood carefully tugged the drawing free and saw the Stonehenge design was for a gateway in a giant wall.

"This is the gate you said you've built on the Pathe lot," he said.

"Yes. That was our director's idea, Nate Tannen, who's currently clearing things with your pal Stagg. He said the Stonehenge look would tie in thematically, since our movie is ostensibly an Arthurian tale, and those stories have Celtic origins."

"Then your movie *is* involved in the Taylor case, just not as you and your 'Dark Eminence' thought." He tapped the drawing of the Stonehenge gate. "This looks like the *I Ching* hexagram for the number twelve. That is the number of Yttle Elumi's card and the Egyptian numeral for twelve on it. This wicket in the corner here, remember? Also looks like a gateway.

"Your Mr. Tannen's intentions in set dressing may have been superseded by a larger design not his own. Listen to the significance of the twelfth hexagram. I copied this from my volume of the *I Ching*," Ravenwood pulled a note card from his inside coat pocket and read:

*"Heaven draws away from earth. The self-willed will rule and the arrogant shall stand. Beware love and its appearing. Know no fear. Hold fast to your integrity in the hour of trial."*

"'Beware love's appearing'?" Arneau asked. "Now, that's a hexagram I can't get behind. Not with the lovely Miss D'Arromanches' recent appearance in my life."

"Hank, I know it's difficult, but try to get your mind off Anne D'Arromanches." Ravenwood raised the palm of his hand and spread his fingers. "For five minutes, that's all I'm asking. Work with me.

"The twelfth card in the tarot deck is typically 'the Hanged Man' which signifies a change of situation. You 'just happen' to have built a giant hexagram for the number twelve. Tell your 'Dark Eminence' that something pivotal to the case is going to happen at this gate."

"That's your professional opinion?"

"That's my professional opinion. One more thing: my master stressed that I turn the twelfth hexagram back to the eleventh. Its formation is the inverse of the twelfth. This is its meaning," he said, reading again from his notes:

*Heaven descends. The Great Ones return. The Arrogant is made to pass in flame. Peace, now, and good fortune.*

"So it's not all bad news; splendid!" Arneau said, clapping his hands together. "Now, I really must get ready for breakfast. But first…"

Arneau pulled open a desk drawer, took out an envelope, and handed it to Ravenwood. "I still want you to go to Los Angeles to confer with Murphy Fort," Arneau said. "I want you to take the cards. Who knows? He's an occult buff; he might have some insights into both this Major Arcana and the Yttle Elumi cult.

"I'll call ahead to tell him something new has been added. And I still want him to fill you in on the history of *The Ordeal.* Synchronicity or not, I'm inclined to think those tarot cards ended up in the same lot as the movie scenario for a reason. Agreed?" he said as he returned the cards, including Stagg's, to the steel briefcase."

"It's a definite possibility. Sure, we'll talk about the opera and why its single production was aborted. I'm rather curious about that just on a personal level."

"My automobile is waiting to drive you to the airport. You can leave yours on the lot until you return." He handed Ravenwood the briefcase. "Your reservations at the Roosevelt are in that envelope with the plane ticket. Please note that it is a round trip to Hollywood. First class. I'll make contact when I and the rest of the movie crew fly over to the West Coast. We'll all be staying at the Roosevelt as well.

"I want you to know that you have my complete confidence, Ravenwood."

"Very well, then, Arneau," Ravenwood said and the two men shook hands. "See you in Hollywood, then."

"See ya on the other side, Stepson of Mystery."

As the door closed behind him, Arneau was sliding his suit coats down the hanging rod until he came to one with a slight bulge in the side pocket. He tapped it, looked back over his shoulder toward the door Ravenwood had just closed, and began to chuckle. He then turned back to the closet, and selected a crisply ironed shirt to go with the coat.

# CHAPTER NINE:
## *"Beware Love
## and
## Its Appearing."*

A freshly shaven Arneau looking sharp in a black, pin striped three-piece suit, entered the Astoria Room, the studio commissary, and overlooked his domain. He frowned, tapping the tiny box inside his coat pocket. Anne D'Arromanches was not at his table.

Then from the corner of his eye he saw her waving broadly, smiling at him. She was seated with the extras and grips. Arneau bit his lower lip as he walked over to her table.

"I hope you don't mind my starting without you," she said, "but after my workout this morning, I was famished." She pointed at the chair across from her. "Please be seated. After all," she said, sweeping her fork out in an arc as though it were a wand, "it's your studio."

"Nice of you to remember who's in charge," he said as he slid into the chair.

"I do," she said, pinning the egg with her fork and looking down at her plate as she sawed with her knife. "When it comes to where I wish to sit down to breakfast, I am."

Her knife and fork clinked against the plate as she set them down and looked him in the eye. "If you think back over our conversation earlier, I never agreed to meet you at your table. But, of course, if this is all strictly business I suppose I do have to sit where you order me to." She put a hand on each side of her plate.

He quickly placed his hand on one of hers. "It's *friendly* business, Miss D'Arromanches. Please stay right where you are."

She smiled at him, raised her fork to her lips and took another bite of egg. "Have you noticed," she said between swallowing and taking up her cup of coffee, "that you and I both have French last names but speak with Midwestern accents? From where do you hail, Mr. Arneau?"

An Italian waiter in white tux hovered at Arneau's elbow, pouring him a cup of coffee. "Black, just as you like it, sir," the waiter said.

"Thanks Gio," Arneau said. "I hope your child is doing well?"

"As of yesterday, my boy's brace come off. No more the other boys make fun. Ha! He give the last one a bloody nose, though. Thank you so very much, for what you do for my family, Mr. Arneau."

Arneau smiled. "My pleasure, Gio. Wish I could have been there to see that bloody nose."

Gio bowed and left. Arenau took a drink, and, from over the rim of his coffee cup, saw that Anne's bright blue eyes regarded him under arched brows.

"I despise a bully," he said as he lowered his cup.

"No," she said, "it's more than that." She poked her fork at him. "You, Hank Arneau, are a philanthropist."

"You mean 'pugilist,'" he said and smiled. "I taught the kid to punch. The philanthropist was the specialist who agreed to do the operation *gratis*."

Anne watched Gio pouring coffee table to table. "Gio doesn't look like he moves in the same circles of those kind of specialists."

"What say we talk about something else," Arneau said, tapping lightly the delicate skin of her slender wrist. "Like you were saying something of how we are fellow

French expatriates or something?"

"Well, I'm only from French Quebec...as far as I know."

"But your name means Anne of Arromanches. So you have some idea from where your family migrated."

"'Anne of Arromanches,'" another voice above them repeated. Arneau and Anne looked up to see that, as he had done earlier that morning during the contention with Inspector Stagg, Nate Tannen had appeared as though from nowhere. "You know," Nate continued, "your name indicates your ancestors are from the Normandy area, land of the Norse men. May I say it shows?"

"You're our little Viking princess, Anne," Arneau said.

"And beyond her Viking progenitors were people from the utter North," Nate added.

"Eskimos?" Arneau said. "Sorry, Nate. I don't see it."

"I mean Hyperborea," Nate said, looking at Anne. "Are you familiar with it?"

"I can't say that I am. Won't you please join us?" Anne asked, looking around the room for a chair.

"It's the Atlantis of the North Pole," Nate said, "from a time when the pole was green and verdant. The entire civilization was frozen in an instant. And, no thank you. I just dropped by to inform Mr. Arneau that our little problem with the law has been resolved in our favor. That skeleton will be on its way to LA with me on the next plane, just as planned."

"Splendid," Arneau said. His forefinger went back and forth from Anne to Nate. "You two know of each other, but you haven't been formally introduced, have you? Anne D'Arromanches, future star, meet Nate Tannen, star director."

Anne shook Nate's offered hand. "How do you do, Anne?" he said.

"Very well, thank you," she said. "And Mr. Tannen, regarding my earlier comments about that skeleton...I did not intend to make things unnecessarily difficult for you or the production, but for a moment I honestly believed what I said...and if there had been a murder, or someone missing...that person probably has loved ones, so..."

Tannen smiled and patted her hand before returning it to her. "Just the sort of uncompromising integrity I would expect from the woman who played Claire Taveral so convincingly. If I had any lingering doubts, your response assured me you were the one. I could tell your own virtue was projecting from that character, and that was exactly the quality the audience must see in our heroine in *The Ordeal*. As well as your bravery in performing your own stunts. Please, don't let those eggs get cold."

"Thank you," Anne said.

Arneau looked at his wristwatch. "Nate, isn't it about that time? You and, you know, 'Boney?' The plane?"

"Hmmm? Oh yes ..."

"Look up Ravenwood. He'll be on the same flight."

"Ravenwood?"

"Dark-haired young man who was with me this morning when the ambulance showed up."

"Carried an umbrella with no cloud in the sky?"

"The same."

"Is he involved in this production in some capacity of which I was not informed?"

"Oh, no. He's having my tarot cards I told you about, uhm, 'authenticated' for me. Queer thing; I just completed that Major Arcana today. Ravenwood recovered the missing card. Actually, you won't believe this, it was in the possession of that stout police inspector you entertained earlier."

"*Inspector Stagg*?" Nate asked.

"The same. Turns out nine years earlier, and, one suspects, a hundred pounds lighter..."

"Mr. Arneau, really," Anne said, trying not to grin.

"I forgot I was talking about your boyfriend, Anne. I beg your pardon. Anyway, Stagg was on the scene of the William Desmond Taylor murder. He chased a suspect who had apparently stolen this tarot card from among Taylor's possessions. Stagg lost the suspect, but recovered the card and has held onto it all this time."

Anne rested her chin on folded hands and gazed at Arneau. "It's like that card made its way back to the others," she said.

"That's *exactly* what I said," Arneau said and pointed at her with his fork. Then, to Nate: "I suspect they're quite rare, perhaps one of a kind. Besides their age, the tarot iconography isn't completely typical."

"Yes. That sounds most interesting. Well, lovely to meet you at last, Miss D'Arromanches. I look forward to working with you."

"And I you."

Nate flicked a salute off his forehead and began to make his way across the room.

"Now," Hanks said to Anne. "Let's talk about our little club some more. Were both your mother and father French?"

"I never knew my father or my mother. But she could only speak French, according to the ladies who ran the orphanage in which I grew up."

"She abandoned you?"

"Yes. But I've never known her story. I try not to judge her."

"I'm very sorry Anne."

When she lifted her coffee cup this time, Hank noticed she held it around the bowl with both hands; a most child-like manner in contrast to her hard stare into the cup's wisps of steam unfurling and undulating before her.

"That farm made a bit of a tomboy out of me," she said, taking a sip and setting down the coffee. Her formerly pensive eyes suddenly again all bright and cornflower blue, she said, "When I headed out to try and get in the flickers, my upbringing served me well. When they asked a crowd of extras if there was a girl who wasn't afraid to ride standing in the saddle, or walk along the edge of a building, I always raised my hand. That's how I was noticed for *The Jaundiced Claw*."

"That's how you were noticed by me. I can't wait to introduce you to the public: 'Anne D'Arromanches, the bravest girl I've ever known.'"

Anne tucked her head and stirred her coffee. "Oh, I don't know about all that."

"I'm not just talking about Anne D'Arromanches, serial ingenue or stunt woman. I'm talking about the girl who had the pluck to walk away from that orphanage on her own and not accept the first marriage proposal that would have kept her taken care of."

She looked up at him. In her eyes, he could see both the consummation of years of yearning for affirmation, and, now that it had arrived, her incredulity at its source. For a moment. Then she laughed. "I was hardly a girl when I left. Trust me. I've never really known my actual age. But based on what the doctor said who examined me when I first came to the orphanage, I should be around twenty-eight."

"It suits you."

Anne took a sip of her coffee, and, with a faraway stare, said, "I wish I knew more about my heritage. It's not like I'll ever get to France, let alone Arromanches."

"When you're a star, you'll go places, Miss D'Arromanches. If you wish, France will be one of them. But first, I have something for you...." He reached into his coat pocket.

Anne pushed back in her chair from the table. "Oh, no, Mr. Arneau. Breakfast on your dime is one thing but..."

Arneau produced a small jewelry box. "This is just a gift in celebration of the journey we're beginning together."

"No, really. Please respect my wishes. I'm starting to like you...Hank. Don't spoil it."

With a smile, he withdrew the box. "You called me 'Hank,'" he said. "Miss D'Arromanches, I came bearing you a gift, and you gave me one, instead."

She smiled back at him. "Then here's another one: please keep it 'Anne'... Hank."

# CHAPTER TEN:
## *Airborne Evil!*

Ravenwood had put nearly half a continent behind him before he realized danger had followed him into the air.

His thoughts had been preoccupied with the fate of the Nameless One. Startled as he was by his unwilling rapture, the Nameless One's parting words nevertheless made it clear his master understood why he was being taken and by whom, and that he expected to be tried in a manner he clearly dreaded. Yet, the cryptic words of the twelfth hexagram to which his mentor had pointed implied the Nameless One's personal trial might be superseded by a universal one, with heaven withdrawing to allow for the rule of the self-willed and arrogant. How could that *not* also apply to what the Nameless One felt was the threat of Yttle Elumi's return?

Ravenwood had been staring at the back of the chair of a man who now turned and scowled at him, making a quick nod of his head toward the tarot cards' steel briefcase in Ravenwood's lap. Ravenwood realized he had been drumming his fingers on the lid while deep in thought, and his fellow passenger had reached his limit. The Stepson of Mystery smiled apologetically and ceased the drumming. With his upper lip still curled, the man turned back around.

The surly fellow had done Ravenwood a favor: with the breaking of his train of thought, he realized for the first time that there was a metallic taste in his mouth, a psychic harbinger suggesting the type of danger involved.

And that the bringer of that danger was with him on this flight.

He thought of the steel he had all *but* tasted the night before at the hands of Madame Thothmes' anti-Yttle Elumi league. How had they

"I wish I knew more about my heritage."

picked up his trail? Of course: Stagg had identified himself as an officer of the law to Madame Thothmes and her swordsmen, and then he had returned to the *Club Samedi* in that capacity. Easy enough for them to get his stocky countenance lodged firmly in their minds. This secret society's agents, then, would have watched the various precinct headquarters until Stagg appeared, and they must have followed him to Astoria Studios that morning and right back to Ravenwood.

*Hang the man!* Ravenwood thought. *Even at this altitude and with half of the country between us, he* still *manages to make himself an obstacle in my affairs!*

Could the anti-Yttle Elumi league possibly have any knowledge of what he carried in the metal case? Or were they simply following him because they believed him one more follower of Yttle Elumi in need of erasing from the earth?

When a stewardess passed down the aisle, Ravenwood took the opportunity to turn his head as though debating whether to call her back while in actuality surveying his fellow passengers. Only one individual stood out: Nate Tannen, the director of *The Ordeal*.

Hank had failed to mention they would be sharing a flight. Just as well. For the director's safety, Ravenwood didn't wish Madame Thothmes' agent to associate them. Tannen had his head down, reading and occasionally marking what were probably script pages. Ravenwood quickly turned back around before the director might raise his head and recognize him from earlier that morning.

Once the plane landed, Ravenwood immediately began pushing his way into the aisle, always keeping his back to Tannen. Then, claiming his luggage, he stepped out into the spring-like temperature of a mid-January morning in Los Angeles and hailed a cab. His bags were loaded in the trunk by an airport attendant, but Ravenwood held onto the steel briefcase.

The metal taste in his mouth told Ravenwood his adversary was still near. As he took his seat, he asked the driver if he knew where any of the homes of the stars were located.

"There's a lot up in Whitley Heights," the sandy haired, freckle-splotched driver said, eyeing Ravenwood in the rearview mirror.

"Don't hesitate to give me the scenic route," Ravenwood said, hoping to shake his pursuer. "There's an extra buck in it for you beyond the fare."

"You want to go up as far as Topside; the Francis X. Bushman place?" the cabbie asked.

Ravenwood grinned: he could scarcely be secretly followed up a series of steep hills and winding roads. His pursuer would either abandon pursuit or reveal himself. In the latter case, should he choose to attack, he would not find Ravenwood unarmed.

Passing the driver a dollar bill from the back seat, Ravenwood said, "If the air isn't too thin up there, straight to the top, my good man."

"Yes sir!" the young man responded as he took the dollar and pulled out of the airport.

Turning the corner at Hollywood and Vine, the cab drove for almost a mile before beginning the climb up Whitley Heights, its steep topography ornate with Mediterranean style homes. The terrain they passed was one of mansions with raised tile roofs, overarching doorways, enormous picture windows, courtyards, and balconies with balustrades thrust over a bright, Californian abyss of green grass, multicolored flowers and palm trees. The demarcation line between celebrity and average man could hardly be more pronounced: large, looming wrought iron gates secured this opulence and shut out the Great Depression.

The metallic taste no longer in his mouth, Ravenwood congratulated himself on losing his pursuer. Then he thought again: was it possible he was not being followed because his assassin somehow knew he would end up at the Roosevelt? Time for a change of accommodations on his own dime...after his meeting with Murphy Fort.

"All right, my good man," Ravenwood said. "If you'd now be so kind as to carry me over to Universal Studios."

Less than half an hour later, bearing the metal briefcase, Ravenwood arrived at Universal's front gate.

"Listen," he said to the cabby as he withdrew a small stenopad and pen from his inside coat pocket and began writing. "I want you to get to the nearest phone. Dial this number and ask for Inspector Stagg. Just say you have information related to the attack on his person last night, and they'll accept the charges. Tell him that Ravenwood said that the anti-Yttle Elumi league..."

"*Who?*"

"I'm writing it down. He'll know what I mean. Tell him that Ravenwood said the anti-Yttle Elumi league still has a bullseye painted on his broad back side, and he should watch it. Love and kisses, etc. Here is another couple bucks for your trouble. And if you would see fit to return here afterward and wait for me, I have absolutely no problem with your meter running while I see to my business inside."

The cab driver smiled and nodded. As he drove away, Ravenwood informed the gate guard that he was there to see Murphy Fort on the behalf of Hank Arneau, head of Astoria Studios.

The guard made a call, and, appointment confirmed, he told Ravenwood an automobile would be sent for him. The vehicle duly arrived and soon Ravenwood was being whisked along the expansive studio on a hill that Carl Laemmle had built. They passed a large billboard heralding a film due out in just a few weeks: *Dracula*.

*That's the movie whose screenplay Fort was working on,* Ravenwood thought. *Don't know if that fellow Lugosi's grimace makes him look frightening or constipated.*

The driver let Ravenwood out in front of an office building. Locating Fort's office, he looked through its open door at a screenwriter in his early-thirties, one with leading man good looks behind large round lens glasses, sitting at a wooden desk. Fort's fingers clacked away at the keys of a cast metal typewriter. He eyed intently the paper scrolling before him.

Ravenwood knocked on the door. "Mr. Fort?"

The clacking stopped immediately, and the man looked up at him.

"I am Ravenwood." He held up the steel carrying case and said, "I have the Major Arcana Hank Arneau wishes you to examine."

Fort smiled. "Yes, Mr. Ravenwood. Wonderful name you have, sir. Please come in. Be seated." He nodded at a wooden chair on the other side of his desk. "I'd be delighted to have a look at William Desmond Taylor's personal tarot deck."

# CHAPTER ELEVEN:
## Out of the Aeons, Coming Soon To a Theater Near You...

"**O**nly the Major Arcana," Ravenwood repeated as he sat down and placed the metal briefcase on the desk. Fort straightened himself in his chair and clapped his hands together as Ravenwood lifted the lid and gently placed the stack of cards before him.

Fort looked at the zero card carefully, put it aside, then lifted card one: the Egyptian brandishing the staff. Ravenwood saw Fort's magnified squint behind his large lenses. He drew the card closer to his eyes.

"James," Ravenwood said. "We figure it's the name of whoever owned the card before Taylor. The second card has the notation Angel under the image of a woman dressed to represent Thoth. That connection is easy enough to get."

"You mean, they correspond as messenger entities."

"Right. I checked through the other cards on the flight over, and none of those have any notes penciled in."

Fort now examined the second card, then held the two side by side. "Both of these were written in the same hand," he said. "If Angel has significance to that card's image, so should James. Hmmm.

"Wait a minute, wait a *minute*." He held the card back for fresh regard, then smiled, turned the card to Ravenwood, and gently tapped the staff the figure held. "Not James but *Jannes*. This tiny lettering has bunched the two 'n's together so that they look like an 'm'"

"Jannes? Is that an alternative name of an Egyptian deity?"

Fort rose from his chair and went to an overloaded bookcase, then ran the tip of his index finger bumpily across the rows of book spines. "Did you ever attend Sunday School, Ravenwood?"

"At a mission in India."

Fort pulled a Bible from his shelf. "Well, you probably know the story, just not the name. It's not even given in the *Old Testament* where the story appears," Fort began flipping to the back of the Bible, "but in the *New Testament*. A bit obscure, but here it is from the Apostle Paul, in Second Timothy 3:8—'Jannes and Jambres opposed Moses.' Jannes was the name of one of Pharoah's court magicians who had several showdowns with Moses."

Ravenwood remembered and pointed at the card. "Jannes' staff turned into a *serpent...*"

"As did Jambres'. But Moses' staff swallowed both of theirs whole," Fort added with a grin.

Ravenwood looked at Fort. "You're familiar with Apep, the evil serpent god?"

Fort nodded. "You're suggesting Jannes' staff turned into a manifestation of Apep?"

"Could Jannes have been a worshipper of the serpent god?"

"Hmm. Members of the Apep cult were usually hiding out to keep from being whacked to pieces, not performing for the royal court. But as obfuscated as Egyptian history of that period is, a dynasty might have emerged that accepted Apep as a legitimate god if only to sharpen its distinction from the dynasty it had supplanted."

Ravenwood now quickly began putting aside the other cards until he came to the twelfth. "Look at card twelve. You'll notice this is not the correct infiguration of Osiris Rising. It upset a tarot reader named Madame Thothmes so much that she began smashing underfoot serpent images of Apep, but what she said was, '*Yttle Elumi* will not rise.'"

"Yttle Elumi?" Fort asked. "I've never heard of that deity, but she clearly associated it with Apep."

"Yttle Elumi is actually a title, not a name," Ravenwood said.

"Yes," Fort said sibilantly as he took his glasses from his face with one hand, leaned back and gnawed the end of one of the ear pieces. "Yttle is Caananite for... enemy, if I recall correctly, and elumi echoes Eloheim—'gods' but always used with a singular verb and adjective in Moses' writings. Yttle Elumi could mean either enemy of the gods or enemy of God."

Fort slid his glasses back on, and then he placed the Jannes and Angel cards side by side. "These two are connected, you know."

"How so?"

"Numerology: cards one and two, the yang and yin of male and female come together," here he held up the card of Yttle Elumi rising, "to make twelve. That wicket like an archway is the Egyptian twelve."

"So, they not only meet *at* the gateway, they also, in some sense, *are* the gateway," Ravenwood said, hand to his chin. "A gateway where Yttle Elumi rises from his death bier." Ravenwood thought of the gate on the Pathe lot resembling the *I Ching*'s twelfth hexagram. Something significant to the case was going to happen at that Stonehenge like structure, he had promised Arneau. That significance seemed to be quickly superseding merely solving a murder.

"Mr. Fort, I don't think I will be completely changing the topic at this point to ask you about *The Ordeal*," Ravenwood said.

Fort leaned back and steepled his fingers. "Well, historically, *The Ordeal* is an important evolutionary link to Wagner's final opera, *Parsifal*. You see, he initially wanted to write a play based on Buddhism which he also abandoned called *The Victors*. It dealt with reincarnation and the denouncement of desire. The lovers, who have each rejected the other in different incarnations, find oneness in following Buddha. Wagner picked up on those themes in *Parsifal*, but *The Ordeal* is when he actually first merged Buddhism with Arthurian romance.

"He *also* drew source material from the occult author whose novel *Rienzi* was the basis of Wagner's first great success."

"You mean Edward Bulwer Lytton."

"Yes, but this time he only borrowed 'the Dweller of the Threshold' from Lytton's *Zanoni* for the opera's final act."

"It would be odd if the Order of the Golden Dawn wasn't familiar with all of Lytton's works," Ravenwood observed. "And Wagner's themes could hardly have been anathema to them. What shock could possibly provoke them to abort the play when it was practically over?"

"Well, the very end was probably not Wagner's, but his posthumous collaborator Joseph Wright's work. That would appear to have been the general consensus of the Golden Dawn, anyway. Arneau told you about the last page in German of the libretto being cut out?"

"Yes, but not the English version of that scene on the facing page. And since The Golden Dawn left the English intact, then apparently the offending element *doesn't* translate back from the English into the German. Correct?"

"Well, enough comes through that is egregious enough. Do you wish to hear the story? I promise I won't sing."

"Sour notes and all please…I'm all ears."

# CHAPTER THIRTEEN:
## What The Golden Dawn Saw

"The Ordeal is the story of a beautiful princess of Camelot named Lita Clerval. Wright cast his mistress in the lead, by the way, a mezzo-soprano named Odette de Lyss. Anyway, Lita Clerval's lover was a knight who died in battle in search of the Holy Grail. He comes to her in a vision and tells her not to mourn him: he is in eternal bliss in Monsalvant, the paradise of the grail company.

"She wants to join him there, so she bobs her luxurious, long, golden hair in denouncement of worldly vanity and passes herself off as a knight to follow the path that will ultimately lead her to Monsalvant and reunion with her lover.

"After a series of adventures, she comes at last to the gateway through which she can see Monsalvant in the distance, this beautiful castle. As she eagerly approaches the gate, a hermit suddenly appears, played by Joseph Wright himself, by the way, and says, 'Beware the Dweller on the Threshold! You're not ready to face it; despite your great deeds, you are still imperfect in fear and desire. Come under my tutelage that you may mortify flesh and blood, love and fear. For the threshold is also an altar where the final sacrifice is made before you pass through the gate to Monsalvant.'

"And so Lita goes on a twelve day fast during which she wears nothing but chain mail against her bare skin and drinks nothing but bile. And on the twelfth day when the hermit tells her that her flesh is mortified by this ordeal, she starts out to make the final sacrifice to join her lover. She returns to the gateway accompanied by the hermit to find on the threshold a covered altar. And there's something on the altar under that covering.

"Now, at this point, for some reason, the members of the Golden Dawn are becoming uncomfortable. They look at the libretto, and back at the stage, and nothing's changed, but it's suddenly like they're reading and watching a very different opera than the one they started.

"A lizard-like woman appears and perches on the draped figure. She looks at Lita and laughs and skitters off the altar, drawing the covering away with her, and it reveals a human skeleton...that of Lita's dead lover.

"And now the hermit is laughing, too, because *he,* not the lizard woman, is the Dweller on the Threshold. During his time with Lita he's got her number. She fears that passing beyond the flesh could never *really* be the key to reunion with her lover in eternal Monsalvant. Annihilation of their bodies? Of carnal desire? How, then, can they love each other?

"The lizard woman is Lita herself. Or the externalization of that secret part of her that has not let go of her fleshly lust. The part that has now betrayed her. It's the inverse of *The Victors*, where the lovers denounce their passion each for the other to join Buddha's path to self-denial.

"In the English translation we're left with, the Dweller on the Threshold, who is being played by Wright himself, remember, cries out, 'Rise! Rise! Walker after death! Contend with God in the earth!' which, in the restored German is *'Erhebe ich! Erhebe ich! Aptrganger! Kampfer mit Gott in der erde.'* 'Earth' in this context simply means 'ground,' as in 'grave.' And the skeleton, at this point, *begins to move!*

"The Dweller on the Threshold is attempting to resurrect Lita's lover and bind them both in maya. He's saying, 'Struggle against God to rise from the dead and return to corporal life.' 'Aptrganger' means 'after goer' or 'walker' as in 'walks after death.'

"And Lita mounts the altar and wrenches at the skeleton, like she's trying to resuscitate him! She symbolically embraces the lower self, a mutable existence of decay, as superior to the immutable one in which her id is eternally annihilated. The Dweller of the Threshold triumphs! It's all very anti-Wagner, let alone Buddha. So, this ending must be Wright's work.

"You see, he and his mistress had recently lost a bid for leadership in the inner circle of the Golden Dawn. Somehow, they were planning on getting back at them with this final scene, but the Golden Dawn managed to cut them off in time."

Ravenwood looked at the tarot cards on Fort's desk. "*The Ordeal*'s ending seems to parallel the relationship of the first, second, and twelfth tarot cards, doesn't it? The hermit and Lita come to a gateway where a skeleton rises to life just as the Jannes and the Angel join at the gate where Yttle Elumi rises from his funeral bier."

"You're suggesting the end of this opera is much older than *The Ordeal* and that Joseph Wright had some knowledge of this very esoteric Major Arcana?"

"I am. And I'll tell you something else, Fort. The opera's truncation and expurgation may have left things unresolved, but I think they're about to be. And I don't mean on stage or in a movie. I believe this time it's happening for real."

Fort's eyes widened. "How can that be?"

"I saw this skeleton they're using in Arneau's movie. It's ancient. The production borrowed an archaeological find. There's a prophecy that Yttle Elumi would surface in the Indian Ocean. Some expedition must have dredged him up. But he's not alive again. Not yet. But with his bones headed for a gate they've built on the Pathe lot, his cult must have access, or are about to have, to all they need to usher him into the land of the living. Maybe even that uncut libretto you mentioned to Arneau. Perhaps what was lost in translation is the spell to raise Yttle Elumi."

Ravenwood slowly shook his head. "His resurrection represents a threat we cannot allow to be realized. The problem is we still know practically nothing about him...not even his name."

He snapped his fingers. "Fort! Have you actually read a copy of *The Ordeal*'s libretto?"

"It was expurgated, but yes."

Where did you get it?"

"From the same person who gave me the details of the performance: Sally Chesney-Waite. She's part of the British colony here in Hollywood. She was active on the English stage and was part of the Order of the Golden Dawn."

"I understand William Desmond Taylor's background was similar. Did she know him?"

"Yes, she did. In fact, they reconnected here in LA."

"Do you think she might talk with me about him if she knew Taylor's murder case has been reopened? Other lives are at stake, and I need to know everything she knows about him, including any past associates he may have had in Hollywood who are still active in the occult."

"I can't imagine why she wouldn't want to have a part in all this drama. Just the opposite; you'll understand when you meet Sally."

"I just hope my other potential ally responds to my overtures with such alacrity."

"'*Other*?' Who do you have in mind?"

"There's a secret society that has existed for millennia to exterminate the Yttle Elumi cult. One of its members has followed me from the East Coast because he thinks I'm one of them. He intends to murder me."

"Don't you think you ought to alert the police?"

"No. I want him to come to me. If I can convince him we're on the same side, then perhaps the entire anti-Yttle Elumi league can be mobilized on our behalf. Who knows the numbers we might need to fight his cult?"

Fort let out a quick burst of breath, shook his head, and said, "That's taking an awfully big risk, Ravenwood."

"I have little choice. Like I said, Yttle Elumi's followers could have all they need to resurrect him."

"What?"

"Except the Angel to join with the Jannes. Not if she's the actress playing Lita who's a blonde just like the woman on 'the Empress' card. It's a possibility I can't ignore, for her safety if nothing else. Do you think Carl Laemmle will mind if I use your phone to halt a rival studio's production?" Ravenwood asked, gathering up the tarot cards and returning them to their metal carrying case.

"Please, feel free to use the phone on Uncle Carl's nickel."

Ravenwood snatched up the receiver and began to dial.

"But," Fort said, "you *have* considered someone in the production is a plant for the Yttle Elumi cult?"

"And with this call I'm risking tipping them off that I'm wise to their scheme? Of course. But if I can connect directly with Hank Arneau..."

Arneau's office phone rang continuously while Ravenwood drummed his fingertips on Fort's desk. Finally, he hung up. "He's apparently left for the day, and it's too chancy to leave a message. I'll try his penthouse number."

Neither was he there, but out with Miss D'Arromanches for the evening. Ravenwood stressed to Arneau's butler the importance of Arneau not letting Anne out of his sight. "Tell him not to try and reach me at the Roosevelt," he added. "I'll explain when I call him back."

*Keep her close, Hank,* Ravenwood thought as he hung up. Then he realized Hank Arneau may have already sent him further instructions; if so, they would be at the Roosevelt, where his would-be assassin may well be watching for him. He would have to risk this person picking up his trail and following him to what he had hoped would be a safe haven.

Well, hadn't he said he needed to make contact and convince him they were on the same side?

"What is it?" Fort asked after a few moments.

"I'm going to have to find a hotel. Get in touch with your friend, uhm, Sally --?"

"Chesney-Waite."

"Right. Do you have a card that has your phone numbers? So I can reach you?"

"Certainly. Here."

"I'll call you as soon as I'm settled to see what you've been able to set up," Ravenwood said, already heading out the door—steel tarot case in one hand, umbrella in the other. The automobile which had driven him to Fort's office now returned him to Universal's front gate.

The taxi was still waiting as agreed. Within fifteen minutes it was in front of the Roosevelt. Once again telling the cabby to keep the meter running, Ravenwood, carrying the briefcase with him, ducked inside the Roosevelt. Wishing to keep up the appearance that he was staying here, he took the room key and asked if he had any messages.

"Yes, sir. I was just about to hand you this." Ravenwood took the offered piece of hotel stationary and read:

*Meet me at the* Pig n' Whistle *next door to Grauman's Egyptian theater. 8:00 p.m. Bring the tarot deck.*

"Can you describe who gave this to you?" Ravenwood asked the clerk.

"The clerk on the previous shift wrote it down. That's all I know. I'm sorry, sir."

"All right, then. Thank you."

*So,* he thought, *apparently these cards have more significance regarding Yttle Elumi's resurrection than we've suspected. But is this note from my would-be assassin or the Jannes himself?* Watching for anyone who might be watching him, he returned to the cab.

"Where to now, sir?" asked the cabby, who was enjoying a very good day indeed.

"I think I'd rather like another tour up that hill we took earlier."

"*Again?* Not that I'm complaining about the fare, sir. But there's more to Hollywood. It's already twilight. If you'd like to see something different..."

"Once more to Whitley Heights, my good fellow, before we lose the light."

Ravenwood kept his eyes trained on the rearview mirror during that steep climb to see if he was being trailed.

Once again, he was not.

Still, he was taking no chances. He asked the cabby to take him out of Hollywood by the most out of the way route, and also for the recommendation of a hotel with a suite with a private elevator.

"But you're staying back at...oh. I get you. There's a tomato involved. The Biltmore should have at least one suite with a private elevator."

"To the Biltmore, then, sir, by the most circuitous route possible."

They arrived after dark. Stepping under a high, Moorish sculpted ceiling flecked with twenty-four-carat gold, Ravenwood paused by the lobby's marble fountain. Before him, twin stairways converged from either side to form an archway atop which was a large doorway of Spanish Baroque revival bronze. Its pendant astrological clock read 7:15. He was beginning to push his rendezvous.

A suite of the type Ravenwood required was indeed currently available. A valet removed his luggage and clothing bags from the cab and dollied them through the large lobby, but Ravenwood was careful to keep the steel briefcase on his person at all times.

He realized simply ducking out of the Roosevelt might prove insufficient to dodge an assault. Perhaps he had ceased to be followed because the anti-Yttle Elumi league already had multiple assassins undercover as staff at every hotel in Los Angeles and its surrounding areas. In fact, with the stakes so high, both pro and anti Yttle Elumi secret societies might have posted agents everywhere with a room to rent. But at least here, with a single, private elevator entrance to his room, he could see them coming. He tipped the valet at the elevator's gate and took the ride up solo.

He had been debating on what to do with the tarot cards until he had ascertained this mysterious individual's intent. His or her insistence that Ravenwood bring the cards seemed like an attempt at reverse psychology so that he would leave the cards "secure" in the hotel vault. But he didn't trust any hotel's safe as impenetrable to those who coveted this Major Arcana. Best to keep the cards with him.

After hanging up his clothes, Ravenwood removed his coat and checked the pistol holstered on his left shoulder.

*Just in case verbal negotiations break down.*

He slipped his coat back on, tucked his umbrella under his unholstered arm, took up the metal briefcase, and left for his rendezvous at the *Pig N' Whistle*.

# CHAPTER FOURTEEN:
## *Wrath of the Calf!*

Ravenwood arrived at the *Pig n' Whistle* a few minutes before eight and took a moment to survey the restaurant's famous neighbor, Sid Grauman's *Egyptian Theater*. Over the entrance to the movie palace's 150-foot long courtyard, the marquee read:

BUSTER KEATON IN *FREE AND EASY* WITH ANITA PAGE PLUS *HEAD OVER HEELS* WITH MABEL NORMAND (R.I.P) ADDED SUBJECTS FEATURING HAL ROACH'S OUR GANG   AND *THE FATAL WARNING* EPISODE THREE: *THE CRASH OF DOOM*  TWO SHOWS 6:00  8:00

The east side of the courtyard was lined with store fronts, each with its own Arabic awning. These had all closed for the night. At the far end of the courtyard was the theater with its façade of twenty-five foot high Egyptian columns. The roof, incongruously, was Hispanic pan style. Ravenwood noticed what looked, in the dark, like a large dog sitting on its haunches up there, perfectly still. Some sort of decorative statue he thought, shrugged, then stepped over to the *Pig N' Whistle*. He opened one of its glass doors and stood under the restaurant's high ceiling with its exposed beams of ornate woodwork.

He had to dodge and dart through couples dancing over the checkered floor to a phonograph recording of *The New Yorkers* by Red Nichols and his Five Pennies. The music issued from a state of the art Audiophone, a large wooden cabinet with two modestly-sized round speakers on either side of the enclosed turntable.

Ravenwood checked his wristwatch as he sat down at one of the restaurant's small tables that had been pushed back to clear the dance floor: eight o'clock sharp. He looked over the long polished bar that ran along the wall to his right as he set the steel briefcase on the table before him. Each of the bar's high-back wooden chairs was filled. No one sitting there expressed any interest in his arrival. He drummed his fingers on each side of the briefcase.

He had, however, drawn the attention of the barkeeper who finished wiping up the counter, then walked over and nodded at the briefcase. "Your name Ravenwood?"

Ravenwood's drumming ceased, and he grasped his carrying case by its sides. "I am Ravenwood," he said, his chameleon eyes changing, one blue and the other gray as the steel he touched.

"I was told to look for a well dressed guy with a metal briefcase," the barkeep said. "Probably an umbrella, too, whether it looked like rain or not. The guy you're waiting for said he'd meet you in front of the *Egyptian*. He said he was taking in the six o'clock show and was going to stick around and watch the *Our Gang* short again when they reran it for the eight o'clock. Said he's a sucker for Hal Roach's rascals. Box office is closed by now, but it's just a one-reeler, you know. You won't be standing out there long. He promised." The barkeep jerked his head toward a side door. "That door opens right on the *Egyptian*'s courtyard."

Ravenwood suddenly tasted the same metallic bitterness he had on the airplane and he flashed psychically on the figure he had seen on the theater's roof.

He licked his lips and swallowed. "What did this person look like?"

"Stetson. Business suit. Briefcase; not metal, though. Movie producer or wanting to look like one. We see that type walk through the door fifty times a day here."

"I see. Thank you, sir."

"No problem," the barkeep said, pulling a cloth from his front shirt pocket and wiping up a circle of moisture left by the glass of the table's previous occupant. As he started to leave, he stopped and turned around. "Oh, yeah, there was one more thing he asked me to do...." Ravenwood, however, was in a meditative state that shut out the sound around him, even that of his own fingers tapping again on the side of the metal briefcase.

The barkeep shrugged and began making his way over to the Audiophone.

Ravenwood smiled. *All right. Whoever you are. Time we got better acquainted.*

As he rose, *The New Yorkers* came to an end. He did not notice the barkeeper slide a nickel into the Audiophone and set off the carousel-type machinery encased in the bottom of its cabinet. A phonograph recording of *Get Happy* came up, the record needle connected with the spinning platter, and out blasted the Victor Orchestra conducted by Nat Shilkret. The giddily receptive couples began dancing again as the male chorus enthused, *"We're going to the promised land..."*

Briefcase handle grasped firmly in his fist, Ravenwood used his umbrella in the fashion of a cane and began navigating his way across the floor.

*"...It's oh so, peaceful on the other side..."*

The *Pig N' Whistle's* door closed behind Ravenwood, the sounds of music and stomping feet thrumming against it. He began making his way toward the movie theater, feeling the expanse of the darkened, empty court, and always keeping his eyes trained on the statuary on the roof. Ravenwood stopped exactly at the spot where, if toppled, it would strike him.

The large, heavy figure tipped forward, just as Ravenwood had foreseen. On cue, he stepped back easily to safety. The statue struck the pavement, the ringing of metal reverberating down the court. Ravenwood searched the roof for any trace of movement. Unclear whether who had just tried to crush him was in the "for" or "against" camp concerning Yttle Elumi, he still couldn't afford to let the opportunity slip if it was the latter.

"Hello up there!" he shouted. "What happened at the *Club Samedi* was all a misunderstanding. I assure you, I wish to stop the return of Yttle Elumi as much as you! We should be working together!"

Only silence from the roof.

On the pavement before him, a grating of metal.

Ravenwood's eyes widened.

The metallic figure the size of a large dog was a primitive, pagan representation of a bull with an upright disc etched with Egyptian hieroglyphs between its horns *and it was rising to all fours*, tossing its head creakily from side to side. The Taurusparion scraped a forepaw on the courtyard pavement, striking sparks and thrust forward lowered horns aimed for Ravenwood.

He sprang aside, just avoiding an impaling. The bull was halfway down the courtyard before its metal paws regained traction, spraying sparks in a welder's arc as it rounded itself back toward him.

Ravenwood quickly put the theater façade of twenty-five foot columns between him and the raging Taurusparion and began tugging and beating on one locked theater door after the other, only to find the lobby apparently deserted.

He looked over his shoulder to see the metal bull pawing, tossing its head and the projectile on legs fired itself at him again.

*It would be like being struck full on by a cannon ball with horns.*

He began dodging from one column of the *Egyptian*'s façade to the other, throwing off the Taurusparion's focus and forcing it to lose its lethal momentum. It pursued him now in a series of staggered rushes as he emerged from behind one side of a pillar to draw its aim, then darted from the other side to take shelter behind yet another column.

Ravenwood dropped his umbrella. His sword, as well as his shoulder-holstered pistol, was useless. His only weapon was the steel briefcase in his hand. With it, he might cripple the thing. He doubted he could knock a leg off, but if he could bend it sufficiently, this alchemically enlivened automaton would be incapable of charging.

Now it was anticipating where he would momentarily be vulnerable when he crossed the spaces between pillars. It charged and he leapt back, again taking shelter behind the column he had just left. Clearly, this strategy was played out. And to achieve what he wished, he was going to have to provoke the Taurusparion into a lengthy charge.

He sprinted from behind the column, the 150 feet of the courtyard stretching before him to the sidewalk of Hollywood Boulevard.

Immediately, the Taurusparion was after him. Could he make the street? No one was loitering on the sidewalk just ahead, but he would risk injury to others should it follow him down Hollywood Boulevard. Head for the *Pig N' Whistle*? It'd crush him against the door...flatten it...trample him...then turn loose on the crowded dance floor.

Now halfway up the courtyard, he dodged aside as he simultaneously drew back the steel briefcase in both hands.

The Taurusparion flew by him, carried by its momentum. Throwing all the power of his muscular arms and broad shoulders behind it, Ravenwood swung the steel briefcase at the metal bull's left foreleg, hoping to make it fold inward under the torso. Instead, he struck the automaton on its side, the force of the rebound sending him staggering back toward the theater.

A wave of numbness shot up his arms and into his fingers from the blow. Even as he sought to retain his grasp, the briefcase became heavier, its weight pulling him to the ground.

He struck the pavement hard on his knees. He had landed in execution position with his back to the Taurusparion. Ravenwood refused to yield his slipping grasp on the briefcase and was still struggling to rise when the blow to the back of his head came.

He flew forward across the courtyard, prostrate, arms spread wide, the metal briefcase bouncing away from his unfeeling fingers.

A moist heat oozed through his hair as flint sparks flew against a veil determined to settle over his eyes.

He managed to blink back that dimming veil long enough to see a well-dressed man step quickly out of one of the theater doors, grab up the metal briefcase, and walk past him and the now still Tarusparion, up the *Egyptian*'s courtyard, and onto Hollywood Boulevard.

Only now were people rushing out onto the court from the *Pig n' Whistle* and the *Egyptian*. The sound of combat that had unfolded in hardly two minutes had been drowned by the dancing music in the restaurant and the movie in the theater. Ravenwood managed to roll over on his back, eyes blinking, hearing voices.

"Somebody get a doc!"

"What happened?"

"Where did that thing come from?"

"...toppled over at last..."

" … left over from the premiere...DeMille's *Ten Commandments*..."

"...was there a wind?"

"...on the roof for decoration..."

"...up there for years..."

"...thought it...taken down by now ..."

"...the golden calf..."

His eyelids in feeble paroxysms, one last, futile protest against the dying light, Ravenwood lost consciousness.

# CHAPTER FIFTEEN:
## *A Princess of Arromanches*

*H*ank Arneau doesn't have enough tailored suits to cover what a boor he is.

So thought Anne D'Arromanches as she waited for Arneau to pick her up for a visit to the Metropolitan museum. She had spent an hour on her hair and judiciously applying make-up which she literally could not afford to waste, then choosing her outfit; not out of abundance but meagerness. She had finally decided on a double-breasted blouse with large buttons and a pleated skirt, all powder blue, with heels to match. The winning dress had the advantage of being the only one for which she had a matching purse.

*"...rounded itself back toward him."*

But now Hank was over an hour late. Only when it was almost closing time for the Met did he appear at her door in his coat, long white scarf, and top hat.

"What took you, Hank?" she said. "It took me hours to get ready, and when we get there we'll be lucky to have a whole fifteen minutes to..."

"Easy, Anne, easy. I had to take care of some business. Wrapping it up took longer than I expected."

"Could you possibly offer a more vague excuse, Hank?"

"I'll be specific then. I went to *The Club Samedi* for a meeting."

Anne arched her eyebrows. "Hank! If that's your idea of some sort of sly euphemism, and you're brazen and callous enough to tell me *that*'s why you're late for our date...well, then I'm not going *anywhere* with you!"

Hank held up his palms. "Anne, it's not like that at all. This was a business meeting ..."

"There was no *respectable* place you could have met?"

"Look, Anne. The *Club Samedi* wasn't my idea. I happen to prefer the *Cobalt Club*. But I had no choice of venue. And it *was* purely business..."

"*Funny* business...," Anne said, hand on her hip and looking away.

"There was *nothing* funny about it. Look, I'm truly sorry I'm late. You... you really look great, you know...

"Thank you," Anne said, still looking away.

"I'd be proud to have you on my arm. And I promise all will be more than made up for if you will still consent to accompany me to the Met tonight."

She turned her head back toward him and glared. "It's all but closing time now, Hank."

"We have plenty of time. Please, do me the honor, Anne."

Anne let out a heavy sigh. "Okay," she said, shaking her head in disbelief at her own, not Hank's, behavior. "You're exasperating, you know."

"But never dull," he said and grinned.

"I don't suppose you'd care to share what you've obviously cooked up," she said, as he held the passenger's side back door for her, and she slid inside.

"That would have the effect of rendering null and void the surprise, so... no." He rounded the car and joined her in the back seat, then tapped on the limousine's ceiling. "Drive on, Jenson."

Anne pursed her lips, drummed her freshly manicured nails on her knee, and elected to stare silently at the back of the chauffeur's head rather than look at Hank. But after a few minutes of this, she decided to at least try to be an adult and make conversation.

"Have you been in touch with your man, Ravenwood?" she asked, still staring straight ahead.

"I figured he could use some rest after his flight and making his contact. Don't worry about him," Arneau said. "He's a disciple of oriental philosophy, you know. Those types relish an opportunity to withdraw from the world. He has been well accommodated."

The limousine pulled up just short of closing time before the broad stone steps that led to the pillared porch of the Metropolitan Museum. No sooner had they reached the doors than a uniformed guard intercepted them: "Closing time, folks," he said.

"Everything's jake," Hank said. "I'm a friend of Rockefeller." He passed the guard a note, and the man immediately recognized the signature.

"Certainly, Mr. Arneau," he said. "You and your young lady take your time. I'll pass the word along."

"Thank you, my good man," Hank said and tipped his top hat at him.

"This is your surprise? An after-hours tour? *Alone*?" Anne asked as they stepped inside.

"Miss D'Arromanches, I assure you my intentions are honorable," he said as he led her by the hand to a fourteenth century statue of the Madonna and child from *Cernay-les-Reims*. "Here's something French and it was sculpted not too far from where your ancestors lived."

"It's beautiful," Anne said softly.

She envied it, this thing from a remote place and time, somehow still cherished under the current Modernist paradigm. She had often felt herself also out of time, but had yet to find anyone who would truly cherish her. Even her own mother had...

"Are you ready, Anne?" Arneau asked.

"I suppose," she said.

"Then follow me."

She sighed, and, holding her purse behind her back with both her hands, walked after him with the attitude of a duchess much put upon by the help.

Hank led her to a roped off corridor in the back, clearly marked "Do Not Enter." Hank unhooked the velvet cord and nodded for her to go forward. After reattaching the rope, he steered her down the long corridor that opened onto a large, enclosed loading dock redolent of oil and gasoline.

"Hank Arneau," Anne said as she regarded the deserted work area in which loomed detached truck trailers of cavernous depths, "I do not pretend to begin to understand you. You bring me to the Met, then drag me past priceless treasures of antiquity to show me a glorified garage."

"I assure you, Miss D'Arromanches, that this is nothing less than the V.I.P. tour." He led her over the concrete floor, Anne careful to guide her freshly polished heels around the smears of oil there.

A throaty grating rumble sounded from the other end of the loading dock. Both Anne's and Hank's heads turned in the direction of the largest; meanest German Shepherd Anne had ever seen. Anne's nails sank into Hank's upper arm, biting his flesh even through the thick fabric of his coat. She stepped behind him, wide-eyed as the growling dog began trotting towards them.

Hank looked for a weapon, a crowbar or hammer left lying around, and found none.

Now the dog charged. Arneau felt Anne lurch away from him.

He spoke in a commanding tone that welded her powder blue heels to the floor: "Anne, stay *right* where you *are*."

Hank could feel her quick breaths brushing the back of his neck as he allowed the dog to get within ten feet of them. Anne was near screaming when Hank locked eyes with the dog and shouted out:

"Beast! Be *quiet*!" The authority in his tone brought the dog to a stop as though he had encountered an unexpected wall. Its hair peeled up in bits on the back of its neck, and its threatening roar suddenly lowered into a subdued growl.

Hank's eyes never veered from direct contact with the Shepherd's. "*Be quiet!*" You are but a beast, a brute. Your spirit is broken! *Fear me!*"

Could Anne had seen his eyes, she, too, would have feared Hank Arneau; from them emanated something that struck the dog head-on like magnetic waves of force.

The dog suddenly yelped. And then, its head downcast but careful to keep eyeing Arneau, it shied away for a few feet, then turned and fled.

Hank took a deep breath, and grinning, turned to Anne. "He must have not gotten the memo," he said, jerking his thumb in the direction of the departed guard dog.

Anne's body slumped against his. She looked up at him. "Why do I feel like I'm the girl back in that movie serial when I'm with you?" she asked, looking up at him. "And who *are* you, Hank Arneau? How did you do that to that beast?"

"Knock around the orient for a while. You'll pick up some things. C'mon," he said. He took her hand and led her up the ramp and deep into the back of one of the detached truck trailers.

There a tarp covered something of great size. He flipped up the covering and exposed large cut blocks of stone. "C'mere. Touch it. Touch your past, Anne of Arromanches."

Stepping forward, Anne extended her hand and found the rock cool. "Is this from Arromanches?" she asked.

"This, no," Arneau said. "But you may have heard that the Met has purchased some land on the northern part of the island. These stones are from one of the medieval French monasteries being reassembled there,The Cloisters, they're going to call it. It'll be a few years before they have it all ready, but I didn't want you to have to wait. You said you would probably never get to France...well, here's France, and ancient France at that, brought to you."

Anne looked up at him. "Hank...," she began. There were tears shining in her eyes. "Why?"

"You've had a tough time. Probably felt sometimes like you didn't count, but you do, kid, believe me. Now, come with me. This has all been just a side trip, a little something extra. Let me show you why I *really* brought you here tonight."

He led her out of the truck trailer, down the ramp, onto the dock and back into the museum. Turning into a small hallway off the main rear corridor, he nodded at a room to the left. "There's something or you in there. Not to keep, mind you. Just to borrow for a few minutes tonight. Something that *is* from Arromanches. You'll, uh, want to shut the door behind you," he said, scratching his jaw.

Anne looked at him, a pleasant perplexity in her eyes. She slipped into the room, flipped on the light, and immediately clapped both hands over her mouth. "Oh, my," she said.

On a mannequin, very close to her size, was a gown: not a costume, but a real gown that would have been worn by a noble woman of Arromanches in the Middle Ages. It was white satin, embroidered with gold, its girdle studded with emeralds.

She fingered it gently, wondering for whom this garment was made so very long ago. She found it was as exquisite to the touch as to the eye. She saw that she had not yet closed the door, but before bringing it completely to, she smiled with her eyes at Hank through the crack.

Once she had put on the gown and was inspecting herself in the room's mirror, she decided to go for the full effect. She took the pins from her hair, shook her head, and sent a tumble of reddish gold over her shoulders to the small of her back.

She came out of the room with tentative steps, head tucked, looking up at Hank with hooded eyes.

"Miss D'Arromanches," he said, "your beauty is not of an age but for all time; if you'll pardon the paraphrase."

She spread the skirt out with her hands and smiled as she regarded it. "No apology needed. Thank you. I...I do feel like Beauty ..."

"Then what does that make me?" Hank asked with a crooked grin.

"I think I'll let you fill in that blank," Anne said with an arch of her brow. "But ...thank you, Hank. For a girl who's been hoping all night you wouldn't notice there's thread in my blouse that doesn't quite match the rest of the material... I'm just telling you *now*, so you'll know, how special you've made me feel. If just for a few minutes. But I suppose it's time to turn in my glass slippers, hmmm? I won't be long."

Hank called after her: "There'll still be a limousine out front when you're done; not a pumpkin. I promise."

Back in the dressing room, Anne looked in the mirror at herself in the gown one more time. She shook her head slowly from side to side. "No. Stop it," she said to the girl in the mirror. "*Stop* it, Anne D'Arromanches. You're *not* going to fall in love with Hank Arneau."

# CHAPTER SIXTEEN:
## Of The Coming of the White Lodge and the Call of Aunoch

*H*ere, *my son, time turns into space...*
Ravenwood opened his eyes on a cherry orchard. Blossoms floated in the air, and he could hear water rippling along at his feet. On the other side of this brook, between two trees, sat the Nameless One.

"Come to me, my son," the Nameless One said.

Ravenwood stepped over the water without hesitation, breathing deeply of the orchard's air and finding it sweet. The trees hummed from the milling of bees among the blossoms.

"You did it, didn't you?" he said to the Nameless One. "You brought me to the cherry orchards of your youth. Or...have I lost my marbles?"

The Nameless One smiled and produced a small cloth bag with a draw string. "If so, I have found them," he said. "Pee wees, steelies, aggies, and cat's eyes, I believe."

The Nameless One passed him the bag. Ravenwood took it, began to tug at its draw string, and immediately the Nameless One clasped a hand over Ravenwood's. "No, my son. You must neither see nor touch what is inside. Not until the moment is come. That moment you will know."

Ravenwood looked about the orchard again. "Did you bring me here from the *Egyptian Theater* courtyard? Because, with all due respect, your timing could have been a *little* better." He touched the back of his head, which he was surprised to find not sore at all.

"Only your consciousness and mine are met at the outer rim of Elyon. Your body is in a hospital bed. And mine is assumed to Aslem-Beth. Yes, 'twas the Seven Unseen by Men, the same I planned to approach through my dreaming mind, who took me corporally instead to them. Now listen to me, my son, and see with me the history of Yttle Elumi just as I received it from the Seven."

"Speak, my master."

"In the long ago, in the epoch of lost time, the earth's North Pole was verdant, lush, and the site of a happy civilization: Hyperborea, the seven ascending cities of the seven plateaus which rose as steps toward the polar lights. Through these cities' flagstone broadways, flanked by white colonnades, lumbered shaggy mastodons bearing the land's yield of precious stones and crops which were brought daily to market. Men looked down on these processions of abundance from the parapeted terraces of rose-veined marble towers and minarets connected at their highest reaches by arched bridges.

"Once the people of Hyperborea had lived under martial dominion. It was King Tor the Pitiless who used the vantage point of his domain on the highest plateau to conquer those beneath. For no city's wall could protect it when he loosed his catapults, hurling down his thunder stones from above.

"But when the hour of doom came upon Hyperborea, there were none with living memory of that dark time, or a time when the White Lodge, the dwelling of the source of Hyperborea's subsequent felicities, had not set at the edge of the highest plateau; none, that is, save one."

"Yttle Elumi," Ravenwood said.

"He was not always 'Yttle,' not always 'the Enemy,' my son. No, he was once the chief agent of the White Lodge. With the White Lodge, his fate was bound and is so bound to this day, for Yttle Elumi forged his own bonds.

"What is this White Lodge, Nameless One?"

The old man smiled slightly. "I will show you. We are at the outer rim of Elyon where all time simultaneously exists. From here, should we wish, we might, as your Western philosopher Boethius has said, 'see at once, in a single glance, all things that are, or were, or are to come in the eternal present.'

As the Nameless One spoke, the orchid's boughs bent with a great wind, and blossoms blew loose and swarmed in a column about Ravenwood, as though he were being wrapped in a pale vermilion carpet, a magic one to transport him to another place. Ravenwood threw his arm over his eyes. And when he lowered it as the wind ceased and the blossoms unswathed him, he saw now that he and the Nameless One stood on a plateau where the blossoms fell to the ground and faded like pink dew on the early spring grass.

Rising far above them, as far as they could see before a dense cloud enveloped its highest reaches, the mountain was snow riddled with gray: the exposed crooked ridges of granite running along its sides. The snow blushed in patches of rose and blue with the coming of dawn. "It's like a Maxfield Parish painting," Ravenwood said. One hundred feet before it met the plateau, the mountain's side was exposed damp stone from the eternal trickling of the melting at the snow line.

"The men of Hyperborea long believed that all that was divine or called god was remote beyond reach and dwelt among their mountain's mist shrouded peak of ice and snow. From there issued, on the mountain's other side, the Ifing, a mighty torrent of a waterfall which flowed over and watered each plateau.

"We are in the days of King Oordin, Tor's heir-son, on Hyperborea's highest plateau. The long polar night is just ending. Look above, my son, for something wonderful is about to happen..."

As Ravenwood craned his neck upward, a perfect marble cube, twenty-one stories high with a single entrance of thirty foot tall gates of gold, cleaved the heavy mists that hid the mountain peak above and slowly descended, riding gravity, coming to rest on the western edge of the seventh plateau.

"The White Lodge," Ravenwood said, his voice small.

"Let us move closer in space and time...after this event has been reported," the Nameless One said, and in an instant they were surrounded by a crowd of people in robes as well as martial attire such as hauberks, leather jerkins, armor, and helmets. Those wearing the latter bore broad swords and battle axes.

"These Hyperboreans cannot see us, for all these things we shall behold are done and neither can be added to nor subtracted from," the Nameless One said.

Cries flew up from the crowd as the sustained bourdon note of warning from deep feline throats and the sound of the speedily turning of great chariot wheels arose among them. The people parted in a panic, and, holding the reigns of two sabretooth tigers the size of horses, King Oordin drove his chariot forward. He slowed the great cats and brought them to a halt a good fifteen feet away from the Lodge.

Dismounting his chariot he gave a command, and both sabretooths dropped to the ground on their bellies, paws stretched out before them. Oordin patted the head of one of them in passing, his eyes trained on the Lodge. As soon as he had removed his hand, the sabretooth he had petted immediately began a worried cycle of licking her paw and grooming with it the hair Oordin's touch had disturbed.

Oordin was lanky and muscular with long blond hair and beard, wearing a black leather jerkin that fell to his knees. Over the jerkin was a hauberk of silver chain and his feet were clad in boots of mammoth fur. His bare limbs displayed various and sundry ugly scars, and being on the battlefield under the unrelenting sun of Arctic daylight had prematurely wrinkled him about the eyes and browned his skin.

He swaggered as arrogantly as ever as he approached this wonder descended from the unbreachable realm above, and his band fell in behind him. Hand at the hilt of his sheathed broad sword, he examined the gold gates which were carved as two giant winged bulls with crowned human heads. Facing with an austere countenance those who would enter, they rested on their haunches.

Swiftly, the gates swung outward on their own, bringing the sabretooths back to their feet, only to cringe back, planting their forepaws in the ground and bending to raise their haunches as bits of their fur dropped from them. Oordin and his band fell back. When nothing emerged and he commanded they enter the Lodge with him, the fear of the king's men was obvious, but just as obviously they feared more to fail to obey.

"Come, my son," the Nameless One said, and he and Ravenwood followed.

Inside, a single, vast chamber of alabaster hue was empty except for five pillars of white marble on either side reaching from floor to ceiling.

"So men first saw the ten Assyur," said the Nameless One. But nowhere was there inscription in runes or words to explain the descension of the White Lodge.

Then one of Oordin's men spoke and Ravenwood was surprised that he could understand him: "Remember, O king, that in the days of your father Tor, the seer Vanr spoke of a Lodge neither hewn by human hands, nor made for the glory of the kings. To it would the people gather, not to the king or his descendants, and he leveled this very spot for its coming. Then Tor came forth in his chariot pulled by sabretooth tigers. And he loosed his great cats on Vanr, and they slew him where this Lodge rests. Today is Vanr the prophet vindicated before the house of Tor."

Oordin drew his sword at this reproof of his lineage, and Ravenwood lurched forward before the touch on his arm by the Nameless One reminded him that "nothing could be neither added to nor subtracted from" what they observed.

"This man did not speak this of himself," the Nameless One said, "but of the Effulgence who even now is filling the White Lodge."

"It feels like the air pressure is dropping in seconds, "Ravenwood said, and a dread crept over him.

"Quickly my son let us take our leave for even the shadow of the Effulgence is holy, and we are here unbidden."

Oordin and all with him also sensed the gathering presence; this alone spared the life of the soldier who had spoken as they all fled the Lodge.

The gold gates closed behind them, and Ravenwood realized they had moved through time as well as space again, for, to judge by their weary appearances, the king and his men had been keeping vigil outside the Lodge for hours. At last, the gates again flew open. In tentative steps, Oordin and his men moved forward to enter, but the Nameless One led Ravenwood past them, and they went inside first. "There is nothing to fear now, my son," he said.

"Nothing's changed," Ravenwood began. "No, wait." He approached one pillar and saw that it, as now did each Assyur, bore a distinct glyph. "What do these mean, father?" he asked.

"None could read the glyphs which were written on the pillars, and all Hyperborea was troubled, and King Oordin not the least," the Nameless One said as he led Ravenwood back outside.

"So Oordin inquired of the Lodge who might understand what was written inside, and he cast lots before its gates, one for each province of Hyperborea. And the lot fell on the province where the least literate of their people dwelt in huts of mud and straw.

"To this province came the king, and the lots that had been thrown before the White Lodge's gate were now cast on the heads of each family.

And a family of herdsmen was chosen. And when the lots were cast on this family, the chosen was the oldest, who was lame of foot. He leaned on a staff and could not defend his father's flocks against the wild sabretooth cats that in those days prowled the utter north. So he lived among the people while his brothers were in the field.

"Auroch was the name he was given by his father in bitterness when he saw his first born son's deformed foot while the babe yet nursed on his mother's breast. During her lifetime, she was ever kind and gentle to her child, but taught him not to pity himself but others of their misfortunes. So Auroch gave no thought to the lameness of his foot, but ministered to those who suffered both more and less than he.

"When the lot fell upon him, he paled with fear, for Auroch could neither read nor write in runes, nor the common tongue. He wished nothing more than to escape from the company whose eyes now all fell upon him. But King Oordin told him he would either consent or be taken by force to the White Lodge. Trembling, Auroch submitted to the will of the king.

"Days have passed now, my son. Behold. Auroch comes limping on his staff before the closed gates of the White Lodge."

Ravenwood and the Nameless One now stood among a greater multitude than had assembled before at the White Lodge. They all parted for the limping young man. The gates of the Lodge swung open from inside, and when Auroch stepped on the threshold, a blaze of white light surged forward to seize him.

The crowd screamed. Immediately the blaze receded, and they beheld the Lodge filled with a diamond brilliance at the heart of which shimmered an emerald light, an emerald so vivid that it made that of the polar lights forever pallid by comparison to those who had seen both. From a thick cloud which hung in the Lodge's vaulted ceiling, burning coals hailed and scattered upon the threshold while cinders swarmed as angry hornets in the luminance. From the Lodge's deepest reaches came the sounds of trumpets calling and answering in the distance, as when the armies of Hyperborea went to battle on the plains.

"The people fear attack," the Nameless One said. "Yes, even Oordin pales on his armored horse while he holds his army ready to join in battle, but he knows that already he has looked upon his doom."

Then the gates closed on Auroch.

"It is now the fifth day since Auroch entered the Lodge," the Nameless One said, and Ravenwood noticed the crowd had suddenly thinned considerably. Among those that had remained until now he heard grumbling about also leaving and whispers that Auroch had certainly been consumed as a sacrifice and would not be seen again. Others murmured that he hid inside, having learned nothing, and fearing to come out and face Oordin.

"These fools do not understand," the Nameless One said. "But mark how King Oordin keeps a stony vigilance, though his inward man still trembles at the wrath revealed when the gates of gold stood open. He knows, had those gates not shut when they did, all Hyperborea would have been consumed. And Auroch's fate he ponders."

Then the gold gates flew open. The horses reared and Oordin, who had been leaning on his spear, raised it, ready to thrust it through the air, but the Effulgence they saw no more; rather a figure no longer lame but standing straight and without a staff. And there was beauty in his face, and polar light scintillated on his forehead like an anointing.

"Ah," the Nameless One said. "It is now the seventh day. And Auroch begins to teach the people the meaning of the glyphs just as he has received them. In sum, that if the people of Hyperborea should always love the Effulgence who chose to show his favor by lodging with them, and should each esteem their fellow before themselves, henceforth there would be no premature death among them, nor would their cattle fail to deliver their calves or a horse lose a foal. And the cycle of sowing and harvesting would remain unbroken.

"Every year they should show their love by obeying the Effulgence and gathering at the White Lodge to rehearse the glyphs as a people, bringing a choice portion of their abundance. This offering is to provide for the poor in the coming year and also he who now stands before them: he who was no longer Auroch, but Aurochel, hearer and speaker of the divine."

Ravenwood watched King Oordin's expression as he heard these words and saw Auroch no longer lame but whole, and the glory of the Effulgence lingering on his face.

"He is thinking of the wrath on whose cusp he and his nation has tottered," the Nameless One said. "And as he considers this grace they have received in its stead, the glyphs of the Assyur are burning into the king's heart. Behold!'

Before his people, Oordin halved his spear across his thigh, and bowed before the gates of the White Lodge.

"Henceforth, I will no longer teach my subjects fear, but I will love them and learn mercy," the king said.

The Nameless One nodded at the crowd. "And not only Oordin, but all those of Hyperborea who heard the words of Aurochel that day felt the glyphs that were burned into the stone columns of the Lodge burn within them as well."

# CHAPTER SEVENTEEN:
## Of the Rise and Fall of Aurochel

Aurochel then called to whomever would come and spread among all Hyperborea what the Effulgence had written. Ravenwood moved aside, forgetting he was among shadows as a large group of women came forward, women in whom the glyphs had burned at Aurochel's words. These Aurochel pronounced Angels of the Presence.

"They will spring like harts throughout the seven plateaus of Hyperborea," the Nameless One said, "taking up tambourines and making sounds of joy as they pass through the seven great cities. And the people of Hyperborea will receive and hear them gladly.

"Yearly, the Hyperboreans did gather as had been ordained. Aurochel would enter the White Lodge and upon his radiant emergence, the glyphs were rehearsed. And, of a truth, neither man nor woman failed to live to a ripe age, and their flocks and fields were fruitful and without fail. The Hyperboreans loved the Effulgence and each other, and, for generation upon generation, they knew peace.

"As for Aurochel, he was blessed with an extension of days far beyond the allotted mortal span of his fellow Hyperboreans. For Aurochel alone partook directly of the Presence in the White Lodge. Yet he remained mortal.

"Then a generation arose that could not remember a time without the White Lodge or Aurochel or peace and prosperity. And since the Effulgence was no more seen, only the glimmering on the brow of Aurochel when he came from the Lodge, the multitude at the yearly gathering began to say among themselves, 'He is like a god.'

"When this word reached Aurochel he rebuked the people. Yet inwardly he took pleasure at this flattery, for age at last had begun its wear on his body, and the old deformity was returning to his foot. But the saying of the people confirmed he had successfully concealed this, for who with a limp had ever been called a god?

"Still, he knew the day must come when he could neither enter nor exit the Lodge without leaning on his old staff, and he contemplated this time with shame. Finally, when he was no longer able, a successor would be appointed by the Effulgence to enter the White Lodge and rehearse the glyphs before the people. Old and bent, he would suffer the humiliation of watching as another, young and handsome, came forth from the White Lodge with the glow of the Effulgence upon *his* face.

"Thus did Aurochel purpose that none should ever possess the glyphs but him.

"On a certain day, he entered the White Lodge before the appointed time, in the absence of the Effulgence, bearing a chisel and hammer. And from the ten pillars he cut away the glyphs and fashioned ten stone rings for himself. From these rings he felt a power grow in himself, for the glyph of each ring was the finger work of the Effulgence, and their stone was no longer unliving mineral but a quickening thing, and immediately his foot was straightened.

"Invigorated with power, Aurochel haughtily displayed them on his fingers before the people and declared *he* now bore the glyphs where he would. Henceforth they should assemble to where he would gather them, for where he was, *there* was the White Lodge.

"It is said the Effulgence suffered these things and all that would follow to try the hearts of the people of Hyperborea.

"And on the appointed day the next year, the Effulgence filled the White Lodge as before. But only the Angels of the Presence attended where they should. Look, my son: the rest of the people stray to Aurochel."

Now the Nameless One and Ravenwood stood among a crowd which looked up eagerly at Aurochel where he had taken his place on a mountain outcropping that made a natural elevated platform. Then he began to read the glyphs on his fingers as *he* would.

" For these," he told them, " are not etched in stone as they appear, but are living things. And these oracles, even these, are themselves ruled by a greater law, that all that would survive must ever change forward."

The Hyperboreans cheered as one. "This generation, my son," said the Nameless One, "takes as their entitlement the blessings of the Effulgence and so receive these new oracles gladly. But, look…"

The Angels of the Presence, in number one hundred and fifty, were marching into Aurochel's assembly. Standing as a group, they looked up at Aurochel. Then their leader, Ariastella, stepped forward and said:

" Thus says the Effulgence of the White Lodge, 'When you were humble in your own eyes, and knew you were weak, yet ministered to the needs of others instead of seeking your own things, I brought you into the White Lodge. Whole I made you, not you yourself, and gave you days extended beyond your fellow Hyperboreans because you never said in your heart, 'It is because I am better than they.' But now you esteem yourself higher than you ought, and have become a thief and usurper.

"Therefore, so says the Effulgence: 'No more are you 'Aurochel,' hearer and speaker of the Divine. Henceforth, your name is 'Maelgaltyr' because you pervert my glyphs according to your own will and the will of the people."

But Maelgaltyr said, 'Who knows but this 'word' from the Effulgence is naught but what you discussed among yourselves? Perhaps you tire of being my handmaidens and wish to usurp my place. The Effulgence does not shine upon you as it did whenever *I* came out from the Presence before the people. How is it that you speak for it as though *you* now possess its oracles?'

And Ariastella, Star Song, who shone brightest of the women of the Presence, said, "How might we claim to possess the oracles of the Effulgence when you have taken the glyphs into your own hands that are less than a miser's, since you hoard that for which you have not toiled?"

Then Maelgaltyr rose up and ordered the crowd to seize the Angels of the Presence. Ravenwood caught himself as he lunged to intercept those who would grab the Angels closest to him.

"Father, make me solid. Allow me to help stop this miscarriage of justice."

"The miscarriage is *done*, my son," the Nameless One said, firmly grasping his stepson's arm. "But fifty escaped, including Ariastella. The rest, Maelgaltyr, perverter of the glyphs, he who had been Aurochel the kind, threw in a dungeon save one. Listen as he dispatches his messengers to reach King Freyr, great-grand son of King Oordin, before the Angels might:

"Warn him that the women of the Presence have openly challenged my own authority before the people," said Maelgaltyr, "and they will not think the king's throne beyond them. Say I will come hastily to him with my counsel on this matter."

Immediately the Nameless One brought them to the throne room of

King Freyr's palace where Maelgaltyr stood privately with the king. He told him the Angels of the Presence had tried to seize control of the White Lodge, and how, being forewarned by the Effulgence of their mutiny, he had chiseled the glyphs from the pillars and placed them on his hands to safeguard the oracles.

"But one I have secretly brought for interrogation, my king. I have her hidden in the inner council chamber where we must needs retire. Unfortunately, we cannot speak further openly for even those of your own palace cannot be trusted to know what is said or what our counsel will be, for among them are kin to Ariastella, who leads the Angels in their revolt."

"And because Maelgaltyr still appeared to King Freyr as Aurochel, fair of appearance and speech," said the Nameless One, "he went with him into the inner chamber. And there Maelgaltyr drew the short sword he had concealed on his person, and he thrust through the trusting Freyr, slaying him. He splattered the woman of the Presence with the king's gore which ran down the walls. Then he unsheathed the king's own sword and slew her.

Ravenwood clinched his eyes closed against the cries of Maelgaltyr for aid. "He's going to blame the woman for the murder, isn't he? And he's going to get away with it. Like you said: 'it is already done.'"

"When the guards arrive," the Nameless One said, "Maelgaltyr will say that as he counseled the King, this woman of the Presence took them by surprise and slew the king with her short sword. But before she escaped, he took up the king's blade against her. 'Can there be any doubt that this Angel was dispatched by Ariastella, who has come in and out of the palace freely and is so trusted she has learned the way to the inner chamber of the king's council?' he will ask.

"And the Hyperboreans will be in one accord that, since King Freyr had died without issue, Aurochel, as they continued to call Maelgaltyr, should take the throne to most effectively protect the people from the Angels of the Presence and their rebellion.

"Now as priest-king, he ordered the castle of the heir-sons of Tor razed and his own citadel hewn out of black onyx be built as *his* seat of power. This was the beginning of the Black Lodge.

"Maelgaltyr initiated his Lodge with the blood sacrifice upon its threshold of those captive Angels of the Presence who were flayed alive before him."

"He *what*?"

"My son…"

"Take me there."

"There is nothing…"

"*Take me there!* Give me substance, so that I can…" Then he caught himself and bowed his head, his cheeks burning. "Forgive my impudence in ordering you, father. But you have to understand…"

Suddenly they stood on the blood-slicked floors just inside the threshold of the Black Lodge. Corpses of naked women were sprawled over it, limbs entangled. Only tatters of skin hanging here and overlooked patches there were all that were left on forms of exposed red, raw muscle.

"I *meant* take me here when I could still …"

"Do something?" the Nameless One asked calmly.

"Father, how can you be so detached?"

"The past is done, my son. I show you these things for the *present* threat. So that you will understand the fullness of Maelgaltyr's sins. His judgment is at hand. And you shall have your part in it. But you must remember that the wrath of man will not work the righteousness of the Effulgence, or you *will* be ineffectual against Maelgaltyr's evil."

Ravenwood sighed so that his shoulders slumped. He shut his eyes. "Please take me out of here before my anger grows so great I will never again find my center."

In an instant, they stood amidst the long, whispering grass of that plateau where across from the White Lodge lurked its mockery. From a distance it looked like a great, dark opening into the mountain. Instead, it projected out from it, a deep shadow made solid and impenetrable: the Black Lodge.

"So men abandoned the White Lodge," the Nameless One said, "and the Effulgence entered it no more. Maelgaltyr then ratified the revival of the old druidic order from King Tor's day; for there were those already who had returned to that faith, but secretly did they practice in their hidden groves. These druids schooled him in the *Diet of the Wyrm*, and he received this knowledge gladly, and through its application perverted the use of the glyphs to create the Dark Wisdom. This he taught the people, and even the druids, his teachers, became his disciples.

"Then Malegaltyr enthroned himself at the top of the world. On his fingers were the keys of life and death, and by them he grasped as his scepter the cursed flail of nine thongs. And he decreed Tor's catapults, which had been long dismantled, to be rebuilt with the threat that if a city of the plateaus was found to harbor the Angels of the Presence, then would he bring down the thunder stones of old upon it.

*"You...have become a thief and usurper."*

"But Ariastella in a robe of falcon's feathers met Maelgaltyr on the threshold as he came out from his Lodge on his high day. She halted him there and said, 'So speaks the Effulgence: as long as your threat lingers over the world of men so shall a remnant of his handmaids remain to resist you. Into the outer darkness you shall be cast, a Dweller on the Threshold you will become, and of our blood will be the door which will allow you no ingress. On the burning ground we will meet, though the disciple be consumed. The judgment is set. But from now on, you shall not see one of our faces until that appointed time.'

"And when Maelgaltyr would have seized her, a hail of burning coals drove him back, and all the people fled for shelter. As for Ariastella, she drew her cloak of falcon's feathers over her and passed under the fiery hail without the singe of a single pinion. But Maelgaltyr and his men could do nothing until Ariastella had removed herself safely.

# CHAPTER EIGHTEEN:
## *Of the Destruction of Hyperborea*

"In those days," the Nameless One continued, "men entered the White Lodge carelessly, but Maelgaltyr would not permit the pillars of the Assyur to be molested, for he did not understand whether or not the stone rings drew power from their source or were independent of them.

"Yet he allowed his druids to break open the floor of the White Lodge to take of its precious marble for their own palaces. The druids thus discovered on the Lodge's foundation inscriptions to and images of the goddess Tashalia. Then they said that the White Lodge had certainly not descended uncut by hands, but had been built upon the ruins of an older temple whose religion the followers of the Effulgence had unknowingly retained. Thus, Tashalia's worship they revived.

"Wanton grew the people of Hyperborea and more wicked, yet their life spans were not shortened save those babies they themselves slaughtered in sacrifice to Tashalia, whom they now called the wife of Maelgaltyr. Yet, still did the livestock not fail to breed, and sowing and harvest continued unabated. And the Hyperboreans said these were the boon of King-Priest Maelgaltyr and Tashalia, Queen Consort, and they worshipped them both.

"Maelgaltyr continually sought for his rivals, the Angels of the Presence, but could not find them or their followers. For in a dream, the Effulgence commanded Ariastella, 'Go out from Hyperborea that you do not partake of her portion when it has reached its fullness.' Then the Angels and their disciples took ships by night, some only to the green land of the immediate South and others far, far into the southeast.

"When he could not find his enemies, Maelgaltyr feared the Angels of the Presence had been removed by the Effulgence because judgment was nigh upon Hyperborea. More, the people had begun to murmur against him, for pestilence was now not unknown in the seven plateaus.

"Maelgaltyr promised the Hyperboreans that he would retire into his Black Lodge to commune in solitude with the glyphs as he had at the beginning when Hyperborea's happiness was uncheckered. Then he would come forth again to right all their ills.

"But he told his closest followers; druids who still trusted him without question, that he feared a conspiracy had loosed this pestilence to turn the people against him. To outwit his foes and forestall any attempt on his life, he would enter a sarcophagus, and, in disguise, they were to transport him by night through the streets, as was the Hyperborean custom for the dead, to a small craft and sail south until he emerged from his self-induced trance. Then he would show them where his wandering mind had found the cure for the pestilence. Thus would he save his people, and having regained their favor, he would foil his enemies' schemes.

"So Maelgaltyr escaped Hyperborea.

"Then on a polar spring morning when the husbandman rose early to prune his vineyard; and the bridegroom's eyelids flew open with anticipation; and the fond mother made her child's bed so that it would be ready for him at the evening toll; and men arose to eat of the yield of their fathers' fathers' fields....

"On such a morning, a great groaning was heard throughout the land of Hyperborea. And men saw the White Lodge lift from the razed floor of the temple of Tashalia which the men of old had leveled at the word of Vanr the seer. The White Lodge rose into the sky where it hovered for twenty-four hours."

Suddenly they were in the midst of a multitude of Hyperboreans. Some had thrown themselves on their faces to the ground, bodies heaving in great sobs. Others knelt, heads bowed to the earth, lips moving, then stopping, starting again, and then stopping, over and over as they discovered that while they could say words, they had lost the capacity for prayer. The majority raised shaking fists at the ascended Lodge and cursed it.

The Nameless One squeezed Ravenwood's arm as the Lodge withdrew from sight into a bright cloud which immediately became a leaden gray. And the entire North Pole flash froze, quickly slaying both humans and beasts.

Ravenwood and the Nameless One suddenly stood among ages-old glaciers and canyons of ice, a wasteland through which gusting arctic air whipped snow in whirlwinds and sleet pelted the deep drifts and tinkled faintly about them.

"Thus are the people of Hyperborea confirmed in their will forever," the Nameless One said.

"And Maelgaltyr got away again," Ravenwood said.

"The mind of Maelgaltyr saw what he had wrought, only the ascension of the Lodge was withheld from his vision, for this was a witness against the people of Hyperborea," the Nameless One said, "and he laughed at its great desolation and caressed the rings still upon his fingers.

"But the druids who carried Maelgaltyr away saw their home destroyed from afar. They wailed at the loss of their loved ones and knew he whom they bore had foreseen Hyperborea's ruin, and might have spared their wives and children. And because his mind was distracted by the destruction he had brought about, Maelgaltyr in his coffin did not perceive the thoughts of those he trusted until they had thrown his sarcophagus into the sea. Then they tossed themselves into the icy deep after him.

"When he understood that he was betrayed, Maelgaltyr sank deeper into his trance so that he need not draw a breath for days. And over the ages, as his sarcophagus slowly crept, but at times was violently wrenched, along the ocean's floor, he sent out his thoughts to men, calling to them, but their dreams were distorted, and in their minds he became Apep, the serpent who devours the dead, and Typhon and Vitra; Shaitan, Sutekh, Ahriman and Erlik Khan.

"There were some who had sailed with the Angels of the Presence who, though they had fled Hyperborea for their lives, were bitter in their hearts against the Effulgence because of the destruction of their homeland. These recalled the Dark Wisdom Maelgaltyr had taught them when he perverted the glyphs, and they made disciples of the people who dwelt in the far southeast, which became known as Chaldea.

"To these disciples his thoughts were most finely tuned as he directed his dreams from his sarcophagus in the sea. To them he vowed he would come one day, and they would rule with him in his new kingdom in the south. He gave instructions of how, should he perish in his coffin, he might be brought back to life. And though he hated the name 'Maelgaltyr,' it was now his true name and only 'Maelgaltyr' could initiate the ritual to raise him. At the moment of his resurrection was he to be so called, and in Chaldea he was first given the title "Yttle Elumi" by which his true identity would be hidden from the Angels of the Presence and their disciples.

"But Maelgaltyr could not control where his sarcophagus would drift over the millennia, so in the end he did not come to Chaldea. And when he realized this would be so, he discarded his followers there, though his cult continued to worship Yttle Elumi and look for his rising from the sea, even after they no longer recalled his name.

"Maelgaltyr now saw he drifted toward what would be called the Bay of Bengals, and his roaming mind discovered those indigenous to India whose thoughts, though they had never known him, were as tuned to his as had been his followers in Chaldea. And while still in his sarcophagus, he began to prepare him a people in the Himachal Pradesh. 'Dugpas' he named them, and so they called themselves. To them he gave his name and the ritual to raise him should it be required. And they waited for he who would rise up from the sea and teach them the Dark Wisdom."

# CHAPTER NINETEEN:
## Of the Slaying of Maelgaltyr

Now the Nameless One removed them from snow ridden and glacier locked Hyperborea to the tropical forests of the Himachal Pradesh, where steam crept along the base of the tree trunks, the vapor seeming more ethereal than their astral selves. Among the trees jutted from the ground a great black stone.

"It is now the fourteenth century of our own era," the Nameless One said, "Maelgaltyr has sent visions to his dugpas to come to the Bay of Bengals and draw him forth. They took him into their ship and opened the sarcophagus and for the first time in millennia, Maelgaltyr breathed fresh air and woke himself from his sleep. They wondered at him and at the stone rings on his fingers and what the glyphs might mean.

"For all his power, Maelgaltyr was yet mortal and his physical strength abated from all that he had endured. See, the dugpas come carrying him on a litter. And while he recovers, he will give orders on how that they should hew his new Black Lodge out of this dark, monolithic stone before us."

The pressing forest was suddenly cleared and on leveled land now arose Maelgaltyr's new temple.

"This version is a lot smaller," Ravenwood said.

"But no less a locus of evil," said the Nameless One.

"When Maelgaltyr's strength returned to full measure," he continued, "he called his ten chosen dugpas into the Black Lodge and openly shared with them the power that comes from the Dark Wisdom. But Maelgaltyr did *not* share with even his chosen ten the secret of his stone rings. And his ten suspected these were the wellspring of Maelgaltyr's power and coveted them, but they feared their new master while relishing his teachings and what power he did grant.

"When they believed Maelgaltyr to have taught them all, the chosen ten conspired to slay their master and lead the dugpas themselves, each with a stone ring on his hand. And on a set day, they met him inside the Black Lodge, and the ten drew knives and thrust him through repeatedly. However, Maelgaltyr did not die quickly, and they fled the Lodge while he yet writhed on his own altar…"

The doors flew open, startling Ravenwood, and the panicked ten burst out, the last only lingering momentarily to close the doors behind him before rushing from the site of their deed.

"They told the other dugpas the master is ill and has gone into a healing sleep such as he was in when they drew him from the Bay of Bengals," the Nameless One said. "Thus, he must not be disturbed. This lie bought them time to take counsel. For they now feared Maelgaltyr had power to heal himself and waited inside for them to return for his rings.

"Finally, the ten agreed that whoever would first enter the Lodge should have two rings, for he bore the risk of facing Maelgaltyr's wrath should he live. Yet he still should take but one ring if the master were dead. Then the others who followed would take a ring, and lots would be cast to determine who should give up his prize.

"See now: it is the dugpa Ghantal who first goes in and finds Maelgaltyr is dead indeed. He comes out with not one but *two* rings on his fingers for he knows his fellow dugpas' hearts as his own, and so claims his due before one of the other nine would be called upon to surrender his.

Ravenwood watched as Ghantal brandished his hand in triumph. Seeing but eight rings remained, the other nine jostled each other in their rush inside the Lodge to plunder the corpse of Maelgaltyr.

"Then the dugpa Ki was sullen, for no spoil was left for him," the Nameless One said. They watched as he approached the other nine, frowning and gritting his teeth.

Ki said, 'Why should I have no ring? Did I not also slay Maelgaltyr?" He pointed his finger at the dugpa Dai, and said, "When I thrust from the front between Maelgaltyr's ribs, Dai held back and did not stab from behind until he saw the master fold in his agony. Why should Dai, the coward, have an equal share? Let him surrender his ring to me. Or let Ghantal give me one of his two rings and then let us cast lots, as he knew we were agreed when he took two for his own. And if the lot falls upon me, then I will return the ring, but if on another, let *him* yield.'

"I will not yield what is mine by right," Dai said, his face burning because Ki had exposed his cravenness.

"Nor am I fool enough to believe that you would give up the ring once it is on your finger *should* the lot fall upon you, Ki," Ghantal said.

With a cry, Ki drew his sword and charged Ghantal. Ghantal's blade met Ki's, but then Ki feinted and was swift to seize the opening and run Ghantal through. Ki withdrew his sword, and Ghantal had barely collapsed to the ground before Ki fell upon the corpse to pry from its finger one ring. He held it up with a smile before the others. But his countenance quickly fell, for they were all looking, not at Ki in his triumph, but the remaining ring on Ghantal's still hand.

So heated became their argument over who would possess it that, as Ravenwood and the Nameless One watched, they attacked each other with their swords.

"They're going to wipe themselves out!" Ravenwood said.

"Each died with a glyph of the White Lodge of Hyperborea upon his finger, never understanding what it was he bore and for what he had died," said the Nameless One.

And now the jungle had reclaimed the land, its vines and tendrils of overgrowth overrunning the Black Lodge, and the tall grass the skeletons of the ten.

"When the other dugpas found Maelgaltyr slain on his altar and the ten slain outside the Lodge with his rings on their fingers," the Nameless One said, "they believed the rings bore Maelgaltyr's curse. So no one dared touch them. And of the stone rings, the fate of five is known; that of the others remains unrevealed; no, not even the priest kings and queens of Aslem-Beth have knowledge of *those*.

"Then the dugpas fled the Black Lodge, never to return, and dared never speak or write the name 'Maelgaltyr.' It became to the dugpas what is called in Latin *Magnum Innominandum*, that which sorcerers fear invoking at risk of great peril. Thus did the name of the chief dugpa pass from the knowledge of his followers.

"Only one group remembered it but these were the enemies of the dugpas, the Ascended Chieftains of India. For one of their number, a great warrior, and proud, had turned back Maelgaltyr and the dugpas from Shamballah, and he would not allow the name of his chief adversary in this great deed to be forgotten.

"So, when the Ascended Chieftains knew they were dying, and they passed their history by couriers to the Order of the Golden Dawn, the personal name of Yttle Elumi was made known to the inner circle. But only with the strictest warning that they burn the paper on which it was written after committing it to memory and pass it to their successors only verbally with the injunction that it never be written again. Thus has the name 'Maelgaltyr' survived in the world."

"My father," Ravenwood said, "so have his bones. I have seen the skeleton of Maelgaltyr, even where the blades of his murderers chipped his ribs. It is being taken to a gateway in the form of the twelfth hexagram. I was knocked unconscious so that my attacker could steal some tarot cards that are relevant to Maelgaltyr's resurrection. I believed it was an enemy of Yttle Elumi who stole the cards. But with the bones en route to the very type of gateway where the ritual must take place, the theft could mean everything is coming together to revive him, *if* a member of Maelgaltyr's cult assaulted me instead. In that case, I fear, along with the cards and his bones, they have also rediscovered his name and the spell to return him to life."

"My son, should Maelgaltyr pass over that gate's threshold, great will be the woe upon mankind." He nodded at the bag in Ravenwood's hand. "Only what you carry there can weaken him significantly so that he may come under judgment. Then turn the twelfth hexagram back to the eleventh and to this beacon the Great Ones will come."

"We do have another defense, master: an Angel of the Presence has continued in the world in accord with the prophecy; I know who she is. She…"

"'And on the burning ground they will meet, though the disciple be consumed!' My son, these words carry the weight of doom for me and for you. They speak of a thing into which I will not go further. As for the Angel, she will face the Dweller on the Threshold, and her courage will fail her. The way *will* be opened for Maelgaltyr. Only then are you permitted to strike with the contents of the bag.

"And then, my son, you *must* turn the twelfth hexagram back to the eleventh before he passes through the gate. Now, the time grows short. Awake."

"Wait, father, Nameless One…. 'Turn it *back*?' How?"

"To the beacon they will come. The time is upon us! In that dark hour, on the burning field, fail not to remember that I love you always. Now, again, I say to you, awake, my son! AWAKE!"

# CHAPTER TWENTY:
## Sally Chesney-Waite

"**Y**ou're awake," the pretty nurse taking Ravenwood's pulse said as his eyes fluttered open.

"I am Ravenwood."

"Yes you are. That's a good sign for someone who took a blow to the head like you did, hon'. Good to have you back with us, Mr. Ravenwood."

"How long have I been out?" he asked.

"Since the night before last. Seems the golden calf left over from DeMille's *Ten Commandments* premiere fell off the roof of the *Egyptian Theater* while you were standing in front of the movie house. They said the wind must have pushed it toward the edge over the years. Then along came a big gust and …well, *you* know."

"Yes," Ravenwood said, gingerly touching the back of his head and wincing. "'The wind.' I don't suppose I've had any visitors?"

"Sorry, hon'. No."

"Could you get me a phone, please? And my wallet?"

"I thought these were your priority," the nurse said and held up the draw-string bag from his dream. She swung it back and forth over him and grinned.

Ravenwood's eyes widened and he snatched the bag from her hand, feeling the heft of the objects inside. But, of course, on the physical plane things *would* be more weighty.

"Easy!" the nurse said. "I wasn't going to keep your precious pee wees, steelies, aggies and cat's eyes. I brought them to you."

Ravenwood cocked his head and squinted an eye up at her. "How do you know about these marbles?"

"You kept repeating them in your sleep. I dunno…something that important to you, I thought maybe subconsciously you'd realize you had 'em next to you, and you'd relax. Like a kid and his teddy. I found this bag among your effects and had a look inside."

"You *looked inside*? You shouldn't have…"

"I've seen a lot more than your pee wees since your stay with us, hon'. All in a purely clinical context, Mr. Ravenwood, I assure you. Now, please lie back down while I let the doctor know you're awake."

"Madame, I believe I asked for a phone and my wallet, please."

"Mr. Ravenwood, it's important that you…"

"So is this. Life and death. I am not kidding you. So, either you bring a phone and my wallet to me before you get the doctor, or I will get up and start looking for them."

"Okay, okay!"

Ravenwood had just reached Astoria Studios on the phone when the doctor walked in.

"Mr. Ravenwood? Good to see you're awa…"

Ravenwood waved him off. "I see. Then please leave a message for him at the Roosevelt that he and Miss D'Arromanches must wait for me there together. He mustn't let her out of his sight. Thank you."

No sooner had Ravenwood put the receiver back into its cradle than he had lifted it again and was dialing once more.

"Mr. Ravenwood," the doctor said. "If we could have a moment of your time?"

"I'm sorry, doc," he said. "But there's someone who has no idea where I've been the past couple days, and it's paramount or, I should say, universal, that I contact him immediately."

Seeing that his patient would not be deterred, the doctor moved around and began examining the back of Ravenwood's head. "You had a terrible blow. I hope you're not planning on going anywhere."

"Sorry again, doc," Ravenwood said. "But I am. If someone will fetch my clothes. And I had an umbrella and a gun…wait. Did the police take my gun? Hold on. Hello? Could you please put me through to Murphy Fort. I am Ravenwood. I assure you he'll want to hear from me. Yes, I'll hold...doctor, my gun?"

"The police took it, but the permit in your wallet was in order. All of your personal effects have been returned. You *do* understand that if you leave now, and choose not to remain under observation, you'll be fully responsible if..."

"Understood...ouch!" Ravenwood pulled away from the doctor's probing fingers.

"You see? You're still tender, Mr. Ravenwood."

"Yes, I'm really quite delicate. Now, get my pants. Fort! Please accept by apologies. I'm calling from the hospital. Yes. I'm fine now," he said, looking up at the doctor who shook his head from side to side. "I'll explain when we meet. Were you able to get in touch with your acquaintance? She penciled us in for yesterday? Fort, would you please call her again and explain things to her. Remind her it's urgent that we speak. Things are quickly coming to a head," he said, touching his own again and trying to hide his wince from the doctor.

"What time is it?" he asked the nurse. "One, you say? Okay, Fort. I can meet you at the studio within the hour. If she can speak with us as soon as possible after that, that would be swell. See you soon, Fort."

Ravenwood shaved, showered, dressed, and holstered his pistol under his arm. With his umbrella under the other and the bag of marbles in his inside coat pocket, he signed the release forms, then hailed a cab to take him back to Universal Studios. On the drive over, he wondered how he was going to explain his sojourn in the hospital as well as the loss of the tarot cards to Fort.

Although Fort was open to the possibility that an ancient sorcerer might be resurrected, an attack by DeMille's prop golden calf might be a bit much. Better to simply say that he was knocked on the head and the cards stolen.

"That was no random attack," Fort said when given this explanation. "Don't you believe it was the man who was following you?"

"I *hope* who I *thought* was following me ended up with the cards. At least the anti-Yttle Elumi league he represents would destroy them. But if my attacker is part of the Yttle Elumi cult, and *they* have the Major Arcana...."

"Fort, I believe William Desmond Taylor was reassembling that Major Arcana because he was part of the cult. I think those cards are as necessary to the ritual of raising Yttle Elumi as is whatever the Golden Dawn expurgated from *The Ordeal*'s libretto. I just hope your friend might have some knowledge from her association with Taylor that will help us find the Hollywood chapter of the Yttle Elumi cult."

"Well, Sally is waiting for us," Fort said as he took his coat from a hook behind his office door. "Shall we?"

Fort drove them off the Universal lot, and Ravenwood soon recognized the climbing topography and Mediterranean architecture of Whitley Heights. Fort pulled up to a tall, iron-barred gate. Ravenwood could see beyond it a mansion under a raised tile roof, its huge picture window overlooking a long front yard with strategically planted palm trees, their leaves now brown and forlorn.

Fort buzzed the gate's intercom, announced himself and the gate opened. They drove up a lengthy cement driveway, circled a dry fountain in the midst of which a parched Cupid the color of teal blue seemed to hold up his water jar imploringly, then pulled into a capacious wood-paneled garage beside an ivory colored stretch of a limousine inlaid with pearl.

Ravenwood noted a spacious back seat upholstered in leopard skin. Curtains could be drawn around the rear windows when the passengers wished to enjoy the mini-bar mounted in the back floorboard. If Ravenwood had encountered this vehicle on the highway, with its display of extravagance and indulgence combined with the drawn window curtains, he would have thought it the most decadent hearse he had ever seen.

As Ravenwood and Fort stepped out of Fort's car, the door that connected the garage to the mansion opened, and Sally Chesney-Waite's butler, in a crisp black tux and immaculately white gloves, greeted them.

"If you will follow me, gentlemen," he said, "Madame will see you in her solarium."

He led them down a broad, thickly carpeted hallway, along which hung framed, signed photos of legendary personages of the British stage; Sarah Bernhardt, Ellen Terry, and Henry Irving. And there were other notables on the wall, the poet Yeats and the self-proclaimed Great Beast, Aleister Crowley. The same winsome young woman with the freckled tom-boyish face also appeared in each of these photos. This was Sally Chesney-Waite in her youth when she was a member of the Order of the Golden Dawn.

They entered a glass-enclosed room filled with potted plants much better attended than the palms in the yard. Miss Chesney-Waite was reclining on her side on a divan, thumbing through movie magazines that were piled on the floor beside her. Within reach, on a small art deco designed table, stacks of scripts set beside an empty china tea cup.

"Miss Chesney-Waite? Messrs. Fort and Ravenwood."

From under the fashionably bobbed but gray hair, the eyes that Ravenwood could now see were one blue, one green, peered up at him, as unabated in their youthful gleam as they were in the old photos. But this timeless quality was compromised by the ruts of her laugh lines and the wrinkles that had resisted a thorough rouging.

Sally Chesney-Waite rose to greet them in her royal blue satin dowager's gown with pearls strung down a flapper's flattened bosom. On her feet were oversized, cushy leopard skin bedroom slippers.

Arms spread wide and above her head, she walked toward Fort. Though he and Ravenwood were the ones who had entered the room, Sally Chesney-Waite was the one making an entrance.

"Murphy, darling," she said, bringing her hands down on his shoulders and kissing each of his cheeks. "When was the last time, my dear?"

"You were privately screening *The Jazz Singer*, and we all chimed in, right on cue, when Jolson said, 'Wait a minute, wait a minute, you ain't heard nothin' yet.'"

Sally tossed back her head and laughed. "That was the death toll for a lot of lovely young faces, wasn't it, my dear? But good news for those as you and I who are stage-trained in the spoken word."

Ravenwood glanced over at the stack of scripts and wondered how many actually had a speaking part for Sally Chesney-Waite. Sound had come too late to the movies for her. There could only be so many dowager parts in Hollywood, which, even with the advent of sound, still continued to thrive on lovely young faces.

"And this gentleman," she said, turning to Ravenwood, giving him her hand, and staring into his face, "has the most peculiar eyes I have ever seen."

She threw back her head again and laughed at the ceiling. Decades of tea consumption had given her teeth the same brownish tint of the pearls she wore. She locked her arm with his and walked him over to the divan. "We exceptional optical types must stick together, mustn't we, dear? You'll sit beside me, Mr. Ravenwood. Murphy, if you'll take the wicker chair there."

"It will be a pleasure, Miss Chesney-Waite," Ravenwood said.

She waved him off. "Please. It's Sally," she said as they were all seated.

"Now, where do I begin to tell you what I know about the life and death of William Desmond Taylor. Well, first of all, he is not."

"'Isn't...dead?" Ravenwood asked, looking at Fort to see the same knit of the brow on his companion's face as his own before he turned back to Sally.

"No, he is not. At least, not the last I heard."

# CHAPTER TWENTY-ONE:
## *The Strange Case of William Desmond Taylor*

"**B**ut, Sally," Fort said. "You *know* he died nine years ago..."

She looked first at Fort and then at Ravenwood. "I knew William Desmond Taylor when he was a young actor on the British stage, and I can most assuredly tell you that the person dead on that bungalow floor was *not* he."

"Then who? Sally, why haven't you ever said anything of this to the police?" Fort asked.

"I was afraid I might endanger myself by coming forward. He warned me at the start that my role as his confidante was a potentially perilous one, best kept secret. I've been silent all this time, but, if other lives are now in jeopardy as you say, how can I remain so?"

"*Who* warned you to keep quiet, Sally?" Ravenwood asked.

"William Cunningham Deane-Tanner," she said. "The man Hollywood knew as William Desmond Taylor. But he *wasn't*, you see. William Desmond Taylor was a different man. I knew them both during our days in London's West End, when William Cunningham Deane-Tanner was acting under the name Cunningham Deane."

"You're saying this Deane-Tanner took Taylor's name when he came to Hollywood?" Ravenwood asked.

"Name? Darling, Tanner took his *identity*. No, that's not accurate. Taylor *gave* Deane-Tanner his identity. Deane-Tanner was already halfway there. Their resemblance was uncanny, though Deane-Tanner, or Cunningham

Deane, as he called himself then, was younger, around eighteen or so, and Taylor twenty-one. And on stage, certainly, no one could tell the difference. After essaying a small part in Sir Charles Hawtrey's *The Private Secretary*, Cunningham Deane became William Desmond Taylor's understudy.

"Taylor had begun as a character actor with a genius for make-up. What that boy could do to transform himself. Even the late Mr. Chaney couldn't compress his spine to adjust his height as Taylor could. He graduated to 'juvenile male lead' and could have had quite the West End career, had he not become a courier between the Ascended Chieftains of India and the Order of the Golden Dawn. Oh, yes: even the Ascended Chieftains used the post in some form in those days.

"The prudent manner in which he carried out his duties granted him the invitation to stay in India and sit at the feet of a Yellow Hat monk. This was quite an honor for it represented something of a prep school for those who one day might become proxies in the West of the Ascended Chieftains themselves.

"This meant that Taylor's look-alike Cunningham Deane who was also involved with the Order of the Golden Dawn, but much more on the fringe of things, waiting tables and so on was set to step into the limelight.

"Unfortunately, his participation in *The Private Secretary* had already come to the attention of his father from whom he had run away. That was it for the London stage career of 'Cunningham Deane.' His father was scandalized that someone of their family name and standing was performing on the stage; disreputable profession, you understand. Papa Deane-Tanner aborted Cunningham Deane's West End career and sent him off to work on an American horse ranch to get the acting bug out of his system.

"That was the last I saw of him until, at a party years later, darling Mary Pickford introduced me to William Desmond Taylor, Hollywood's fastest rising director. I, as an actress, am a trained observer. Even given their resemblance, and the years that had passed, I recognized who he really was.

"At the earliest opportunity, I took him aside and asked, 'And how are you *really*, 'Cunningham Deane' ...or should I say, Mr. William Cunningham Deane-Tanner?' He made a feeble attempt at denying it, then quickly surrendered. He implored me that his true identity should remain our secret and promised to explain as soon as we might arrange a private meeting."

"Well, who could resist that sort of intrigue? Certainly, no woman. I insisted that we meet for noonsies the next day and play catch up. He said he would cancel his luncheon with Jesse Lasky at Paramount and gave me his address."

"That day I learned that William Cunningham Deane-Tanner had never returned to England, but remained in America, rambling about in various and sundry professions including a return to the stage. He finally settled down in New York and married the officially prettiest chorus girl there; so designated by no less an authority than *Broadway* magazine. That was quite the conquest, enough alone to make him the envy of any man, but he was also set up by his father-in-law in a profitable antique business.

"However, the old wanderlust and discontent began to manifest itself after a while. And at this propitious moment, who should come into his antique shop but his old colleague, William Desmond Taylor? A man now fleeing for his life from a demon."

"A *demon*?" Ravenwood and Fort said in unison.

Sally looked at them. "My dears, I assure you both I was trained to annunciate so that those in the back seats of the balcony could understand me. Yes, a *demon*. What had happened was this: at the end of the preparation period with his Yellow Hat mentor, Taylor had applied for admittance among the Ascended Chieftains' school of proxies with intent to eventually return to England and lead the Golden Dawn. His selfish ambition, however, proved him unfit.

"This rejection offended him severely, and so, despite the offered opportunity to reapply once he had learned humility, he opted to leave in pursuit of a quicker way to power. He joined another eastern cult, one which followed the left-handed path: the Red Hats, also known as 'dugpas.'"

Ravenwood leaned forward, his eyes shifting colors, one to black and the other to gray.

"Well, that certainly got *your* attention, Mr. Ravenwood," Sally said. "I take it you are familiar with these creatures?"

Fort was looking at him now as well. Ravenwood leaned back. "By reputation only. But enough to know that if Taylor threw his lot in with them, he had truly embraced the darkness."

"Indeed. Well, Taylor proved as overly ambitious with the dugpas as he had with the Ascended Chieftains. He attempted a failed coup, and, as a punishment, the dugpas marked him to attract the voracious attention of their destroying demon Adharma. Watching the devouring of a captured enemy highlighted the dugpas' year of jubilee."

"Wait! They 'marked him?'" Fort asked.

*"Who warned you to keep quiet, Sally?"*

"Shaved his head and tattooed him with some sigil. As Deane-Tanner related it to me, Taylor said, 'The dugpas put me in a cage to await my fate. There, I was to be eaten alive by their demon while *they* feasted on my fear and suffering. The temporary opening that allows Adharma ingress to our universe occurs at a certain stellar alignment that only forms every fifteen years. The waiting, knowing it was inescapably coming, was part of the punishment, you see. As it was, I would not have to wait for long: the latest period was almost up at the time of my imprisonment.'

"'But I had a predecessor in that cage, someone who had displeased the dugpas seven years before. And it takes only *one* sacrifice per manifestation to glut Adharma. Apparently he has the digestive method of a python and is still processing things when his time is up and he is compelled to exit the universe until the next alignment fifteen years later. Although Adharma wasn't obligated to take my predecessor first, *he* had rather plumped up over his confinement. And I was able to escape shortly thereafter.'"

Ravenwood and Fort looked at each other: Sally was no longer just relating what she had been told; she had gone into Taylor's *character*. A small shake of Fort's head warned Ravenwood against interrupting and risking offending Sally who was so desperate to perform. Ravenwood sighed. At least he was getting the facts along with the theatrics.

"'And you've made it to the states,'" Sally said, turning her head from Ravenwood to address thin air. He realized she was *now* speaking as Deane-Tanner. 'But, I take it that while you've eluded the dugpas...'

"'This sigil on my head remains a honing beacon to Adharma. Quite,'" Sally said, resuming the Taylor persona.

*She's actually playing* both *men in conversation?* Ravenwood thought. *She's going to expect applause when she's done.*

"'And I can't just have the thing removed without passing it on, or it will come back,' Sally said, continuing on as Taylor. 'There has to be a willing substitute, some cosmic law even the dugpas can't get around. So listen, old man. I have a proposition for you...'

"'William, do you think me mad?'

"'Not at all, old boy. Now, *listen*. While the mark draws the demon, what makes one *vulnerable* to suffering harm from such an entity is that the demon knows one's real name.'

"'Yes, I recall that from the teachings of the Golden Dawn.'

"'Right. It's standard demonic lore. You know that. Now, neither Adharma nor the dugpas know William Cunningham Deane-Tanner by name or otherwise. Should you agree to a skin graft of my flesh bearing the sigil onto your own scalp, you will become the demon's target. But because Adharma does not know your real name, he will prove powerless to harm you.'

"'But why me, William? How many years have you lost hunting me down? Surely you could have approached someone else.'

"'Who could be my twin? Adharma *does* know what I look like. I didn't wish to be obvious about how I've tricked him. That might set him on the course of discovering my substitute's true name. No, this way everyone involved is safe.'

"'Still, with that fifteen year gap narrowing, how many are left?'

"'Adharma is not due again until 1922. So, I've only used up one year. Really, old boy, you weren't that hard to find at all. And this isn't one-sided. If you accept my conditions, I have the power to set you on the path to realize the dreams you've always cherished, that this antique business cannot satisfy.'"

"What could possibly be in all this for Deane-Tanner to trust Taylor to be his understudy for a role cast in hell?" Ravenwood asked, seizing the moment to get Sally off track of her one-woman show.

Sally stared at him, jaw slack, obviously a bit miffed by the interruption. After a moment she said, "Why, it was the classic Faustian deal, Mr. Ravenwood. The real William Desmond Taylor was not without powers of his own. They were enough to grant Deane-Tanner's theatrical wishes: more specifically, a place in the newfangled 'photo' plays, a medium whose potentialities had excited him creatively. Taylor could grant that his endeavors in the flickers would lead him to the top. Deane-Tanner simply had to walk away from his old life with no explanation to anyone, become William Desmond Taylor, and all this would be his.

"With the demon thus decoyed upon his eventual emergence, the real Taylor would have unlimited time to search the globe for a greater source of power to avenge himself upon the dugpas."

"And Deane-Tanner deserted his family simply on Taylor's word that he could do all he promised?" Ravenwood asked.

"Though not an active participant in the occult world, Deane-Tanner had seen from the fringe things that would convince anyone but those dedicated to skepticism on principle, not lack of evidence, that there are those who may bless or curse with efficacy. He recognized Taylor as such a sorcerer with certainty, for Deane-Tanner went off to attend the Vanderbilt Cup sailing race one day and never came home. He registered in a hotel as one man and left it as another.

"Now, as Deane-Tanner was making the transition from actor to respected director, he would receive small packets from Taylor to hold for him. Tanner was not forbidden to open these envelopes, postmarked Cairo, Alexandria, Istanbul, Jerusalem ...all over the Middle East...and they all contained cards, sometimes one, sometimes more...of some ancient Egyptian tarot deck. Taylor warned Deane-Tanner to guard them carefully, that they were involved in a resurrection spell for someone called 'Yttle Elumi,' who was once a great power in the East. Taylor believed this sorcerer, if revived, would, out of gratitude, be persuaded to ally with him against the dugpas.

"Taylor knew that if any possessed knowledge of Yttle Elumi, it would be the Ascended Chieftains of Shamballah, the same who had rejected him. They were allegedly long-lived, but not immortal, and he knew their impending sense of their deaths was why they began entrusting the Golden Dawn with their knowledge in the late nineteenth century. Now it was almost the second decade of the twentieth. Perhaps they had by now passed and their archives open to plunder. Indeed, the last of the Ascended Chieftains was dead by this time, so Taylor entered freely where before he had been forbidden; the remote, now deserted, inner sanctums of Shamballah. There he learned that not only was Yttle Elumi known to the Ascended Chieftains, he had become their arch foe in the fourteenth century when he had founded none other than the dugpas!

"That was irony, wasn't it? Taylor's search for an ally led him to the establisher of his enemies' cult...a founder that they had apparently feared so much that they slew him. If he could but resurrect this Yttle Elumi, he would certainly share Taylor's desire for revenge on their mutual foes.

"He was able to find documents in the archives of Shamballah to help him locate a place called the Black Lodge. When the Ascended Chieftains had sensed a loss of the master strategist's guiding hand in their battles with the dugpas, they were emboldened to seek out Yttle Elumi's seat of power, this 'Black Lodge,' to confirm what they suspected. Indeed, they found and identified his bones inside. Apparently in a dugpa coup, Yttle Elumi had been slain on his own altar. The Chieftains sealed up the Black Lodge, and Yttle Elumi's throne room became his tomb.

"But what Taylor did *not* find among the Ascended Chieftains archives was the personal name of the dugpas' founder Yttle Elumi being a title, you see. The name of the revenant must begin any resurrection ritual. If the Ascended Chieftains had known this spell and the accompanying dread appellation, they had destroyed any written record of them.

"At any rate, Taylor had long been demanding money from Deane-

Tanner's Hollywood earnings to finance his adventures. Now he needed funds to mount a proper expedition where he did not dare venture himself, into the Himachal Pradesh, dugpa country, to take the bones of Yttle Elumi from the Black Lodge. Deane-Tanner's pockets were not bottomless, of course, successful director or not. The real Taylor's quest was bleeding the *faux* Taylor dry. Deane-Tanner realized he needed a production far more extravagant than social melodramas or comedies to obtain the necessary budget for funds which he could then channel into Taylor's project.

"Now, Deane-Tanner had enjoyed some great success with the 'William Desmond Taylor production' of *Huckleberry Finn*. Even Mark Twain's daughter was impressed. With one prestige adaptation to his credit, he now turned to opera and Wagner's *The Ordeal*. He was well aware of its notoriety. Are you, Mr. Ravenwood?

"Fort filled me in."

"I attended that single performance. Deane-Tanner knew my copy of the libretto was expurgated, but he had all he needed from which to adapt his scenario and titles. He planned to promote his film as 'the until now unseen, penultimate work of Wagner.'

"Meanwhile, the real Taylor was back in England, persuading a professor, a man in desperate need of a find, into leading an expedition into the Himachal Pradesh for the remains of Yttle Elumi.

"The expedition was successful. When Taylor saw photos taken of the skeleton as they had found it on the altar upon opening the Black Lodge, he immediately thought of the skeleton on the altar in the opera the Golden Dawn had not allowed to play out. The very opera, which, of course, Deane-Tanner was raising money to turn into a film."

"You said Deane-Tanner was aware of *The Ordeal*," Ravenwood said. "And now Taylor. Did either of them actually attend its performance?"

"Oh, no. Taylor was but a courier, remember? And Deane-Tanner was practically sweeping up after our socials. But they heard the details of its truncated finale.

"Given the similarities of the contents of Yttle Elumi's tomb and the mise en scene of *The Ordeal*'s last act, Taylor became convinced that somehow in the German, at the very end of the play, the ritual incantation that could raise Yttle Elumi, including his name, had been written. He believed the inner circle, who were the living repository of the Ascended Chieftains' total knowledge, realized what was happening and stopped this mock resurrection of their late masters' archenemy.

"Taylor's interpretation of the events was spot on. The composer Joseph Wright and his lover Odette de Lyss were part of the Golden Dawn's inner circle and had learned both the details of Yttle Elumi's tomb and his true name from the Ascended Chieftains.

"Bitter over a loss of promotion within the inner circle and intent on revenge, Wright sought to learn what even the Ascended Chieftains did not know and certainly would have not passed on if they had: the resurrection incantation and what devices were required to effect it. Wright obtained that information from an East End Palestinian with whom he was consorting.

"Wright had written into Wagner's libretto some word play that signified to the inner circle the unspeakable name while simultaneously concealing it from the rest of the Golden Dawn. By presenting a skeleton 'coming to life,' he gave them good reason to believe Yttle Elumi's resurrection spell was about to be chanted up there by Wright himself in the role of a hermit. Their temple, where the opera was being performed, would be defiled and the inner circle given a poke in its collective eye.

"Before he could go any further, the curtain was unexpectedly dropped. Wright was able to slip away in the confusion, but he abandoned his lover Odette, who played the opera's heroine. Wright knew that when the inner circle interrogated Odette, she would sing, not like the proverbial fat lady, but a canary."

"Was she your source for this information on Wright's plan?" Raven-wood said.

"My indirect source," Sally said. "I was never part of the inner circle. But, yes, he *wanted* her to tell them all, including that he indeed possessed the resurrection spell for Yttle Elumi, that he had rewritten Wagner's ending to incorporate it, and he meant to speak it over Yttle Elumi's actual bones which he planned to recover from the Black Lodge. Wright said the next time they saw him; he would be at the left hand of the chief of dugpas, bringing down vengeance on the Golden Dawn as the heirs of the Ascended Chieftains.

"To this end, Odette said Wright and his Palestinian cohort were seeking a special tarot deck with certain alchemically-treated cards. When these were applied to Yttle Elumi's remains, together with the calling of his true name and the proper incantation, the dugpa would return to corporal life. His quest paralleled William Desmond Taylor's all these years later."

"So, the Golden Dawn send out a hostile current against Wright to preempt his reintroduction of this horror into the world," Fort asked.

"Oh, we uttered some incantations aimed his way," Sally said with a mischievous roll of her eyes. "But Wright was actually murdered by the unsavory types with whom he was consorting in the East End, trying to obtain those coveted tarot cards. Both his body and that of his Palestinian were found bobbing in the Thames. Apparently there was some element as opposed to the raising of Yttle Elumi as Wright was intent on accomplishing it.

"Odette, understandably miffed at her lover's leaving her in the lurch, did allow the Golden Dawn access to his home for the inner circle to burn Wright's papers on which he had written the forbidden name. But that was the only physical action we took."

"Except for cutting the final German page from every libretto," Ravenwood said.

"Ah, but one went unaccounted for and remained unexpurgated," Sally said. "William Desmond Taylor ordered Deane-Tanner to find that uncut copy of the libretto. He needed that resurrection spell and Yttle Elumi's true name, both of which he was convinced were on the last page in the German. He was certain any translation of the remaining English final page back into German would yield neither or the Golden Dawn would have not left it intact. Yet, try as he may, Deane-Tanner could not produce this uncut libretto. And Taylor really was bringing down the pressure now, because he had moved in with Deane-Tanner in Hollywood."

"Wasn't that one Taylor too many?" Ravenwood asked.

"Oh, but the real William Desmond Taylor was a master of disguise, remember? He became 'Edward Sands,' cook, secretary, valet...and suspect in Taylor's murder. And then Sands, too, was found dead. All, my dears, according to plan."

Both Ravenwood and Fort leaned in toward Sally and she, still a storyteller in her heart if no longer on the stage, savored their suspense to know what happened next.

# CHAPTER TWENTY-TWO:
## *On the Go With Hank Arneau*

While Ravenwood and Fort were in Sally's company, Arneau and Anne were nearing Hollywood via private plane.

Anne D'Arromanches emerged from her freshening up in the lavatory in a borrowed lady's robe monogrammed M.L. Anne's heart had taken a dip at the sight of those initials, similar to the one her stomach took when the plane hit its first air current.

Until then, the flight west had been fabulous. She had particularly enjoyed the sight of the top of the Empire State Building from such a high altitude. Indeed, 'heavenly' was the word until Arneau opened the wardrobe.

"So," she had asked, averting her eyes from his as she took a bathrobe from the hanger, "who's M.L.?"

"Now, Anne, don't go getting the wrong idea."

"What idea would that be, Mr. Arneau?"

"She's a business associate. Look, the plane's borrowed…"

"She let you borrow her plane? Your association must be a close one. I take it you are 'partners?'"

"I assure you, Anne, ours is a purely professional arrangement. Yes, she's great company, but no funny business."

Anne smiled up at him. "It's all right, Hank. It's no surprise that you enjoy other women's company as well as mine. Especially an actress as lovely as Merle Langtry."

"But right now, up in the air over these United States, I'm all yours."

"Umm-hmm. Such a prize." With a cock of her head, she turned on her heel and retired to the lavatory.

Now she emerged, interlocking her fingers and stretching her arms out before her. "Yum-yum," she said. "That felt as delicious as whatever you have on the table smells."

Arneau was already seated at table set for brunch. Anne's plate was ready, and, she noted, that the bacon was limp and the eggs scrambled.

*He remembered.*

"Please, be seated," Arneau said as he affixed his napkin while Anne slid into her chair, spread her own napkin in her lap, and speared some eggs with her fork.

As she was taking her first bite, something caught her eye, something she had not seen before.

Her mouth full of egg, she nodded at his hand, finished chewing, swallowed, and said, "That's an interesting ring."

He laid down his fork, and, elbows on the table, folded his hands and rested his chin on his fingertips, making the ring prominent.

"Would you like one like it?" he asked.

"Is that a proposal?" Anne said, eyebrows arching upward, fork poised at her lips.

Arneau dropped his hands into his lap and looked at her sidelong.

"I was joking, of course," Anne said, shoved a bit of egg into her mouth and quickly raised her coffee cup for a long sip.

"Of course," Arneau said and smiled. "The ring is for another role I have in mind for you after this is over. I hope you'll be game. But 'in the meantime, the in between time…'"

He reached into his own robe's pocket and produced the box he had offered her at the Astoria commissary. Anne's eyes widened. She had never stopped wondering what was inside but would have never presumed to bring it up after having rejected the gift before.

"…I hope you'll reconsider and accept my present. Really, it's a good luck charm that *any* producer with any class would give his leading lady. Please…."

He pushed the box across the table. Anne stared at it for a long moment, then looked up at him. "I acquiesce…but I don't surrender."

He nodded. "Understood."

"For the occasion, then" she said, smiled, then unwrapped and opened the box.

She began pulling out a golden chain piled inside until a golden oriental charm dangled in the air:

"Oh, Hank, it's beautiful," she said. "I'll wear it, of course. Would you put it on me?"

"Of course," he said, rising, and moving behind her as she pulled aside her hair and bared her slender neck.

"There," he said as he snapped the clasp, then reached over, and righted the charm.

"Always wear it in that position," he said and smiled. "That way, it's the *I Ching* hexagram for the number eleven, the T'ai. It indicates auspicious circumstances which we could all use on this production. You don't take it off until you hear me say 'it's a wrap.'"

"Don't you think this Chinese symbol will look odd on a medieval maiden of Arthur's court?" she asked and grinned.

"We'll shoot around it," he said as returned to his chair.

"Well, 'in the meantime,'" she said, "the in-between time, as you say, what do we need to do to be prepared for our arrival in Hollywood?"

"You'll continue working on your lines. How are they coming along?"

Anne put the back of her hand to her forehead, "'Oh, Aurlianus, why did you ever set forth on your quest? Were not my lips grail enough that you could not find your bliss, your paradise there?'"

"Holy cow," Arneau said. "Wagner wrote that kind of corn?"

"The title page of my script reads, 'The Ordeal by Richard Wagner...with additional dialogue by Bob Smith.' I'm betting that line was one of Smith's contributions. What about you?"

Arneau sipped his coffee and shook his head. "I wanted to be sure this highbrow stuff would play in Peoria, but I have to say, if that was an example of Smith's work, even Max Factor couldn't make your lips gloss that kind of dialogue. Just skip the corn when you come across it. When we land, I'll find another writer, preferably one who can work fast."

"Oh. What about Ravenwood? You must be looking forward to meeting with him."

Arneau stared pensively over the rim of his coffee cup as Anne looked down at her plate and sawed at her bacon. "Oh, yes," he said. "I most assuredly will be checking in with Mr. Ravenwood."

# CHAPTER TWENTY-FOUR:
## Who Serves Maelgaltyn?

"This would have been about...hmm...," Sally Chesney-Waite paused, lips hovering over the edge of her tea cup, "...two years before his murder." She took a sip, looking from Ravenwood to Murphy Fort, then set the cup on her deco table. "Taylor was compelled to take on the invented identity of 'Edward Sands,' valet to William Desmond Taylor to share in the life he had created for Deane-Tanner in Hollywood."

"Wait a minute," Ravenwood said. "The papers said that 'Edward Sands' was a confirmed pseudonym of someone else. Some miscreant with a record who was working as Taylor's or, I should say Deane-Tanner's, valet."

"You're thinking of one Edward Snyder," Sally said. She shrugged. "I wager in actuality Snyder was a man whom Taylor paid to assume the Sands identity to decoy the authorities. It would fit Taylor's *modus operandi*, and this 'miscreant,' as you put it, Mr. Ravenwood, would have been game for a scam.

"In any event, no one saw Edward Snyder, or 'Edward Sands,' again after the murder of, as it were, William Desmond Taylor. Unless it *was* Snyder's corpse discovered in a Connecticut freeze with a bullet in the head. The authorities reported Sands a.k.a. Snyder was dead. But due to the condition of the body, no one who had known Snyder could positively identify the body. Convenient, what?"

"Very," Ravenwood said.

"Convenient was not the word Deane-Tanner would have used to describe sharing a domicile with Taylor as Sands, I can assure you. A distressed Deane-Tanner told me that the pressure was becoming intolerable. Taylor was continually demanding he produce that uncut libretto and, in private, helping himself to whatever he wanted.

"Is it any wonder Deane-Tanner developed a stomach ulcer that required surgery? When his doctor told him to go abroad for recuperation, the real Taylor grudgingly agreed to Deane-Tanner leaving the country for a rest. After all, Taylor needed him alive and healthy. He did insist upon and receive a signed blank check before he left, though.

"Deane-Tanner did not trust what Taylor might do in his absence, so he removed the Major Arcana cards from the false drawer bottom where he and Taylor had hidden them and secreted them in various spots around the house."

"Their locations becoming bargaining chips to, to mix my metaphor, put Taylor on a leash," Ravenwood said.

"If need be. Hiding the cards was a back-up plan, actually. You see, Deane-Tanner had arranged to swap residences for the period of his vacation with the playwright Edward Knoblock. Knoblock was going to be writing the screenplay for Fairbanks' *The Three Musketeers* at Paramount. Knowing Taylor would have a conniption at the news of this arrangement, having planned to have full reign of the house in Deane-Tanner's absence, Deane-Tanner waited until he was half-way to his port of departure in New York to cable him with the news. Deane-Tanner was praying that Knoblock's arrival with his expectation that 'Sands' keep up his supposed servant's duties would make things so uncomfortable for Taylor that he would abscond with that blank check. For his own reputation's sake, he didn't wish his strange friend around Knoblock during his stay.

"Indeed, Taylor as Sands told Knoblock that he was 'going on his honeymoon,' of all things, in Catalina. He promised Knoblock that he would be back by the time his 'employer' returned. Knoblock noted that it was quite a large trunk that 'Sands' was packing.

"Taylor called Deane-Tanner at Knoblock's England residence, and, far from being upset, informed him that, unshackled of his 'Sands' identity, he was going to enjoy the lifestyle of Hollywood's William Desmond Taylor on a tour of the States while Deane-Tanner was overseas."

"Well, as Deane-Tanner's homecoming neared with his manservant nowhere in sight, Knoblock called the hotel in Catalina where 'Sands' said he could be reached. Of course, Knoblock was told he had never been there.

"Upon Deane-Tanner's homecoming, Knoblock immediately informed him of Sands' actions, and they rushed to Deane-Tanner's bedroom to find most of his clothes gone, as well as jewelry and money. Even one of his autos was missing from the garage!

"He also discovered Taylor had cashed the blank check he had left with him for $4500. Of course, none of this truly surprised Deane-Tanner; Taylor had informed him of his plans to relish the good life of 'the' William Desmond Taylor in his absence.

"In fact, Taylor *never* returned to resume his life as Sands though Deane-Tanner still expected Taylor to come for his precious Major Arcana. But not as Sands. No, Deane-Tanner had no doubt Taylor would return to the bungalow *as* William Desmond Taylor while Deane-Tanner was away on location or on set. What better way not to arouse suspicion?

"But Taylor took a different means of reasserting his presence.

"Deane-Tanner received a letter signed Sands, telling him he knew his real name. Of course he did. He always had. To make a point of mentioning it was to insinuate that Deane-Tanner, still bearing the dugpa's mark, would be vulnerable to Adharma's assault, should he give Taylor cause to relay to the demon Deane-Tanner's name. Taylor expected him to bring *The Ordeal* to fruition...or else. That, however, demanded Deane-Tanner complete the nearly impossible task of finding that uncut libretto.

"Deane-Tanner believed himself safe, however. While he did not hold all the cards, he still held the Major Arcana, and Taylor needed them to resurrect Yttle Elumi to annihilate the dugpa cult. The time of Adharma's manifestation was nearing; Deane-Tanner told me the last time we spoke. He had communicated to Taylor that he had removed the tarot cards and hidden them elsewhere. They were to meet in secret to discuss their location *after* the demon was tucked away again for another fifteen years.

"But before that rendezvous could take place, Deane-Tanner was murdered by someone who had slipped into his house while he was outside seeing off the actress Mabel Normand. That denied the villain the tarot deck and the making of *The Ordeal*. All his plans come to naught."

"I'm willing to bet he got a lot closer to fulfilling them than you think,"

Ravenwood said. "Sally, I feel certain that our bogus William Desmond Taylor was murdered by the real William Desmond Taylor. I believe Taylor meant to assume Deane-Tanner's existence as the William Desmond Taylor of Hollywood fame.

"You've told us how he used the wealth Deane-Tanner had earned as Taylor to fund his quest to defeat the dugpas. Once he had what he needed to do that, he would see no reason he shouldn't take out his understudy and take charge of *The Ordeal* himself, using it to orchestrate in the staging the occult geometry and rituals to raise Yttle Elumi. Regardless of his lack of experience as a movie director, he probably remembered enough about acting to reason he could catch on quickly enough. And he would have had plenty of time to quiz Deane-Tanner on the processes particular to film making during his time as Sands.

"And, of course, he would have gotten the location of the hidden cards from Deane-Tanner while the latter would be bargaining for his life at gun point. But someone must have come on the scene who forced him to flee before he could dispose of Deane-Tanner's body and take his place, let alone the Tarot deck.

"The strand of gold hair and the careful way Deane-Tanner's body was laid out makes me suspect it was Mary Miles Minter," Ravenwood continued. "Air tight alibi aside, she adored Deane-Tanner *as* Taylor madly. She would not have allowed his body to be found in an undignified sprawl.

"And, Sally, there was more to Taylor's plan that he would have ever revealed to Deane-Tanner. He would have taken his place a lot sooner, but he was waiting until the proper cosmic convergence or whatever is needed for initiating the raising of Yttle Elumi. I don't believe Deane-Tanner was at his desk when he was shot. The bullet holes in his coat and vest sketch an alternative position, with his hands raised which is standard positioning when one finds one's self at gun point. But you know what that position means in Golden Dawn symbolism."

"Of course. In our rituals it was the sign of the trident, of Typhos triumphant. But we never made that infiguration outside of the context of the rising of Osiris. In isolation, it would be summoning an unthinkable evil."

"Sally, Typhos was one of the pseudonyms of Yttle Elumi."

Her eyes widened. "You're saying Deane-Tanner was murdered while being forced to *invoke* that creature?"

"Taylor was planning to call up someone out of a netherworld of the dead," Ravenwood said. "A sacrifice is the initiation, a preparatory one, for forging an opening for such an entity into our world. Making the sign of Yttle Elumi while being sacrificed made the summoning specific to him. Necromancers generally try to avoid ringing the wrong number. "

"Then Taylor...made a *ritual sacrifice* of Deane-Tanner?" Sally delicately placed her fingers to her mouth and looked away. "That poor boy....Taylor found one last horrible use for him in his scheme."

Ravenwood nodded. "He's pulled off a lot to complete what he started nine years ago, but he's not quite there yet. Sally?"

She turned to the Stepson of Mystery, her eyes misted sapphire and emerald.

"Taylor was unable to claim the Major Arcana the night of the murder," he said. "And the next morning, all of those tarot cards came to light during the mass rifling of Deane-Tanner's home immediately after his body was discovered. All but one of them were part of the same lot, along with Deane-Tanner's script for *The Ordeal*, at a recent underground auction. Then the missing card surfaced.

"I had Taylor's entire Major Arcana in my possession until two days ago when I was attacked and those cards stolen. I'm hoping now that they are in the hands of that element opposed to Yttle Elumi's coming, the ones who put Joseph Wright floating face down in the Thames. I know from personal experience that they're still active in the present day. If *they* took them, they have most likely destroyed them by now.

"But it's possible that William Desmond Taylor has his Major Arcana back at last. He has the skeleton, and, the way things are moving now, I'm betting he has even unearthed that uncut libretto of *The Ordeal*. What he's still missing is Yttle Elumi's true name, without which he cannot call him up."

"But he has that, too." Fort said, "If he has that libretto."

"Ah, but Sally said Wright used word play so that only those who already knew Yttle Elumi's name would recognize it. If he's depending on the libretto to obtain the name, then he doesn't know it already, which means he's going to have to try to decipher it. If I can convince him I have it already, I could initiate some negotiations to set up a sting."

"What if he doesn't buy your bluff?"

Ravenwood smiled. "Who says I would be bluffing?"

"You *know* Yttle Elumi's name *already*?" Fort asked, his jaw dropping. "How?"

"Well, Fort, I'm going to give it to you straight: while my body was recuperating in the hospital, my mind was with my master the Nameless One, who filled me in."

"You're going to need a lot more than that story to convince Taylor," Fort said.

"How about if I can offer to point it out to him in that libretto? Once, of course, we've set things up to nab him before he can use it." Ravenwood turned to their hostess. "Sally, will you trust me with the loan of your copy of *The Ordeal?*"

"If it will help you avenge Willy Deane-Tanner, most certainly. Let me fetch the libretto for you from my library," she said, patting Ravenwood's wrist as she rose. "Excuse me, gentlemen."

As soon as she left, Fort leaned forward, hands clasped between his knees. "What are you thinking, Ravenwood? Her copy is one of the cut ones."

"Fort, everyone has been focusing on the last page of the libretto in German," Ravenwood explained, "as though someone in the inner circle of the Golden Dawn skipped ahead and caught something in the German text before it played out on the stage, all at the last minute.

"But I think it makes more sense that something flashed a red light earlier in the text. Still, Wright wouldn't have wanted to tip his hand *too* soon, so I'm betting it was in the English on the reverse side of the last page in German. And by 'it' I mean

Yttle Elumi's name, concealed to most by Wright's word play, but apparent to the Golden Dawn insiders.

"And before you ask, Fort, 'no,' I'm not going to tell you what his name is. I have to maintain total control of this knowledge. If you don't feel you can go any further without my complete confidence, I'll understand. Thank you for all you have done. Perhaps it is best if you cut out now; you saw what happened to me. This is a dangerous game we've been playing. And it's about to become more so."

Fort smiled. "And I'm still playing," he said and extended his hand.

Ravenwood shook it and smiled back. "Good man. Now is there anyone back at Universal who is fluent in both German and English?"

"Are you kidding? Laemmle is a German immigrant and half the studio calls him 'uncle.'"

"Swell. I want a translation of the penultimate German page back into English."

"That has been done."

"Not with me present. I need to be with the translator when he makes the word choices that reconstruct the English that was cut out with the last page of the German. I have the key, Fort. Trust me. Let's just hope the translation will forge a lock it will fit."

# CHAPTER TWENTY-FIVE:
## *Libretto a Clef*

As soon as they had returned to Fort's office at Universal, Ravenwood had rung the front desk at the Roosevelt. Arneau and Anne were still not there. He left Fort's extension with the desk and emphasized again that Arneau was to call him immediately upon arrival.

As Ravenwood was hanging up the phone, a knock on the door announced the arrival of Hurst Eschenbach, one of the studio's readers for new German fiction that might make desirable properties for Universal.

"Come in, Hurst," Fort said. "This is Mr. Ravenwood."

"How do you do, Mr. Eschenbach?" Ravenwood asked the tall, fit man with closely cropped, sandy hair.

Eschenbach's tie was straight, his shirt and pants crisply ironed, and his black shoes polished. He clicked his heels and made a slight bow. "Very well, Mr. Ravenwood," he answered with a heavy accent. "I hope you are the same. How may I help you?"

"Please, be seated," Ravenwood said as he motioned at the chair beside him and opened the libretto to the desired page. "This libretto, unfortunately, has had the facing English translation of the German cut out. Would you translate for us? Here's some paper and a pen."

"That should be no problem," he said. "What, may I ask, am I translating?"

"Wagner. An extremely rare libretto."

Hurst's blue eyes shone. "A rare Wagner? *Mit* pleasure!"

"Please read and translate aloud as you go along, if you don't mind."

Hurst began:

"*Ich bin der huter der schwelle. Ich werde fragen und du wirst antwort geben: was fur ein gewand tragest du?*

"I am the dweller on the threshold. I will demand and you will answer: what is your raiment?

"*Ein Kettenhemd.*

"A chain shirt."

"Chain shirt?" Ravenwood said. "In English, we would say chain mail."

Hurst shot Ravenwood a bemused smile. "You mean mail like Harvey delivers at the studio? You think this translates into what you Americans call a chain letter?"

Fort grinned, turned, and pulled a volume of the *Oxford English Dictionary* off his shelf. He began flipping through it. "Here we go," he said after a moment. "A different etymology altogether. The mail in Harvey's bicycle basket comes from the Norse language. But mail in chain mail comes from the old French in Middle English: maille for ring."

"Ring...yes," Ravenwood said, staring into space. He suddenly looked back at Hurst. "Go on. Please."

" All right. The Dweller next asks, *Und dein met?* Which translates into... And your mead? And Lita answers *galle* which is gall. Then the Dweller asks:

"*Un was beabischtigst du dich zu nahern?*

"And what would you approach?

"*Dem altar.*

"The altar.

"*Womit glaubst du das recht erworben zu haben?*

"By what right?

Ernst had now come to the last line on the page:

"*Mit dem kettenhemd, mit der galle, nahere ich mich dem Altar.*

"By chain shirt...pardon me: by chain *mail*, by gall, I approach the altar."

Ravenwood tugged the paper Hurst was writing on from under his pen so that a trail of ink streaked across it.

"If I remember my mother's grammar lessons to me," Ravenwood said to Fort, "one wishes parallel construction in English when writing items in a series, and since the meaning remains clear if one abbreviates chain mail to mail...."

He marked through chain and smiled.

*By mail, by gall, I approach the altar.*

*Maelgaltyr.*

"I take it the key fit?" Fort said, leaning over.

"Yes," Ravenwood said. "And it would unlock far more than anyone sane would desire. I need to make a phone call again immediately. If I may?"

"Sure," Fort said, sliding the phone across the desk to him.

"Thank you," Ravenwood said, dialing the Roosevelt again. As the phone rang, he looked at Hurst. "Thank you, too, Hurst. You've been very helpful." He cradled the phone in the crook of his neck, pulled out his wallet with his free hand, and took out a ten dollar bill which he passed to the German. "You may go now, my good man."

Hurst slid back in his chair, looking at Fort who nodded his consent.

"Yes," Ravenwood said, as the hotel clerk picked up, and Hurst was on the way out. "Have Hank Arneau and Anne D'Arromanches arrived? They *have*? Then why haven't I heard from them? Who am I? I am Ravenwood. I left a message… Not where you keep notes? And he said nothing to you? I see.

"…shift change, didn't pass my message on," he whispered aloud to Fort. Then, in the phone: "Never mind. Please ring me Hank…no, Miss D'Arromanches' room immediately."

# CHAPTER TWENTY-SIX:
## *Roosevelt Rendezvous*

Having seen Anne to her room, Arneau had left her to unpack and hang up the dresses he had bought to cover any occasion during her Hollywood trip. When she caught herself staring too long at the large shiny buttons and filmy collar of one dress, she quickly closed the door and leaned her back against it, as though holding something inside at bay.

Hank Arneau had succeeded in sweeping her off her feet, and now she was trying to regain traction, especially after making a fool of herself on the plane with that mortifying hint at matrimony. Add to that how they had just parted, and she was thus doubly gratified at his annoyance when, given all the clothes from which she now had to choose, she insisted on wearing the outfit from their museum outing. That one was *hers*, mismatched thread and all. And unless it was indeed a special occasion or on the set, she would always return to it or another outfit from her meager wardrobe pre-Hank Arneau. Hank would have to continue to understand that he did not own her. When she earned a paycheck, then she would purchase her own new clothing.

No, she would *not* have Hank return and find her going over her lines in anything he had bought for her. She realized she was fingering the *I Ching* charm around her neck. Okay, anything but the T'ai. Still, she wouldn't let him see her wearing it. She tucked the charm inside her blouse. Anyway,

*"And I'm still playing."*

that was no more than what any producer would give his leading lady for good luck. Hank had spelled it out that way himself; purely platonic.

Friends. Maybe...not even that now. She cradled her forehead in her hand and allowed herself enough of a cry that wouldn't leave her face puffy when she saw him next.

Arneau had made it clear he expected her to be able to run four pages with him at breakfast. "And not to be dismissive of your street smarts," he had added, "but you don't know *these* streets. I don't want you wandering around. I can't risk anything happening to you. We're too far in at this point.

"I'm having your dinner catered to your room from *Musso, Franks*, and I expect you to keep the door locked at all times except to let in the bus boy."

"Really, Hank. Why don't we bypass my opening the door altogether? Tell you what: you have him shout 'Rapunzel' from the sidewalk, I'll open the window, let down my long golden hair, and he can use it for a dumb waiter."

Arneau had reached out and patted her hair. "'Gold' is right, Blondie. You're the bullion that's backing the Astoria mint. So I'm not taking a step until I know my investment is secure."

"Investment?" She had jerked her head away from his touch and couldn't help but color. "Don't worry, Mr. Arneau, your investment will remain locked up tighter than Fort Knox."

"Easy kid," he had said, holding up his hands, palms out. "Why so sore? I thought you would feel appreciated."

She shook her head and glowered at him. "Yes indeed. Appreciated. Like a stock or bond. Tell me, Mr. Arneau: what *is* this way you have with women?"

"Way off, it appears," he had said as he had put on his Stetson hat and gave the brim a twist.

Then Arneau had left to track down Ravenwood "to conclude our business," as he had put it, for the man with the chameleon eyes had not been in his room when they arrived.

Composure regained, Anne kicked off her street worn heels, sat down, and began studying her dialogue. She found her lines a welcome diversion from her disappointment and was focusing on them when there was a knock on her door. Expecting her dinner, she crossed the room with her face in the script and opened the door without asking who was there.

"Good evening, Miss D'Arromanches. I hope you and Hank had a good flight?"

She looked up from her script to see Nate Tannen smiling at her, his hat held before him.

"Oh! Mr. Tannen! Hello. Yes we did. Thank you for asking. Please," she said as she stepped back, ushering him inside. "I thought you were the delivery boy with dinner. Hank has me sequestered here, memorizing dialogue. I'd be happy to share my supper if you would consider running the lines with me?"

"Miss D'Arromanches…"

"Please. 'Anne.'"

"Anne, I've actually come down to fetch you to attend to another detail which I wish to settle first: blocking. I'm sorry to whisk you off before you've had dinner; we can grab a sandwich on Hollywood Boulevard on the way to the Pathe lot . . ."

"But...wait. I don't mind missing dinner, but Hank was adamant that I stay in tonight and learn my lines."

"Hank isn't familiar with my process," Nate said. "This is an important scene. You might say the blocking has me blocked, and I won't be able to concentrate on anything else until this is settled."

"Well," Anne said, "you are the director, after all." She looked back at him. "Just let me leave Hank a note."

"Certainly," Nate said, reaching into his inner breast pocket. "I have a pen."

"Thank you," Anne said. She took a sheet of the hotel letterhead from a drawer and wrote down where she had gone and with whom. As she headed for the door, she paused by the closet. There was a bonnet, a lovely blue bonnet. It was from Hank, but the night was cool. It was just the bonnet after all...and it was from Hank.

She took it from the closet shelf, shut the door, paused before a mirror to position the hat just so on her head, then smiled at Nate. "I'm ready."

"Swell. Let's go," he said, holding the door as she stepped out into the hall, then closed it behind her.

The clang and rumble of the arriving elevator drowned out the phone ringing down the hall in Anne's room.

# CHAPTER TWENTY-SEVEN:
## *The Meeting On the Threshold*

Nate and Anne arrived on the Pathe lot, and he parked his car on the side of the dirt road that ran between the facades left over from DeMille's *Chicago*. They walked the rest of the way as the road dipped and then ran up hill to the immediately adjacent set for the same director's *King of Kings*. It was the latter Arneau was refurbishing for *The Ordeal*. Under moonlight, the columns of this *faux* old Jerusalem courtyard gleamed not unlike silver nitrate film when projected. Anne felt she was already on a movie screen, although the first camera had yet to roll.

A set of long steps led up from the courtyard to a gigantic wall in the middle of which protruded the Stonehenge-like gate. In the distance beyond it, directly in line with the wall's opening, scaffolding used to raise the façade of the castle of Monsalvant rose higher than the gate itself. On a platform atop the scaffolding set a large, darkened spotlight tilted down toward a Roman pillar standing incongruously near the medieval castle front.

"That entryway there," Nate said, pointing at the gate as they walked over the open courtyard with its columns, "was originally draped with the giant curtain that veiled DeMille's Holy of Holies...but it's been desecrated now." He grinned.

Anne paused. "What do you mean?"

He took her by the arm and began leading her again toward the gateway. "Surely you recognize the entrance to the Chapel Perilous, Anne. This is where your character has her final confrontation with the powers of darkness. As for who triumphs; did Hank tell you that for decades no one has known exactly how this story ends?"

"He started the movie *without* having an ending?" Anne asked.

"Well, there always has been *an* ending, but it's in the English translation. Things get lost in translation all the time." He held up a bound booklet he had been carrying which Anne had assumed was his copy of the script. "But we now have the only known extant copy of the complete libretto in Wagner's German."

"Wherever did you find it?" Anne asked as she reached out tentatively and touched the edges of the pages with just her fingertips before quickly withdrawing her hand.

"In the personal collection of the originator of your role, Anne: Miss Odette de Lyss. This was the music composer's personal copy. They had been lovers, but she absolutely hated him at the time of his death. Yet, she appropriated his libretto to save it from being mutilated like the others and couldn't bring herself to part with it all those years she survived him. Queer beings, you women.

"She spent her last days in a shabby back room in her sister's house, crammed with mementos from her few-years brush with greatness. She was swollen like a tick with alcohol at the end, a completely forgotten figure in opera."

"Poor, pathetic creature," Anne said softly.

"If you're going to feel sorry for someone, Anne, pity her sister. According to her brother-in-law, Odette was a self-centered, contentious burden on their marriage, one who never once thanked her sister for changing her pissed-drenched bed sheets. Amazingly, her sibling still loved her and actually offered to give me this libretto for free if I would only add in the credits that your role was created by Odette on the stage.

"Her husband told her to shut up, that this was Hollywood, and it was about time that bloated cow paid her back rent. I quite agreed with him. Obtaining this copy at any price was a complete spot of luck for all of us involved in *The Ordeal*. I wouldn't have allowed the production to get this far otherwise."

Anne brought them to a halt and looked at him. "*You* wouldn't have allowed it?"

"Well, of course. How can you do Wagner without Wagner's ending? I would have disabused Hank of that notion a long time ago."

"Do you really think so?" Anne asked as they strolled along again. "This movie is an obsession with him."

Now Nate stopped and looked at her. "Why? Why the adaptation of *this* opera?"

Anne shrugged. "It could be any opera, I suppose. Or anything prestigious enough to allow Astoria to remain competitive with the West Coast movie industry."

"That's all he's told you?" Nate asked.

"What else is there to know?"

"Your mark."

"What?"

"This is your first mark, right here on the bottom step."

"Oh…all right."

"Let's begin. Now, at this point, your character Lita has earned the right to approach the gateway to Monsalvant. But the Dweller on the Threshold does not wish you to pass. He knows your weakness and is going to exploit it.

"Next, you're going to move up to here." He walked her halfway up the steps. "Now at this point, a light will come up on the covered altar there just inside the gateway. There is something under the cover. You don't know what, so you hesitate here for a moment, and then you move forward again. Let's go."

Anne did not move. "This altar…"

"It's in these night shadows. Come closer."

"What's under the covering?" she asked without moving.

"You haven't read the script?"

"Not all the way through, no. I'm learning my lines in order. I haven't skipped ahead. I don't like…to spoil endings."

"Neither do I. You really have no idea at all?"

Anne swallowed and looked through the gateway. "Yes," she said finally, her voice small. "It's that skeleton, isn't it?"

"It is. I noticed your reaction when it was uncovered in front of the Astoria studio. Are you going to be squeamish? It might help if you think of it as a museum piece rather than out of a grave."

Anne took a breath, looked up at him, and smiled. "Well, like Mrs. McCallahan used to tell us at the orphanage, the safest place to be is alone in the middle of a cemetery. No one's going to bother you there."

Nate grinned at her. "That's right. And you're *not* alone. Just continue to follow my direction. I want you to walk up the remaining steps, through that gate and pull back the drapery from the altar."

Anne marched up to the entrance and suddenly stopped, taking in the massive size of the wall in which the gateway was set. She stepped back.

"Anne?" Nate asked. "You mustn't allow your nerves to overcome you. Because your character, Lita, would not. Draw on that Viking blood of yours."

"No," she cut him off. "It's not the skeleton. It's just…isn't this all very large for a *chapel*? What exactly would be on the other side of a wall that big?"

"It's not the kind of wall for keeping something *out*, Anne," Nate said.

"This was DeMille's Jerusalem temple wall, remember? And our *mise en scene* must be on an operatic scale."

Anne shook her head, looked over her shoulder and flashed him a winningly abashed grin. "I'm sorry. I have a recurring nightmare...a giant black shape pursuing me. I just had a crazy feeling it would be on the other side."

Nate shook his head and grinned. "That's okay. It is a little spooky out here at night. But there's nothing back there but any two by fours or electric cables the crew left laying around. The tallest thing is that scaffolding with the spotlight."

"Why is that big light up there?" Anne asked.

"So the crew can work at night. However, *we* couldn't work over all the hammering and sawing racket, so I gave them this evening off."

He nodded her on. She resumed stepping toward the altar. Nate followed, his libretto opened to the final page...

The rumble of a roadster and car headlight beams cutting across the dark Pathe lot turned both Anne's and Nate's heads. The car stopped just short of the remains of the old Jerusalem set, and a man stepped out from the passenger's side.

"I am Ravenwood."

"Well, what are you doing here?" Nate asked.

"Oh!" Anne said. "Hello, Mr. Ravenwood. Are you looking for Hank? I'm sorry; he's not here. He's been trying to find you, though."

"Yes," Ravenwood said. "I went to the *Pig n' Whistle* and ended up in the hospital."

"Oh, dear," Anne said. "Food poisoning?"

Ravenwood rubbed the back of his head. "I was served some veal that didn't agree with me."

"Mr. Arneau is not here," Nate said. "And we're working. So if you'd..."

"Looks like you're blocking the final scene," Ravenwood interjected, walking closer. With a toss of his head he indicated his companion who followed him. "This is Murphy Fort."

Nate crossed his arms. "The man who passed on our screenplay."

"Mr. Tannen," Ravenwood said, "since Fort and I know *The Ordeal's* ending, might we be allowed to stick around and watch?"

Anne put her hand on Nate's arm. "But this is Wagner's authentic ending," she said. "Nate has a copy of the libretto with the final scene in German."

Fort looked at Ravenwood upon hearing this announcement, but

Ravenwood kept his eyes on Nate while crossing his arms and slipping his fingers inside his coat to rest on the pistol holstered beneath it.

"Fort's with a rival studio! He can't stay," Tannen said.

"Mr. Tannen," Ravenwood said, "what Miss D'Arromanches didn't tell you is that I'm a detective in Mr. Arneau's employ. He wants me to keep an eye on Anne when he's not around. Which is what I intend to do. And Fort here is my chauffeur. So, just go ahead and finish your scene there," he said, nodding at him.

"Fine! But Universal had better not be advertising tomorrow that Laemmle is going into production on Wagner's *The Ordeal* with his original, lost ending, or there *will* be a lawsuit. Do you understand, Mr. Fort?"

"No conflict of interests here," Fort said. "Money's too tight at Universal these days for something on this scale."

"Very well then," Nate said and turned back to Anne. He forced a smile.

"Now, Anne, go back to your mark…okay. Now up the steps, over the threshold, pause, and survey the altar. Then look up, and in the distance you see the castle of Monsalvant.

"You faintly hear in the distance the most beautiful music in the world. It's coming from that castle. Your body has a shiver of ecstasy Anne, real spiritual ecstasy, because even from this far away, your soul is trying to step outside your body and go to that music."

Anne closed her eyes and took a deep breath, her lips parted slightly as she trembled. Nate had now joined her at the altar.

"…good, good, but suddenly, you snap back."

Anne's eyes flew open wide.

"You realize to let this go on means that you're saying goodbye to your physical self. But to be unable to even feel your lover in your arms, what kind of union will that be in Monsalvant? You look back down at the altar. And now it's drawing you. You know you shouldn't, but you can't resist. You pull back that covering to just below the collarbone and see what's beneath it."

Anne did as she was told. Her eyes widened even further. She was repulsed by the thing as ever, but she wasn't going to let Hank or Nate down. *Just a museum piece* she told herself.

Ravenwood and Fort had been slowly moving closer while Nate was focused on Anne. They now stopped at a respectful distance but leaned forward to hear.

Nate continued, "Lita says words to the effect of 'Lover, come to me that

I may have the courage to go with you. One final embrace, and I will leave my body on this altar with yours, and our souls will unite in Monsalvant.'

"And here the stage directions say that you embrace the skeleton, Anne."

"I...what?"

"You embrace it and begin to violently try and wrench it from the altar, like you're trying to wrest your dead lover back into physical existence."

Anne stepped back. "Nate, you have to understand why I find that repulsive. Why did this have to be a real skeleton?"

Fort whispered to Ravenwood: "So far, this 'lost German ending' hasn't varied from the English translation we've always had."

But Ravenwood was concentrating on Anne and Nate's argument.

"...because, Anne, a plaster skeleton like something out of a carnival dark ride will undermine the power of the moment. We must transcend mere verisimilitude here. This moment has to be *real*. Real death on that altar and real youthful life in you must come together."

"Nate, I..."

"Look, I suspected you would need time to warm up to the idea. I'm not going to ask that you completely uncloak it yet. Keep the covering between you for now. You won't actually be touching it. Not tonight. All right?"

Anne's bosom rose and fell with one labored breath; she turned back to the skeleton, and fell across it on the altar, careful to raise her body ever so slightly from even the blanket. She closed her eyes against the death's head hollow apertures staring unrelentingly into her face.

If Nate noticed, he did not seem to care. "Then there's a hermit who has joined Lita at the chapel who has this line..."

His eyes riveted on the libretto, he raised his voice:

"Tyvitapep! *Reise! Riese! Aptrganger! Kempfer mit Gott in der Erde!*"

Anne remained poised over the skeleton, waiting for Nate to translate or give her further direction. She opened her eyes and was about to look over and see why he was waiting when something just visible from her position caught her attention.

Ravenwood pressed his fingers to his gun and leaned in to Fort. "Well, there's that line in the original German and it's not exactly what's been reconstructed."

Fort narrowed his eyes as he stared at the frowning Nate intently scanning the libretto. "Indeed. I think I heard...giant?"

"He has no idea he just needs to flip the page back for the name he needs," Ravenwood said and smiled. "Instead, he's trying out a combination of Yttle Elumi's various deity names."

"Not the ending you were hoping for?" Ravenwood called out to Tannen.

Without looking up, Nate said, "You can watch, Mr. Ravenwood, but I'd thank you not to interrupt. We're working here."

Anne rose from her prone position over the altar, turned and held up what she had found beneath the blanket.

"What was this doing in the skeleton, Nate?" she asked. "Is this one of Hank's tarot cards?"

# CHAPTER TWENTY-EIGHT:
## *Into the Chapel Perilous*

Ravenwood immediately drew his gun from his holster and trained it on Nate. Fort stepped back.

Anne's eyes widened. "Mr. Ravenwood?"

"What is the meaning of this?" Nate demanded, setting his libretto on the altar. "You intrude on my set and now you're holding me at gun point? Are you mad?"

"Anne," Ravenwood said. "Please get over here! Now!"

Anne cocked her head at him, knitted her brow, and, still holding the tarot card, stepped forward.

Nate's hand lashed out, grasped her upper arm and stopped her. "Don't, Anne! The man's obviously unhinged. Didn't Hank tell you this movie was going to be made once before but William Desmond Taylor was murdered to stop it? Now it looks like I'm the target and you can be certain he won't let you or Mr. Fort live to talk."

"Who would *ever* kill someone to stop a movie from being made?" Anne said.

"Ask him," Nate said and nodded at Ravenwood.

"Anne," Ravenwood said, "No one was ever murdered to halt this movie's production, least of all William Desmond Taylor. That tarot card you're holding *is* one of the ones Hank sent with me to have Mr. Fort here look over. I was mugged, Hank's cards taken. Under your director's direction, I suffered a blow to the head that put me in the hospital."

"You said...veal," Anne said.

"You see? He can't keep a straight story. You can't trust him," Nate said.

"Nate knows *exactly* how both accounts reconcile. He's a dangerous man, Anne. Get away from him."

She brushed off Nate's hand and extended her own, beckoning with her fingers. "Mr. Ravenwood, if it's my safety you're truly concerned about, give *me* the gun. I'm a good shot."

"Miss D'Arromanches, it's my regard for your safety that will not allow me to lower my offensive stance. Please! Just bring that card over here, and Mr. Fort will verify it is part of the deck Hank sent me to show him."

"Indeed I can," Fort said. "That Major Arcana is unique."

"And as for how that card ended up inside that skeleton; I'll show you where I took a blow to the back of my head when it was taken from me."

Anne hesitated, then sighed. "Fine. I…"

Nate snatched her back, and hugged her tightly to him so that she faced Ravenwood.

"Nate!" she shouted. "What are you doing?"

"By Typhos triumphant," Nate shouted, holding Anne with his right arm while raising his left hand and tracing sigils in the air. Immediately, a powerful wind raised every plank not nailed down along with every loose bit of masonry and sent them hurling toward Ravenwood and Fort.

Before the men could take shelter behind Fort's roadster, they were being pummeled. Grit and dust filled their eyes and mouths. Fort toppled over. Ravenwood held his footing until, finally, a two by four struck his head wound, and he went face forward to the ground. As his gun dropped from his hand, the wind caught it and swept it away.

"What's happening? What *are* you?" Anne shouted over the maelstrom as she tried to wrench free of Nate.

In the subsiding of the whirlwind's cacophony, he wrapped both arms around her and said, "The question is who are *you*?" Anne flinched as his hot breath brushed her cheek. "And what is your connection with that skeleton which you've sensed from the moment you first laid eyes on it?"

"You're an Angel of the Presence, Anne," Ravenwood called out, gingerly touching the back of his head as he and Fort rose to their feet.

Nate quickly turned his head toward him. "How do you know that title, Ravenwood?"

"Oh," he said, dusting himself off. "I know all kinds of unimportant stuff like that. Like, that card Anne's holding depicts Yttle Elumi coming to life. That's why you had it stuck in that skeleton. It's part of the ritual to bring him back."

Nate stared at him. "Impressive. You seem to have reached the same knowledge as I have but by a different route. What else do you know?"

"Well, first of all, Nate may I call you, Bill? Go ahead and drop the disguise, why don't you?"

Grinning, Nate clawed away with one hand at his face, pulling free putty features and artificial tufts of brows. Anne tried to pull free while he withdrew one holding arm to doff his disguise, but Fort increased his grip with the other so tightly she had to gasp to regain her breath.

Murphy Fort's jaw slackened. "You are the very image of the man!" he said.

"Poor William Cunningham Deane-Tanner, you mean? He was always just my understudy. But when it came time for the real William Desmond Taylor to step forward and claim his Hollywood life from the place holder, someone came calling, and I was forced to flee the premises before I could dispose of Deane-Tanner's body."

"Obviously, you didn't give up *all* your plans," Ravenwood said.

"No," Taylor said with a smirk. "I had worked far too long and hard just to abandon my scheme. I returned in disguise; even compressed my spine to appear shorter, early the next morning. I found the bungalow undergoing a communal pilfering in which I readily joined to recover my tarot deck." He snatched the card from Anne.

"A flat foot whom you know as Inspector Stagg saw me take this one and came after me. I didn't recognize him at the studio the other morning because of age and his significant weight gain, but even nine years ago, he was beginning to carry enough of a spare tire that I easily outdistanced him. I would have kept running and escaped, but he began blowing his whistle which meant he was gathering other cops who would be spreading out, looking for a man answering my description. But I was not unprepared. I had set out that morning with a second disguise on my person in the event my initial false features would need to disappear.

"I gambled I had enough of a lead on Stagg to change my appearance before he could overtake me, but he caught me in an alley with my true face exposed. I escaped by unleashing a violent wind storm on him just as I did you, but I lost this card in the process.

"When I retraced my steps later and couldn't find it, I figured Stagg had returned it to the bungalow, which would mean it had been boxed up with the rest of the Major Arcana by the studio. Turns out he held onto it all these years...until it was ready to rejoin the other cards that had been kept under lock and key."

With a toss of his head, Taylor indicated the skeleton on the altar. "I knew *he* would not allow any of the Major Arcana to be destroyed even if everything else confiscated was. I had merely to plant myself in the proper Hollywood circles and keep an eye out for their emergence.

"So I took on yet a new identity: Nate Tannen, a director 'Taylor' had discovered during his recent European sojourn and arranged to bring to Hollywood before his premature death. I established myself with Taylor's signature, which, of course, was my own, on his letter of recommendation.

"Then I bided my time. After Hank Arneau out-bid me on that lot consisting of my Major Arcana and the script for *The Ordeal*, it became essential that I attach myself to his movie project.

"Fortunately, he was receptive. He even agreed to go to the expense of traveling to Los Angeles to film scenes. I required it. For it was here Deane-Tanner's sacrifice initiated the opening for Yttle Elumi. The metaphysics of magic, as described in *Diet of the Wyrm*, necessitate such rituals of ingress come to completion within the radius of the point marked on the magical grid by the slaying.

"That was a notably different reading of the German of the resurrection scene than has been reconstructed before," Ravenwood said.

"You mean *Erhebe ich! Erhebe ich! Aptrganger! Kampfer mit Gott in der erde* is what you get when you translate Rise! Rise! One who walks after death! Contend with God in the earth! That *does* make perfect sense in the context of the play, where Lita is imploring her dead lover to wrench from God the power of life and come out of the ground as it were.

"But what was written in the libretto's original German, and this was Wright's doing, not Wagner's, were two different words in place of 'Erhebe ich' twice. The first time, Wright used old High German for rise...reise... but the second time he wrote *riese* which is modern German for giant and which inverts the 'i' and 'e' in *reise*. I thought this inversion a mistake and that he meant to repeat *reise* again. The English translation on the facing page as Rise! Rise! supported this.

"Then I realized Wright intended this misdirection in case someone skipped ahead to the ending. Giant suddenly appearing at the end in both German and English with no context with what had gone before would have raised some eyebrows. So he made *riese* appear as a typographical error.

"You noticed, of course, *reise* and *riese* are pronounced differently. But that dialogue was to be spoken by Wright himself in the role of a hermit, so I'm certain during rehearsals he pronounced it *reise* both times so as not to raise questions. But if he had been allowed to speak the word on stage, he would have certainly said *riese* the second time.

"When they expurgated the librettos, the Golden Dawn knew no one would have any reason to think of old High German should they translate rise from English back into the libretto's original language, but the contemporary *Erhebe ich! Erhebe ich!* No one could construe the German word for giant from that. That's why they allowed the English translation to remain intact."

"What made you think *riese* wasn't a mistake? I don't get this giant business. That's not that large of a skeleton on that altar," Ravenwood said.

"Not a literal giant; the key was the phrase 'contend with God in the earth.' Giant' and God contending only come together in *Genesis* 6: 3-4. Wright was playing off the old English translation from the Septuagint in that *Genesis* passage of the name of those who opposed God in prehistory. Giant was translated from the Septuagint Nephilim which means fallen *great one* as in giant among men. In the context of that scriptural allusion preserved in the resurrection incantation, giant still signifies a Nephilim who contended with God in the earth. Apparently it is only necessary to preserve Yttle Elumi's *Ipsissima Vox*, not his *Ispissima Verba*."

Ravenwood looked at Fort. "An acceptable paraphrase would do; his exact words aren't required to revive him," Fort explained.

Taylor jabbed a finger back at the altar. "That skeleton, gentlemen, is nothing less than that of a Nephilim and Wright's interpolation the incantation he discovered to bring him back to life!

"Now, as you've drawn me into answering more of your questions, Ravenwood, I'm going to insist you finally answer mine. The incantation failed because I have not identified the name of Yttle Elumi. Have you found it out?"

Ravenwood sighed. "Yes. I suppose there's no point in bargaining with that information for Anne's release?"

Taylor smiled and shook his head. "You know the answer to that already. The knowledge of the name is pointless without one of her lineage."

"What lineage?" Anne asked her voice small. She suddenly wondered if their parting quarrel would be Hank's final memory of her.

"All will be revealed soon enough, Anne, if Mr. Ravenwood cooperates. You may think we are at a stalemate, Ravenwood. However, I have no problem in torturing Anne until you decide to relieve her misery by giving me the name. And if you think you might try something as foolhardy as you and Fort rushing me...well, you've seen what I can do."

"Surely you don't want to risk one of your wind storms striking me with another loose plank," Ravenwood said, gingerly touching the back of his head. "You'd chance putting me in another coma, and I couldn't tell you anything then."

"Still," Taylor countered, and, still holding Anne to him with one arm, grabbed her head with the hand of the other and twisted it so that she groaned, "you can't possibly reach me before I snap Anne's neck. Don't put me in a position of having nothing to lose, Ravenwood. *Tell me* what I wish to *know!*"

Ravenwood took a deep breath. "Well, Bill, you of all people should know the power of a name. It *is* there in the libretto. Look on the reverse side of the German page you've just read and look closely at the last line."

Taylor released Anne's head, tucked the tarot card back into the skeleton's ribcage, then used his free hand to turn back the page of his libretto on the altar.

"That's right," Ravenwood said. "Lita's last line: by mail, by gall, she approaches the altar: Maelgaltyr is his name."

"'Evil rune wizard?' Why, I do believe you're being straight with me," Taylor said, looking up from his libretto and smiling.

He reached with his free hand into his pocket and produced his car keys. "Mr. Fort, go unlock my trunk," he said, tossing the keys to him. "There's rope in the back. I had planned on restraining Anne, but there should be plenty in there for you and Ravenwood, too."

In a few moments, Fort had the rope and Taylor nodded at one of the columns on the set. "Go over there, Ravenwood," he said. "Fort, tie him to it; then Miss D'Arromanches will do the same to you."

Ravenwood was tied facing the gateway, his arms bent around the pillar.

"*Pull*, Ravenwood," Taylor said. "Strain. I want to be certain Fort hasn't tried any trick knots. Ah, good. You're in for the night." He shoved Anne forward. "Tie Fort now, Anne, on the back side of the column. There you go. And don't either of you think of running for help. If you do, I promise you won't find Ravenwood alive when you return. And Anne, no false hopes about that note you left Arneau back at the hotel. Disappearing ink, you know. "

"Wasn't that conjuring on the cheap for you?" Ravenwood said, noticing for the first time Anne's necklace with the eleventh hexagram. It had slipped out from her blouse during her exertions in tying Fort. Ravenwood caught Anne's gaze and indicated the T'ai with his eyes as she stepped back from the column.

*"So I took on a new identity; Nate Tannen, director."*

"Hide it," he breathed.

She made a slight nod, then, her back still to Taylor, adjusted her collar and slipped the charm back inside her clothes.

"All done, Anne?" Taylor said. "Yes? Good. Fort, if you would be so good as to pull against your bonds so that I can see you're secured as well. Excellent! Now, Anne, come with me."

Anne, chin held high, looked him in the eye as she coiled the remaining rope.

"What are you going to do with me?" she asked as he took the rope and slid his arm through its loop. "Once you've tied me up, too."

"There's something else first. Come along." They again climbed the stairs back to the gate whose Stonehenge design recalled that of the twelfth hexagram. Once there, Anne startled as another tarot card sprung from Taylor's sleeve into his palm: the Angel of the Presence. From his other hand he conjured a safety pin and was moving her collar to affix it to her blouse when he uncovered the T'ai charm.

He clucked his tongue. "No my girl that will *not* do," he said, reaching around her neck and roughly unclasping the chain. He threw it far from the gateway, the charm landing almost at Ravenwood's feet. He looked at the familiar symbol, the inverse of the figure made by the gate. Clearly, the eleventh hexagram was antithetical to what Taylor was attempting to do, he looked up at the gateway, while the twelfth was simpatico.

Taylor finished pinning the tarot card of the Angel of the Presence to Anne's blouse and suddenly her eyes went milky blue, reflecting long ago northern skies along with the electric light streaked ones of Hollywood in 1931.

"This is the appointed moment," she said. She raised her voice: "It's all right, Mr. Ravenwood." She looked again at the skeleton and did not flinch. "I no longer fear him. 'On the burning ground we will meet, though the disciple be consumed.' Maelgaltyr shall not pass. "

"That remains to be seen," Taylor said, pulling from his pocket the Jannes card and pinning it to himself. Then, he and Anne turned, and Ravenwood watched them approach the skeleton.

"Fort," Ravenwood said, "when Taylor pinned that tarot card onto Anne, it did something to her. Her whole demeanor changed. She's fully cooperating."

"Then why did he bring that rope for her?" Fort asked, futilely trying to crane his neck to see.

"I don't know. But they're playing this out like the Egyptian Major

Arcana," he said. "The Jannes and the Angel have come together at the gate where Yttle Elumi is about to rise."

Taylor was now reverently pulling the covering completely back over the skeleton. Then he raised his voice:

"Maelgaltyr! *Reise! Riese! Aptrganger! Kempfer mit Gott in der erde!*"

A yellowish haze began to form over the altar. Suddenly, a shudder ran through the blanket, and Ravenwood realized the altar was trembling. Soon it was in such a violent seizure that it collapsed, the blanket now draping the crumbled altar alone; the skeleton beneath it had vanished.

Ravenwood hoped that perhaps the bones had been ground to dust by the violent shaking they had taken. Taylor seemed taken aback, poking with his toe the blanket and drawing it back with his foot to confirm the obvious.

But Anne, staring straight ahead, pointed beyond the scaffolding with the spotlight atop it.

"Behold! He comes in the form of an old man, hooded and wearing a royal robe!"

Taylor looked at the shadowy shape in the distance making its way toward them.

"He will *not* pass," Anne said.

"You have yet to face him," Taylor said, taking her roughly by the arm. "Come!"

"What's happening, Ravenwood?" Fort asked, jerking at his bonds and feeling the pillar budge. " Ravenwood! Those tremors seemed to have loosened our pillar at its base."

Ravenwood pulled against the pillar and felt it budge further. "You're right. Help me rock it, and we'll see if we can get it to fall on its side. Then perhaps we can crawl along the ground and slip our ropes over the top."

"And then what?" Fort asked. "Our hands are still tied. And even if they weren't, we have no power against this sorcery."

Ravenwood felt the bag of marbles against his chest...

...as he looked at Anne's T'ai charm, which had landed near him properly turned so that it made the eleventh hexagram. Then he looked at the gateway beyond in the shape of the twelfth, and then at the spotlight atop the scaffolding over the castle of Monsalvant façade.

*Turn the twelfth hexagram back to the eleventh and to this beacon the Great Ones will come.*

"I think we do," he said. "Let's get going."

# CHAPTER TWENTY-NINE:
## *Return of the Dugpa*

Anne and Taylor and the figure shrouded in robe and hood converged on the Roman column standing between the gateway and the scaffolding. Under the figure's cowl, parchment colored skin stretched tautly over sharp cheekbones. Beneath a high forehead, sunken back in twin craters, black pupils the size of pinpoints oscillated, regarding the strange man and woman.

"I remember...," the shrouded figure began and stopped, wrinkling the parchment-brow, as though he did not recognize the voice, so long unused, as his own. To Anne's and Taylor's ears, the initial weak vocals sounded like whispers drug from a gramophone record turned by hand.

"I...remember," he began again. "I was...beset by traitors and slain. Then I ...wandered...in arid places...endless wastes of oblivion that stretched ever upward. There was an opening. I heard the name. The name to which I must answer if I would live again. I followed...."

Taylor kneeled, but Anne stood straight. "It was I who called you up, great Maelgaltyr," he said.

"I was...Aurochel," the hooded man said. In that moment, when he seemed not yet completely reformed and his soul naked before them, he trembled at recalling that name.

Then his countenance hardened, pitiless and implacable.

"I am become Maelgaltyr, mighty in the glyphs, the rune magic."

He ran finger over finger, missing for the first time his rings, then spread his fingers before him and frowned. "They have taken spoil of my hands," he said.

Taylor rose to his feet. "Your enemies are mine, Lord Maelgaltyr. I am William Desmond Taylor, your servant who would be your acolyte, first and greatest of the dugpa."

"I do not know you," Maelgaltyr said, turning his eyes on Anne. "But *you*. Your kind did always oppose me."

"I oppose you now," Anne said. "I do not fear you, Aurochel the lame."

Maelgaltyr crooked his head at Anne and smiled, withered lips peeling back to reveal yellow pegs arrayed in pale gums. "Not *yet*," he said, clipping each word. Then his features contracted into a scowl. "You!" he ordered Taylor, seeing the rope in his hands. "Bind her to that pillar."

Taylor obeyed and Anne offered no resistance as her wrists were lashed together and her white arms raised over her head as the rope was pulled and looped through an iron ring fixed above on the column. Though subdued, she was no less defiant. With a toss of her head, her bonnet fell and her hair unfurled like flame down her back.

"You bind me with rope, but it is *you* who are truly bound. You may have reclaimed your body, but you cannot merely tie me here and pass on. My will holds you. You will remain the Dweller on the Threshold! Even if we must annihilate each other, then you will be sent back to…"

"No!" Maelgaltyr snapped. "*You* will be consumed! You *alone*!" He grabbed her head and turned it about in jaundiced, tapering fingers with long, yellow nails. "My banishment is at an end! I return to the world of men, and I *shall* ascend and sit again on my throne at the top of the earth!"

A man's scream for help turned both Maelgaltyr's and Taylor's attention toward the gate.

"Who is that?" Maelgaltyr asked Taylor.

"One of two men who opposed your coming, my master. I bound them that they might be forced to endure the humiliation of seeing you risen in power, and that you might personally judge them."

"*You* see to them!" Maelgaltyr said. "I cannot pass until the interrogation of my handmaid is complete."

Taylor nodded and ran for the gate. He drew a knife he had concealed on his person and smiled. Ravenwood or Fort should have kept his mouth shut. When he was through, neither would have opportunity to shout for aid again.

"Fear me," Maelgaltyr croaked, turning his attention back upon Anne. "You know what I have done to your kind in the past; it was fear of me that made them hide themselves, sent them fleeing from the land. Are you greater than those who opposed me in my hour, little handmaid? And *their* screams went on for a long time as I had them flayed before me."

He drove the nails of each forefinger into her face until blood welled at their tips. "In those days, I had men skilled in such matters. Even with knives, my own efforts would be crude, and I have only my nails. Do you not think they begged me to stop their suffering long before it was done? They, like you, who had been so haughty before? Aye, they were but quivering, cowering fleshless things on the floor until my disgust that such unpleasantness should violate my eyes overcame my pleasure in hearing them plead. Only then did they die."

"But they are out of your reach, now, are they not, great Maelgaltyr?" Anne said her eyes widening as she looked beyond him into the distance. "All that you did then has no more power over them now than a nightmare has in a wakened world. I *see* them, whole and happy. They have not died; they walk in bliss among the ten Assyur in the White Lodge; they, too, have become pillars there. Never again shall they go out…," Anne looked at Maelgaltyr, "…and never again shall you enter…thief. And did you not feel the pleasure you dealt my mothers when the blades were put to *your* flesh, oh slain-by-traitors? Great Maelgaltyr who died the ignoble death!"

Maelgaltyr's upper lip curled, he drew back his hand, and Anne's head recoiled with his slap. "Do you speak thus to me? You who are less than a kitchen drudge? Aye, there's the scent of the gutter on you. Do you think I have not seen? Seen in your mind how you have walked day and night, wandering house to house, all doors closed to you, like a stray bitch. You were driven back into the rain from those shops in which you sought shelter because you looked and smelled of the street. All have turned you away, yes all…even…your *mother*…."

Anne flinched. Now there were tears in her eyes that had not come with the physical torture at his hands.

He grasped the top of her head. Violently, she tried to wrench free.

"You fear…being offered up, the utter abandonment of your own will. Helpless as a babe in another's power, carried off where you would not go. Yes, you have feared this as long as you were old enough to understand your mother gave you away."

"Be quiet!" Anne snapped at him, raising her voice, struggling to free her head which he held steadfastly in the vice of his talons.

Maelgaltyr's parchment brow suddenly wrinkled and surprise shone in the pits of his eyes. "She *sold* you in her place." Now his lips peeled back to reveal again waxen gums, and laughter rattled about in his mouth.

"You have *another* heritage, equally unsuspected, not of your own lineage but one into which you were grafted. Now, little handmaid, I will release what you have long repressed, and I will *show* you a nightmare in a wakened world! "

# CHAPTER THIRTY:
## *The Dweller on the Threshold*

W hile Taylor and Anne were meeting Maelgaltyr, Ravenwood and Fort had succeeded in bringing the column to which they were bound to the ground. So intent was Maelgaltyr on Anne and Taylor on Maelgaltyr that they had not noticed the thud of its landing.

Ravenwood and Fort dug their heels in the ground and shoved themselves along the fallen pillar, rubbing raw the backs of their hands in the process. Finally, they slipped free, though their hands were still tied.

Fortunately, the sliding and friction had worn on their bonds; Fort was able to slip free of his and then untie Ravenwood's.

"Good man, Fort," Ravenwood said. "Now, quickly: change coats with me," he said, taking the bag of marbles from his own coat after slipping it off.

"What for? And what's in the bag?" Fort said, nodding at it as he took off his coat.

"Pee wees, steelies, aggies, and cat's eyes. But never mind that now," he said as he put the bag into Fort's inner coat pocket. "I want you to decoy Taylor so that I can take him by surprise. Which means you have to lie down in front of that column and pretend you're me still tied to it. The coat should throw him off, and he'll assume you're still on the other side. Don't worry; he won't have long to think about it."

He reached out and mussed Fort's hair as Fort put on Ravenwood's coat. "Scream for help, but before he can get close enough to identify you, get your face down," Ravenwood said

"And while I'm staked out like a lamb, what exactly will *you* be doing?"

"I'll be standing in wait at one side of the gate, ready to take him by surprise before he can do any more conjuring."

"And what if Maelgaltyr shows up instead?" Fort asked. "What happens to me, then?"

Ravenwood smiled and tapped the bag of marbles inside Fort's coat which he now wore. "It's all in the bag, Fort. Now, lie down there and prepare to yell for help so loud the demonic duo will hear you."

Fort's face was pale as he lay down in front of the pillar and put his hands behind his back. "I suppose a decoy is the only plan we have," he said. "You just be sure you clock with the first blow *whoever* shows up at that gate."

Once Ravenwood was in place, Fort began yelling. The thudding of Taylor's feet over the ground soon followed.

He stopped short in the archway when he saw the toppled pillar. Inches away from him, hidden by the monolithic gate's left side, Ravenwood held his breath.

"Ravenwood!" Taylor said. "Look at me! Fort! I don't see you. You'd best say something quickly!"

When Fort neither answered nor raised his head, Taylor sheathed his knife, threw up his left hand and began to trace sigils in the air. "By Typhos" was barely out of his mouth, when Ravenwood leapt from behind the side of the gate. Out lashed his hands, one grabbing Taylor's wrist, holding it firmly in place, while the other enveloped the fingers, and in a quick series of crackling twists, snapped each of the sigil-signing digits.

"We'll have no more of *that*," Ravenwood said with the last snap.

Taylor screamed and gawked at his fingers, mangled and splayed at odd angles.

Then Ravenwood brought his fist into his enemy's jaw, sending him to the ground.

He had not noticed the billowing shadow detach from one of the set's columns and glide toward him. Fort thought at first a light tarp left by the film crew was blowing across the courtyard and up the steps, then realized there was no wind.

Before he could shout out a warning to Ravenwood, the ballooning shadow was revealed as a cape that now deflated and draped the form of a tall, hooded man all in black who now stood directly behind the detective.

From beneath the hood, laughter like peals of glee reverberating inside a mausoleum. A startled Ravenwood turned and jumped aside, his fist drawn back. Then he felt himself pale: had Maelgaltyr overtaken him unawares? He was reaching for the bag in his coat when the cloaked figure spoke: "Well, done, Stepson of Mystery. You are Ravenwood. I am the Dark Eminence, your ally."

Ravenwood withdrew his hand. "Hank Arneau's master," he said.

"The same. Now, look at me, William Desmond Taylor," the Dark Eminence demanded, eyes burning in a face draped in darkness. "Face *your* dweller on the threshold, your shadow self: he who calls you into account for your transgressions...*and fear me.*"

William Desmond Taylor knew before him was far worse than any dugpa's or demon's vengeance. Here was one possessed of an uncompromised moral sense both lucid and implacable, ready and eager to strike down the transgressor. In this man's shadow, Taylor stood in a harsh, unforgiving light in which he felt his every sin revealed.

Terror glazed Taylor's eyes as he scrambled to his feet and fled.

More laughter pursued him. "Go, pray in hell to your master! See if he will have you!"

"Report," the Dark Eminence commanded Ravenwood.

"I know this sounds incredible, but Taylor succeeded in raising from the dead a sorcerer named Maelgaltyr."

"Does he have Anne D'Arromanches?" the Dark Eminence asked, apparently taking Ravenwood's revelation of a raised wizard as a rather mundane one.

"She is in his hands I'm afraid."

"Do you know if she still wears the T'ai charm?"

"Taylor removed it."

"Then she's vulnerable." A black gloved finger flicked forward. "Ravenwood, come with me. Ravenwood *only*."

"You'll get no complaints from me," Fort said and sat down on the pillar as Ravenwood and the Dark Eminence passed through the gate in quick, long strides.

Taylor, meanwhile, threw himself at Maelgaltyr's feet.

"Master, help me." He held up his useless fingers. "I cannot make the left-handed sigils of Typhos, and my enemy pursues me!"

"And you led him *here*, fool?"

"Master, I beg you. Share with me your power! Didn't I raise you to life?"

Maelgaltyr's laughter was the rattle of dry leaves in a dead wood shaken by the wind.

"You did only what my mind led you to do. And now you presume upon *my* power?" He slowly shook his head. "You must be mistaken. Henceforth, I do not *share* power. I'll take *yours*!"

The taloned hands clamped onto both sides of Taylor's head, fingernails piercing his flesh so that blood ran down his cheeks. With a crackle and hiss, sparks shot out from Taylor, pitting clothing and raising welts in their wake as they skittered over his writhing body.

Taylor's head, caught in Maelgaltyr's hands as the power gathered between them, was now in a blue blaze. He jerked, turned, and tried to wrench free, a tortured howl issuing from his mouth frozen in agony. Still

Maelgaltyr's hands clamped tightly, even as Taylor's hair singed away in the flame. Anne recoiled at the sight and stench.

Ravenwood and the Dark Eminence were still a ways down the path when Taylor's screams ceased. Ravenwood could see a smile beneath the hood of his companion.

"To you who have sown with the left hand, bitter is the harvest!" the Dark Eminence said.

Back at the Roman pillar, Maelgaltyr released Taylor who dropped face down to the ground. "So shall it be with *all* who intrude upon my dominion!" Maelgaltyr said. "For where I am, *there is* the Black Lodge!"

Now Maelgaltyr turned from the still heaving human wreckage and once again brought his attention to bear on Anne.

"If your friends wounded Taylor, do not take false heart," he said and raised a talon of a finger. "Your fear has betrayed you already." He touched the center of her forehead.

Then Anne's screams began with their palpable despair.

As Maelgaltyr loomed before the bound, shrieking Anne, reveling in her fear, they came into view of the still distant Ravenwood and the Dark Eminence. The latter immediately withdrew twin guns from within his cape and lunged forward. Ravenwood grabbed his companion's arm and pulled him back.

"Stop! That's *not* the way. Maelgaltyr is a thing undead, so he cannot die as mortal men do." Ravenwood pulled the bag from his coat pocket. "Only what is in here will be effective."

"And what *is* in there?"

"More than it seems, but exactly what I do not know. My master the Nameless One has forbidden that knowledge until it's time to unleash the contents. You must have had faith in me and my master to send Arneau to us for help. Have faith in me now."

In response, the Dark Eminence returned his guns to their holsters.

"We need the element of surprise," Ravenwood said.

Does that creature have a human mind?" the Dark Eminence asked.

"Yes. A brilliant one."

"Let us see, then, just how brightly it shines. Under my cloak, I can give us camouflage. Stay close to me, and do not speak."

His hooded head bowed, the Dark Eminence extended his right arm and wrapped his cape around Ravenwood.

# CHAPTER THIRTY-ONE:
## *"On the Burning Ground We Will Meet..."*

When Maelgaltyr had touched Anne's forehead with a talon-tipped finger, he had opened her third eye, and suddenly Anne saw looming behind Maelgaltyr the gigantic black shape of her nightmare.

In the dream, at least, she could run.

Anne began screaming and pushed against the pillar with her feet to strain free. She slipped, and her body yielded to paroxysms of fright.

Maelgaltyr clasped his hands together and smiled. "Your fear opens the way. Now I *shall* pass. Your line has failed! You could not save the world that was; you have not impeded my will in this new world before me. Goodbye, little handmaid. I have given you your nightmare in a wakened world..."

"Now I have something for *you.*"

Before Maelgaltyr there flickered two figures, which, though he was looking at them straight on, appeared as though he saw them in his peripheral vision. Then suddenly, two men materialized in full before him.

Maelgaltyr's eyes and mouth widened, stretching the parchment skin over his skull so that it appeared it might rend. But it was not the men's materialization that alone stunned the Dark Lord: on the five fingers of Ravenwood's clinched fist thrusting into the dugpa's face were five of the stone rings!

As they had neared Maelgaltyr and Anne, Ravenwood had at last slipped his hand into the bag. He felt nothing like marbles inside. What *was* in there had moved of their own accord over his fingers. And he understood at last the "pee wees, steelies, aggies, and cat's eyes": the Nameless One had put a glamor over them so that's all anyone else could see. He could not extend that illusion to his stepson because he had to know them for what they were. Nor could he tell him the contents because Maelgaltyr would have seen them in his mind's eye at the last moment...long enough for him to gain the upper hand.

As it was, stone-ringed fingers smashed into Maelgaltyr's nose and mouth. Ravenwood felt a power that was not his own surge through his arm; the glyphs were glowing, and their force cast the rune wizard fifteen feet through the air. He landed on his back and lay still.

Anne, however, continued screaming at the hulking dark shadow only she could see.

"Why is she still hysterical?" Ravenwood said, keeping his eyes trained on Maelgaltyr who remained flat on his back. "There's no one else here except Taylor, and Maelgaltyr hasn't left him in any shape to threaten her further."

"Her fear has been turned inside out," the Dark Eminence said. He had gone to her immediately and torn away the pinned tarot card. Now he grasped her head firmly so that her eyes met his. "The Dweller on the Threshold is at work here. Do what you must. I will help Anne D'Arromanches."

Maelgaltyr now had risen to his knees, wiping the back of his hand over his bloodied lips and nose. Visions of the flayed Angels of the Presence suddenly lacerating his heart afresh, Ravenwood bellowed and charged Yttle Elumi, ringed-fist drawn back. The sorcerer's hands shot out and blue lightening streaked from his fingertips to strike the Stepson of Mystery head-on. The rings drew and absorbed the power...still, he *felt* Maelgaltyr's blast. His hand went numb, the breath thrust from his lungs, and he went down, his knees plowing shallow trenches into the dirt.

As he sucked in air, still kneeling, his hands resting on his thighs, Ravenwood realized he had failed to heed the Nameless One's warning and acted in hateful self-will; the blow had been Maelgaltyr's, but the Effulgence had allowed this powerful slap on the wrist to rebuke him: *man's wrath does not work my righteousness.*

Maelgaltyr now stood above him, a bent dark shadow:

"Thief! Guttersnipe!"

"I am the servant of the Effulgence whose finger wrote these glyphs. *His* is the power," Ravenwood said between heavy breaths.

Maelgaltyr's upper lip curled, and his eyes were dark pits. "You are my *pawn* who has brought my rings back to *me*! Yield what is *mine*!" he snarled and fired streaks of energy down upon him. Up flew Ravenwood's ringed hand, deflecting the mystic power which turned back on Maelgaltyr, ramming him in his core. The dugpa doubled over and staggered backward, groaning.

By the time he had straightened, Ravenwood was on top of him, the stone ringed hand hammering first one side of the wizard's head and then the other, the rings' glyphs momentarily burning like shame on Maelgaltyr's cheeks. Under his knuckles, Ravenwood felt bone crunch. A lesser being than Yttle Elumi would have had his head taken off.

Suddenly, Maelgaltyr grabbed the wrist of Ravenwood's swinging, ringed fist, stopping it cold, and chomped his teeth down onto the Stepson of Mystery's hand. The jaws clamped unremittingly, and Ravenwood yowled. Immediately, he jabbed his other elbow into Maelgaltyr's stomach, the sharp pain causing the wizard to  loosen his hold and allowing Ravenwood to shove free. But the dugpa's foul teeth scraped blood from the skin of his hand as they drug over it.

The wizard rallied and with a sweep of his hand scatter shot sharp sparks like throwing stars of bluish energy at Ravenwood. Driven by the Effulgence, the ringed hand darted speedily and accurately, deflecting each glowing spur. They flew back, lodging in Maelgaltyr's chest and thighs. He howled until the lingering, piercing sparks winked out like dying blue cinders.

Meanwhile, the Dark Eminence held Anne's head firmly so that her face remained level with his own. "Look into my eyes, Anne D'Arromanches," he began, "and I will lead you back. The Dweller on the Threshold's power over you lies only in your fear. It is the fear of your old dream. I am making the dream lucid...*our* dream. Run, Anne! Run with me!"

"I'm already lost," she sobbed. "It's only because I can wake up that it doesn't catch me. But if I'm *awake* and it's here....!" She began jerking against her bonds, lacerating further her already rope burned wrists.

"I have you, Anne." Withdrawing a switchblade from his belt, he flicked the knife open, cut the rope that held her hands above her head, then caught her in his arms. "We are headed for a gate; a large gate ahead. Do you see it?"

"Yes!"

"The gate will close behind us; we shall cross the threshold and the nightmare will be shut out. We are passing through..."

"It's coming..."

"But we are passing through the gate, Anne!" With his middle and index fingers together, he touched the spot on her forehead where Maelgaltyr had opened the third eye and gently stroked down. "The gate drops behind us. Your Dweller is cut off. Know no fear."

"Safe...," Anne said drowsily, and, from her vantage point, looked up into the face under the hood which she immediately pushed back.

"Hank!" She threw her white arms around his neck and drew herself into him.

"Easy, kid! Don't break my neck," Arneau said and smiled down at her. "Although I know I've more than once given you reason to want to over the past few days."

"Hank, let's never quarrel again. After tonight…"

Arneau looked over at Ravenwood and Maelgaltyr exchanging mystic blasts. Maelgaltyr was in retreat, but was bringing the battle their way. Arneau knew this fight was Ravenwood's and that he could offer no help: the Stepson of Mystery had made it clear his weapons were of no use, and what he was witnessing convinced him this was true. His priority had to be to get Anne away from her tormentor, especially since events could turn and Maelgaltyr get the upper hand. As much as it galled him to flee, he turned and ran with her in his arms.

"Anne, you were in some kind of trance when I got to you," he said as he trotted for the gate. "What do you remember about this evening?"

"Nate! He brought me here…turned on me and…" she pressed her face into Arneau's shoulder at the thought of his fate. "He was an evil man. But to *burn* …"

"Don't waste your sympathy, Anne," Arneau's tone was cool as sepulchre stone. "He once barred the doors then put the torch to a monastery of peaceful Yellow Hat monks. And he was capable of, and did, far worse. Things you don't want to know about." He lifted her chin and smiled down into her large, blue eyes. "Things *I* don't want you to know about."

As the two made their way to the Stonehenge gate, Ravenwood found that now he did not even need to make physical contact with Maelgaltyr: heat lightning blasts of the virtue of the Effulgence flew from Ravenwood's hand as he punched forward in the air repeatedly, pounding the wizard. He noticed Maelgaltyr was no longer firing back but concentrating more on deflecting the surges of energy which left his upheld hands singed.

*He's holding back*, Ravenwood thought. *His reserves are low…or gone.* And, indeed, both Maelgaltyr's own power and that harvested from Taylor were severely depleted from the altercation. He ultimately was no match against the power of the virtue with which the stone rings hummed. For a moment, the Stepson of Mystery thought it might all end here…

Something sharp lanced his thigh just above the knee and hot blood ran down his calf. Ravenwood cried out and looked down to see a grin on the blistered red face of William Desmond Taylor, who still held the handle of the knife plunged into Ravenwood's leg.

Ravenwood went down to one knee, instinctively dropping his ringed hand to Taylor's, struggling with him to pull the knife free.

Maelgaltyr seized the opening and now released the magic he had conserved from his hands in a final blaze of power, but the stone rings acted like lightning rods and drew the mystic flame to themselves before firing it back upon Maelgaltyr in full force.

Enveloped in a burning blue nimbus, a screeching Maelgaltyr went to the ground but caught himself with one hand before complete collapse. As he struggled to stay propped up on that hand until the pain faded, he touched on a rock that filled his palm. Snatching it up, he lunged forward and brought the rock against Ravenwood's temple as he struggled with Taylor over the knife. Ravenwood toppled over, unconscious.

Maelgaltyr went to his knees and began plucking the stone rings from Ravenwood's fingers, then sliding them over his own. His face, swollen by its pummeling, twisted in a grotesque expression of joy.

"Am I...forgiven, master?" Taylor asked, looking up as he lay on his belly. "Have you not seen I am still your worthy servant?"

"Phaugh!" Maelgaltyr hissed as he rose. Already, he could feel the healing power of the virtue of the rings moving through him. But he was currently powerless and far from whole. Still, the opening Anne's fear had given him remained...as did his enemies.

Best to slip away now, to regain his strength, and then rebuild his cult. Only then could he effectively search for the remaining five rings. His upper lip curled as he regarded the unconscious Ravenwood. He could kill him now...but he would not suffer. Better to wait to properly avenge his humiliation.

He began to hobble toward the gate.

Cast off again by Maelgaltyr, Taylor gnashed his teeth and, picking up his knife, began to dig into the wound of the unconscious Ravenwood's leg.

In his lack of lucidity, he had not considered the pain would awaken Ravenwood, nor the consequence. The Stepson of Mystery grabbed Taylor's hand again, then drug his nails over Taylor's singed wrist, scraping away the top layer of burned skin. Screaming, Taylor released the knife and folded into the fetal position.

Fortunately, Ravenwood's wound remained relatively shallow because of Taylor's weakened condition when he had wielded the blade.

Ravenwood then slipped off Fort's borrowed coat and wiped the knife clean on its lining. Then he cut a bandage from his shirtsleeve and wrapped his cut.

He looked at the spotlight atop the scaffolding where the castle of Monsalvant was being constructed; the spotlight in line with the Stonehenge gate in the shape of the twelfth hexagram.

*Weaken him, then turn the twelfth hexagram back to the eleventh....and to this beacon the Great Ones will come.*

"Job's only half done," Ravenwood grunted. But if Maelgaltyr was a Nephilim, a "great one," did that make him the same as those whose return the eleventh hexagram would signal? If so, how could that be a good thing? Putting his faith in the Nameless One, he rose with a groan and began making his way to the scaffolding.

He tucked the knife in his belt loop, then shook the scaffolding to affirm it was secure and began climbing. Frantic to reach the top before Maelgaltyr could cross the Stonehenge gate's threshold, he did not notice the knife slip from his side and fall to the ground.

Pulling himself over the edge onto the platform, he could see the scurrying Maelgaltyr was nearing his goal. The Stepson of Mystery took hold of the spotlight and tilted it up so that the beam would both shine through and fall over the top of the gate.

"DeMille, I hope you're paid up on the electric bill," he mumbled as he flipped the light's switch.

A sudden blast of white, dazzling light...

From the gateway, a wail of anger mingled with disbelief: the cry of Maelgaltyr, who, having reached the threshold of the gateway, suddenly found himself intercepted by its giant shadow, the inversion of the gate's image casting the eleventh hexagram over the courtyard before him:

*Heaven descends. The Great Ones return.*

☩ ☩ ☩

There were giants in the sky, towering far, far above the gate, far over Hollywood. They looked as though they might toss the moon between them, the seven men who looked down in judgment on Maelgaltyr. The priest-kings of Aslem-Beth had descended from the outer rim of Elyon, and their austere countenances burned like bronze hot from the furnace.

The first wore a knee-length tunic of red doe skin over his sturdy, compact frame, and his ruddy hair was bound with a pendant of polished stones. From this a single pearl hung upon his tall forehead. His beard covered his face, and in his hand was a diamond burin. His name is Ukko.

The second was clad in a tunic of lion's skin that hung from one shoulder. His face and head were clean-shaven. In the crook of one arm he held a tablet of clay so that its cuneiform might be read: for the record was open. His name is Enoch.

The third wore only a leather girdle. His countenance was of a young man of Hyperborea. Only his temples and short beard were touched with hair like snow. In his hand was a long staff, carved with hot, glowing glyphs engraved nowhere else but the ten pillars called the Assyur which Maelgaltyr spoiled. This is Vanr.

The fourth wore a crown of flawless silver. He was bearded only about the mouth, the hair of his chin tapering to a point. Baubles of jade and Amethyst hung from his ears, and his piebald robe fell to his feet. In his right hand was a scepter of the same pure silver as his crown. He is called Priest of Salem.

The fifth man possessed the tallest and mightiest frame of the seven. His face was clean-shaven, and his straight black hair fell to his shoulders. A woven cloth of red and blue girded his loins. He is the vindicated vindicator. In his one hand was a burning coal and in another a marvelous stone in which was carved a name known but to two, forbidden to all others to see, for wrongful follies are spoken of him in the Ugaritic shards, and there he is called Dan'il.

The sixth man wore a conical crown of gold. Black was his beard and in short braids. He wore a breast plate of bronze and beneath it a short robe of leather. On the breast plate was a constellation of twelve stars. In his palm he held an olive seed, hard as a diamond, breaking anything which would fall on it, and crushing all upon which it would fall. In his day, the world was sundered. His name is Peleg.

And the last, in a robe of golden silk and a scarlet sash, was the Nameless One.

Ravenwood paused, stunned, in his descent of the scaffolding. "Father?" he said. He reached out with his mind, but there was no communication between them. As with the other six of Elyon, the Nameless One's eyes were fixed on Maelgaltyr.

Ravenwood let himself drop the last few feet, wincing with the pain of impact, then began limping quickly for the gate.

Arneau and Anne stood on the light-flooded courtyard beside Murphy Fort, whose mouth was agape at what he saw in the sky.

Maelgaltyr stood inside the gate, still so weakened and drained from the power of the stone rings having turned against him that the descended kings of Aslem-Beth were able to hold him at the gate's threshold by their wills.

"You have hastened the day of judgment, Aurochel," said Ukko.

"You should have been content to wander in arid places. For now that you have rejoined your body and cannot die again as mortals do, you have hastened the second death," said Enoch.

"The Arrogant is made to pass in flame," said the Nameless One.

"Look on us, Aurochel the lame," said Vanr, "and see what you would have been, had your walk remained humble. This was the portion that the Effulgence had set apart for he whom he loved: that you should have found bliss in the house of Aslem and dwelled at the rim of Elyon with the universe and all time spread at your feet."

"To have moved with the quickness of light, as we do even now, so that you are both simultaneously exploring entire worlds while at rest to contemplate them," said the Nameless One.

Ravenwood, eyes tearing, thought of the man he loved as a father, dwelling in his small room, which had never seemed to confine him— until now. He thought of him on a park bench feeding pigeons: pitiful specimens, surely, compared to whatever beings with whom he was communing now on planets whose light no telescope lens might be ground so fine to ensnare.

"And then," said Vanr, "at the determined call, to depart, as did our sister-queen Makeda, beyond the rim of Elyon, beyond the utter abyss: *there* is the White Lodge."

"Its stones are uncut by human hands," said Dan'il. "Its terraces teem with every beautiful plant and living creature; men and women of all nations bask in the warmth of camaraderie. They enjoy the security of the always same; the novelty of inexhaustible variety. Unsated but satisfied, their appetites are endless; each to his or her art. The door to *that* Lodge is always open, yet none seek to go out but ever inward. And they who once saw only the Effulgence, I tell you, they now look full on into the face of the sun, and they are *not* blinded!"

Ravenwood suddenly realized why his master had been taken from him: the departure of this Makeda of whom the seven had spoken had left a vacancy in their ranks which the Nameless One was meant to fill. Yet his master had not looked upon this election eagerly. There was something involved with it that he regarded with dread.

Maelgaltyr gnashed his teeth. To the seven he shouted: "So, the arrogant shall pass in flame? Was it not also prophesied to me, on the burning ground we will meet, though the *disciple* be consumed? There..." he pointed at Anne, "...is one. And perhaps ..." he now cast his glance about, from Fort, to Arneau...and to Ravenwood who had just limped past him through the gate "...others? Is there one among you whose disciple shall be consumed in the flame with me? That word cannot be broken or altered. Bring down your judgment, then, if you will!"

The Seven made no answer; all turned their backs on the group below, even the Nameless One.

"Father?" Ravenwood said. Again, he found himself shut out from his master's mind.

Fort, who had stood stunned through all this, now bolted for his car. He would not get far.

"Close your eyes Anne," Arneau said as he folded his cloak over her. "I'm sorry."

"It's all right, Hank," she said as she rested her head against his chest, "I understand."

The wall of DeMille's temple erupted in flames; Maelgaltyr, still pinned in the gateway by the will of the seven, bellowed out in a voice that was below bestial; he squatted and beat the ground with his fist and shook his head like an enraged ape. The fire now began to crawl over his robe, and still he pummeled the ground, grunting with rage.

The conflagration immediately fled out over the courtyard; for an instant, all there found themselves in a furnace.

And then the Nameless One turned.

*Here, my son, time turns into space.*

Ravenwood heard the words in his mind; he looked up to see the giant face of the Nameless One smiling down at him...

As though someone had closed a window on a storm, the fire about them, though still present, seemed suddenly remote. Then, after the roar of the conflagration, silence so sudden it rang in their ears. The fire was gone, the night still, the winter air cool upon their fever warm skins. The temple wall still stood except the Stonehenge-like entrance was gone, leaving a large gap in its place.

Maelgaltyr had been taken with the gateway; departed, too, were the Priest-Kings of Aslem-Beth.

On the courtyard, in the fetal position, the Nameless One lay trembling in a coarse robe.

"Father!" Ravenwood shouted and ran to him.

"It's all right, Anne," Arneau said.

She looked up at him. "How? We were incinerated!"

Arneau nodded toward the quivering Nameless One. "I suspect the answer is there."

"He…he was one of *them*."

"Not quite, it appears," Arneau said.

Ravenwood feared what the shock of the sudden fall from transcendence to mortality might have done to his stepfather's mind. "Are you all right?" he asked as he went down on his knees and gently gathered the old man's head onto his lap.

The Nameless One smiled up at him. "My son…," he began, then noticed the blood on Ravenwood's pants, "…you are wounded."

"I'll be okay until Fort can get us both to a doctor."

Then, eyes tearing, the Nameless One said, "I am forsaken. I…failed the test."

Ravenwood smiled and stroked his stepfather's hair. "Personally, I give you an A plus."

The Nameless One frowned. "Do not speak lightly of this thing. I could not sacrifice you, my son, but when I moved the fire through time as a man moves an object through space, I also moved Maelgaltyr."

"Then he burned…"

"No, no, my son. Maelgaltyr was in the midst of the flame, but when I brought it where I would, he was not there. My thoughts were on the fire, where it could be placed without bringing harm to others. He slipped through."

"Where or when did you send that fire, father?"

"Almost eight years into the future. Somewhere between two minutes ago and December 10, 1938…at 8:20 in the evening…Maelgaltyr is already working his evil. Who knows what ills he will cause to pass in the interim? Nor will he forget our part in his defeat tonight. I fear what he has reserved for *you* wherever it is he lies in wait in the future, my son."

"Hey," Ravenwood said, "aren't you the guy who can sit in a Manhattan high rise and see a leaf falling from a tree on the Khyber Pass before it has even budded? You can find him wherever and whenever he is."

"I have no doubt he can conceal himself from my seeking mind. I cannot say that I can do the same should I search for him telepathically. No, my son. Because I could not turn my back on you, I have left unchecked an evil in the world that should have been eradicated this day. I have violated the eleventh hexagram before it was fulfilled; there will be no peace and good fortune now. I have proven myself unworthy to take my place among the priest-kings of Elyon."

Ravenwood colored at this. "Who put them on their high horse? This wasn't requiring anything of them…"

The Nameless One put his hand to Ravenwood's face. "My son, stop: do you not think they faced their own time of testing? That their cups were no less bitter in their day? Now, I can stand. Let us leave this place. I see your leg is hurt. Lean on me."

"We'll lean on each other, like always. Murphy?"

Murphy Fort was leaning against his roadster, staring into space.

"Murphy! Are you all right?"

Fort looked at them. "I just...I'm having trouble comprehending what I've seen here tonight."

"You've had the blind fly up unexpectedly, and the light is overwhelming," Ravenwood said. "You've suddenly seen there is far more at work in the world than there appears; that we exist day-to -day alongside of an unseen reality in which great powers straddle the ages, so that the past, present and future come together. All will be called into account; thus the past is never simply done. And it's the same for us Fort, in our day- to-day life; it's no different for us."

"There's a line in *Dracula*," Fort said. "Van Helsing asks, 'Do you not believe there are things you cannot understand yet which are?' Brother, and *how*."

"And *how*," Ravenwood said with a quick nod.

"I suppose you have your own mode of transportation?" Ravenwood asked Arneau.

"Of course."

"Any reason you couldn't have shown up a little sooner? Or been straightforward with me from the beginning about who you are?"

"To answer your first question, I was occupied with trying to track you down. You can appreciate the maze you cut out for me since you arrived in Hollywood. When I returned to the Roosevelt and found Anne gone, it was obvious where she would be. At that point, I was certain I would find you here as well.

"As for your second question; how do you know I am being straight-forward with you *now* about who I am?"

As Anne leaned on Arneau, they moved past the gap in the wall. A sudden howl of rage erupted from the opening, and raising the knife he had reclaimed from where Ravenwood had unknowingly dropped it, a scorched and blistered William Desmond Taylor hurled himself at Hank Arneau.

# CHAPTER THIRTY-TWO:
## The Price of Justice

Anne screamed as Arneau shoved her back with one hand and caught Taylor's wrist with the other, stopping the knife's downward arc. Taylor cried out at the contact with his burned flesh but, with effort, still gripped the knife.

"So, you survived your meeting with Maelgaltyr," Arneau said. "How unfortunate for you."

"Hank," Anne said, "what do you mean?"

"Silence!" Arneau ordered and the severity in his voice chilled Anne. "Listen to me, Taylor. And remember the cries of your victims...the Yellow Caps you burned...and what you did to the women and their children..."

"How? How could you know about that?" Taylor stammered.

"What?" Anne said. "He did *what*?"

"I said, be *quiet*, Anne!" Arneau commanded. "Listen to *me*, Taylor! I know all your sins: your kidnapping Miss D'Arromanches and almost driving her insane with your pagan rites; your attempt to unleash an undead monster on the human race; the murder of William Cunningham-Deane Tanner; the paid assassination of Edward Snyder; the immolation of the Yellow Cap martyrs...and the massacre of the Buddhist pilgrims at the shrine of Hariti."

Taylor trembled, dipping at the knees.

"Did you think no one heard their screams but you and your fellow dugpas?" Arneau said. "The echoes of their cries reached me at the roof of the world. I did not tarry. On my heels is still the mud you made of blood and dirt when you slew the children before the eyes of their mothers, then plucked out *their* eyes so the fear and agony in their little ones' faces would be their last sight of them. You left the women to crawl and thrash against each other in the dust, each feeling for her own child's remains, until they, too, died slowly from exposure."

"It's true," Taylor suddenly sobbed, dropping the knife, and then, as Arneau released him, falling completely to his knees. "God help me, it's true."

"God? You express remorse only now that you face judgment for your deeds. You'll find no forgiveness from God. Nor *me*," Arneau said.

With a low grating in his throat that escalated quickly into a growl, Taylor, still on his knees, grabbed up the knife, swayed forward and sliced out, trying to cut Arneau's leg. Arneau easily stepped out of range, and Taylor rose back to his knees where he tottered and groaned, still clutching the knife.

Arneau drew his hood over his head and under its shadow what was left of Hank Arneau melted away, leaving only the Dark Eminence. He transfixed Taylor with his gaze. "You know what you must do, Taylor... what I *will* you to do..."

"I...please...no....Don't make me...."

"Murderer of babies and women...the weak and defenseless! You *dare* plead for mercy when you find yourself powerless against another's will as they were yours? Wretch! As you did to them...by the *same* hand, Taylor... as you *did* to them..."

"I ...can...can't..."

"DO IT!"

Screaming, Taylor thrust the knife into his right eye and yanked the blade free, the optical nerve trailing; Anne's shrieks echoed his own.

"DO IT!"

His face awash with blood, and with one last, protesting scream, Taylor drove the blade to the hilt in his left eye where it remained as his corpse pitched forward, the hilt of the knife propping his head up from the ground. Anne threw her hands over her face and screamed again.

The Dark Eminence laughed: "An eye for an eye, Taylor. My only regret is that you possessed but two." He turned to Anne.

"Stay away from me! Don't touch me!" she shouted, tears streaming over her face. "He was already horribly burned all over his body! You could have disarmed him, simply wounded him, but you *made* him...and you *gloated* over his pain!"

"So did he gloat when the throats of little children were slit while their mothers begged for mercy," he said, looking back at Taylor's body.

"That makes you no better than he!" Anne said, heartbreak in her voice.

The hooded head turned sharply upon her. "You equate my rejoicing in the just punishment of the guilty with that of one who inflicts and laughs at the undue suffering of the innocent?"

"Who *are* you?" she asked. "I've...I've never really known Hank Arneau, have I?" Shaking, she began to back away. "You stay away from me. Do you hear me? You...you frighten me. I don't want anything from you! Nothing!"

Sobbing, Anne turned and ran down the road that led to the courtyard.

Ravenwood and the Nameless One, still helping each other along, hobbled over to him. "It's hard not to recognize karma at work here," Ravenwood said. "I suppose you are its agent, but...you *do* have to understand her point of view."

"I'm not compelled in the slightest," the Dark Eminence said. Then: "You won't leave the lot without her? You'll see to her safe passage back to New York? That she has everything she needs?"

"Of course," Ravenwood said.

"And you'll want to be sure to let your friend Stagg know I had a talk with Madame Thothmes at the *Club Samedi*. The two of you are no longer targeted by the anti-Yttle Elumi league."

"Thank you for that."

"I always tidy up things, Ravenwood."

Ravenwood nodded toward the mutilated corpse. "Good luck with this mess. Come, father."

Only then did the Nameless One look into the eyes of the Dark Eminence. "A man is not just if he carries a matter by violence," he told him. "And yet...you would have gone into the flames, would you not, my son, rather than have sent Maelgaltyr into the world?"

"And counted it well worth my time."

The Nameless One nodded. Murphy Fort, shoulders slumped, began to slide into the driver's seat of his auto.

"MR. FORT!"

His face moist and pale, Fort looked up at the Dark Eminence.

"I don't need to tell you that if you try to report that it turns out it was Hank Arneau who murdered William Desmond Taylor, you're going to sound rather foolish?"

"No...no, sir."

"Because, not only has Taylor been dead officially for nine years, Hank Arneau is currently in the Australian back country on a walkabout. Where he was in February of 1922. Perennial sort of thing with him. He has no idea that, until just recently, he was the number one stock holder in Astoria Studios."

"Yes sir. Of course," Fort said, blotting his face with his handkerchief.

Soon the roadster's taillights were in the distance, leaving behind death and shadows.

*"We'll lean on each other, like always..."*

# EPILOGUE ONE:
## *Fiery Finish*

On a late autumn's night near the end of the decade, what had been the temple set of Cecil B. DeMille's *King of Kings* erupted into flames. Seven Technicolor cameras were trained on the conflagration of the giant wall now transformed by new façades to represent Civil War era Atlanta.

So pleased was producer David O. Selznick with this first footage shot for his in-production *Gone With the Wind* that he wrote to his wife, "I was greatly exhilarated by the fire sequence." No one on the set that evening, however, could have been more excited than the special effects crew when, despite an intricate system of valves to control the size of the flames, the redressed wall went into incineration overdrive, far beyond what careful planning had foreseen. Turning back on the valves had no effect. With no retakes possible, the crew bit their collective lip and watched the wall collapse, praying the stunt people in the horse drawn wagon before it would not disappear under a massive wave of fire.

They did not. Control of the flames for the rest of the sequence was immediately reestablished, and a pact was made among the crew in the know that Mr. Selznick would never know any more "exhilaration" over that night's filming than he already had.

When Inspector Horatio Stagg read about the Pathe lot's wall's incineration in his morning newspaper of December 11, 1938, he mumbled that it was a shame they didn't burn the rest of Hollywood to the ground with it.

At least he had been able to close the book on *his* West Coast adventure years ago, when Ravenwood had returned from Hollywood back in '31 and informed him that William Desmond Taylor had been murdered by a worshipper of Yttle Elumi. The villain planned to use their uncanny resemblance to assume the director's identity for his own nefarious ends. The quick discovery of Taylor's body had foiled that scheme, but he had returned to the crime scene in disguise to claim a priceless tarot deck in Taylor's possession. Stagg, it turned out, had faced the murderer that day in the alley.

Unfortunately, in his own confrontation with the killer, Ravenwood had lost Stagg's tarot card. Frankly, Stagg didn't give a damn.

# EPILOGUE TWO:
## Love and Remembrance

Anne drew her bonnet down tightly around her ears and tucked her head against the blasts of a New York winter wind that appeared determine to drive her back across the continent. Dark clouds brooded over Manhattan on this early evening in early February, 1931, and snowflakes were already discernible here and there, wisping through the streets.

Perhaps, Anne thought, she had been too quick to leave California. Her face stung from the wind, her feet throbbed from being on them all day, and her stomach contracted from nearly twenty-four hours without food. What a difference a few weeks made.

Back in Hollywood, Mr. Fort had been a friend in deed: introducing her to people and helping her get a few, small speaking parts in some two-reel Westerns. But her recent misadventure had left her depressed and not in the mood for socializing. Thus, she lacked the aggression for initiating connections to advance a Hollywood career.

The sudden tear drops on her lashes felt as though they'd turned instantly to frost.

She missed Hank.

Why had she ever thought, as the wind stung her face yet again, that she would feel any differently back in New York? At least it was familiar. That's what she had told herself. But that was also the problem, wasn't it? It was *too* familiar. She avoided the Astoria Studio like a leper colony, but earlier today she had found her meandering had brought her unwittingly outside the Metropolitan museum. A sudden gust of bitter wind had driven like a shaft straight into her heart, and she had fled.

Now she was trying to find a flophouse for women that had not already filled for the night. What earnings she had from Hollywood that hadn't been spent on the flight over had been stolen from her hotel room her first night back. She was almost certain it was the cleaning woman, but she hadn't liked the look of the desk clerk, either. In any event, it would have only been her word against theirs.

After tonight, she was headed for the Fort Lee Studios in Jersey. Perhaps enough extra work, should she be able to get it, would reawaken her acting ambitions. And eventually she might be strong enough to venture back across the river and try out for Broadway.

*What you could* really *use, Anne D'Arromanches is a cruise and a romance at sea.* She sighed. *You know. Like in the movies.*

She found herself now in front of a vendor's fruit stand, an oasis of life from somewhere in the world where there was warm sunshine and green fields. It put her in mind of her summers growing up on the orphanage farm, where the fields and trees were always heavy with the season's yield...

Her stomach contracted....

...and you just had to reach out and...

Bracing himself for the biting winter air, the movie producer stepped out of the Manhattan taxi on one final, *essential* errand. He needed a star for his next project, one of mammoth proportions. All the ordinary channels had failed him. But this was New York, after all; Broadway with the Astoria studio nearby at that. The streets had to be running over with out of work actors.

As he surveyed the wintry sidewalk ahead, a voice from behind addressed him:

*That woman at the vendor's stand has a face that should be seen on the big screen.*

"Wazzat?" the director said, turning. He saw only a shadowy figure with a raised collar turning a corner, headed the opposite way. When he looked back, there *was* a girl, but her back was turned to him.

What the heck...he wouldn't mind an apple himself.

# EPILOGUE THREE:
## *Father and Son*

Upon his return from Los Angeles, the Nameless One had immediately sequestered himself in his small room in the Sussex Towers after requesting Sterling leave a bowl of lentils and a glass of water outside his room. For weeks, neither Ravenwood nor Sterling saw or heard him. The only sign of his continued existence was that the empty bowl and glass would appear intermittently outside his door, and, once replenished, would vanish again inside.

On a night when falling snow was oppressing the Sussex Towers, Ravenwood sat in a comfortable upholstered chair in his library reading in the evening paper about Fort's Dracula movie. A phenomenal success since its Valentine's Day debut in New York, the bloodsucker was actually *pumping* life into the studio's Depression era, near corpus. Fort had told him over the phone that Universal had high hopes for *Frankenstein*, Lugosi's follow-up horror movie for the studio.

"Sir, I am sorry to interrupt your paper…"

"Yes, Sterling?"

"You know I am not one to pry, but, frankly, I am concerned about the Nameless One. If I may, what exactly happened in Hollywood that has affected your master so?"

Ravenwood, placed his paper in his lap, leaned back in his chair and looked in the direction of the Nameless One's closed door. He massaged his forehead. "Your concern is duly noted, Sterling, and appreciated. But it's not my place to speak about it. Except he did it for me."

"Did *what* exactly, sir?"

"Sterling, each time I go out to war against Shiva, there is always the chance I won't return, but he has always…*always*…accompanied me telepathically from that little room until whatever end that would come, did.

"I think he could have accepted my loss this time just as he has been willing to do before, except for the fact that *this* time he could *not* be with me when the end came. This time, my abandonment was required for the enemy to be annihilated. Understand, there was some cosmic law at work there that night. It's not so much that he broke that law as it broke him."

"Hello, my son."

Sterling startled with a quick, backward shuffle away from the Nameless One who suddenly stood among them.

"Father!" Ravenwood said, rising. "How do you feel?"

The Nameless One said, "The burden is still great, my son. But…Sterling, I think I should relish some of your vegetable stew."

Sterling, who was smoothing the wrinkles in his tux that were all that remained of his undignified deportment of a few seconds earlier, said, "Light on the lentils, I presume, sir?"

"The world is dew, Sterling. May the savor of lentils be as detached from your stew as we may all hope to be from this insubstantial veil of maya."

"The world is *dew*,' sir? Sterling said, arching a brow at the Nameless One and then shifting his eyes to Ravenwood. "'The world is *dew*?' And yet…"

"Yet what, Sterling?" Ravenwood asked.

Sterling smiled. "And *yet*. If you don't mind sir, I rather enjoy the novelty of being the inscrutable one in this domicile. I should like to enjoy it as long as I may." He turned and exited with a clap of his hands: "Cook! Stew!"

"My son," the Nameless One said, "I have been thinking much of Maelgaltyr."

"As have I."

The Nameless One raised his index finger: "Like the serpent, he coils before he strikes."

"'Coils'...you mean," Ravenwood said and snapped his fingers, "he will first gather his remaining *rings* before he makes a major move."

"He has power, but he cannot be the power he was until he possesses all ten again. He shall seek them out. Since I moved him into the future, you and I inhabit a past he does not share. Thus, we have opportunity to intercept him."

"Or he may be just far enough in the future to have a lead we cannot overtake. Perhaps...he has them already," Ravenwood said, looking out the library window at the snow pelting the glass from a starless sky and gathering in the corners of the panes.

"He is not omnipresent my son; the rings could be scattered over the globe. All the time I have given him might be necessary for him simply to revive and rebuild his cult to the point that he has the resources to support the required, vast network of agents to find the stone rings."

"And should he succeed in gathering them?"

Ravenwood's master's visage for a moment recalled his appearance when he had stood among the clouds with the Priest-Kings of Aslem-Beth. "Should that be the circumstances of our next meeting, I will dare to speak my name, and when I am known, even Maelgaltyr will tremble. Yes, let them *all* tremble."

The Sussex towers swayed as though with a nor'easter's blast and certainly, that's all that it *could* have been, Ravenwood assured himself. Still, he looked with a moment's fear back at his master.

All he saw was the kindliest, simplest of men. A meek elderly gentleman who would be perfectly at home on a park bench, feeding the pigeons.

"Still," Ravenwood said, "we are but two."

"Father and son," the Nameless One said and smiled. "When the hour comes, together we will face Maelgaltyr."

Ravenwood put his arm around the shoulders of his stepfather. They silently watched the snow sifting through a sky like black onyx. It was though, from beyond the outer rim of Elyon, the White Lodge was shedding its beneficent splendor upon a weighty world. A few moments of grace for all who have yet to struggle on in the earth, for whom the ten pillars called the Assyur, though unmovable and certain, remain distant and unglimpsed.

**The End.**

# THE UNSOLVED MURDER OF WILLIAM DESMOND TAYLOR

O n the night of February 1, 1922, respected movie director William Desmond Taylor walked his visiting friend, comedienne Mabel Normand (herself fated for a premature death) to her car. As Mabel drove away, they blew each other kisses. He stepped into his bungalow and was never seen alive again—except, of course, by the person who shot him. The time of Mabel's departure was 7:45 P.M. As he watched her ride off, Taylor could scarcely suspect he had approximately five more minutes to live. Although, another theory, based on the lack of rigor mortis when the body was discovered early the next morning, puts the murder around 1:00 or 2:00 A.M.

Who dunnit? Theories have ranged from a secret order of homosexual Chinese opium dealers which Taylor joined then subsequently incensed by breaking their communal vow to love only each other, to a stage mother who couldn't bear the thought of losing her cash cow of a daughter to a man old enough to be the ingénue's father.

Taylor had traveled a long way from his homeland of County Cork, Ireland to be murdered. He left behind a controlling military father who had no sympathies for his son's stage ambitions; slipped away from a Kansas horse farm to which his father had sent him; walked out on a New York antique business and the wife and daughter that went along with it; and survived a grueling Klondike expedition to enter a just-maturing Hollywood movie industry in which he moved up quickly from extra, to actor, to respected director.

Yet, in a synchronistic twist, Taylor's past caught up with him at the very end of his life: his ancestor Sir Thomas Dean, a major architect of his day, is mentioned in James Joyce's *Ulysses*, and the first edition of that novel was published the very day (February 2, 1922) that William Desmond Taylor's murder became the source of fresh newsprint.

Taylor's body was discovered early the next morning by his African-American servant Henry Peavey—who was expecting Taylor to testify on his behalf in court that day because Peavey had been charged with trying to pick up men for sex. That Peavey took the time to wash dishes after finding his star character witness—let alone employer—dead on his court date is a testimony to how human nature can never be completely reduced to behaviorist formulas. As a novelist, I would be criticized for having a fictional character act as Peavey did under those circumstances. But as someone has said, life doesn't make sense, so fiction has to.

So, believe me, I'm *not* making these parts up: a stranger claiming to be a doctor *did* pronounce Taylor dead of either a heart attack or stomach hemorrhage—and then vanished; Peavey took time to wash those dishes with his deceased employer's corpse just a few feet away; the authorities stood by while the crime scene was pillaged—even the distressed guy that I wrote bumping into Stagg was really there. Why was he so upset? By his own word, he and Taylor had been lovers. And Taylor *did* receive a letter from his ex-servant Sands pointing out that he knew his real name.

And that's not to mention the stranger than fiction stuff I left out of my book like the incident of someone breaking into Taylor's home, helping himself to his kitchen, and taking time to trample his bed sheets under foot...or that mysterious ring of Taylor's keys that was found, their corresponding locks unknown to this day.

Only after his death did the full details of his convoluted—and tainted—past life come to public light. Before this he was a respected, major player in Hollywood. He directed Mary Pickford as well as literary adaptations of *Tom Sawyer* (just one year after Mark Twain's death), *Huckleberry Finn*, and *Anne of Green Gables*. Pulp fans will find it interesting that he even rubbed elbows with Edgar Rice Burroughs and Zane Grey at a meeting for writer's rights in Hollywood.

For those interested in looking further into the enigmatic Taylor's life and death, I recommend *A Deed of Death* by Robert Giroux, and/or Sidney D Kirkpatrick's *A Cast of Killers* (based on the research of Hollywood Golden Age director King Vidor who had known Taylor). Famed cartoonist Rick Geary produced an entertaining non-fiction graphic adaptation of the case. But the hands down best tome on William Desmond Taylor's life and death is the thick *William Desmond Taylor: A Dossier* by Bruce Long. If you find yourself hooked on this unsolved mystery and still wanting more, by all means look up *Taylorology* on the Internet.

Once again, remember that truth is stranger than fiction, but as the great G.K. Chesterton pointed out, that's because we've made fiction to suit ourselves. That's what I did with *Ravenwood: Return of the Dugpa*. I hope it suited you as well.

# ABOUT OUR CREATORS

## *Author*

### MICAH S. HARRIS

I fell in love with Hollywood's golden age –particularly that of Ravenwood's milieu of the 1930s –while I was still a child. The classic horror movies on Saturday night's "Shock Theater" were my major initiation, along with the annual showings of *The Wizard of Oz*, into tinsel town's yesteryears.

Except they weren't quite yesteryear in the sixties and seventies. Many of the iconic actors of the era were still alive, some still active (Boris Karloff in particular was an adopted national treasure, "hosting" his own Gold Key comic book, narrating *How the Grinch Stole Christmas*, and *still* making new horror movies in his seventies!). So these old movies remained freshly relevant to my young mind twenty to thirty years after their initial release.

Besides "Shock Theater" (hosted by Dr. Paul Bearer) programs like the weekday "Dialing for Dollars" and PBS' Saturday night "Hooray for Hollywood" expanded my exposure to the cinema of the thirties, forties, and fifties to include period musicals, swashbucklers, serials, and romantic comedies.

All this was long before home video was available, and young people today probably can't fathom setting your alarm clock for two in the morning to get out of bed to see the late, late show because if you didn't, you had no idea of when you'd have the opportunity to see that movie again. And you were glad for the chance, even without the proper aspect ratio and *with* unlimited commercial interruption.

*King Kong* made the 1930s my period of choice even as a kid. However, Dave Stevens' *Rocketeer*, which appeared when I was in my twenties, inspired deeper research into the era. I grew to love the art deco styles, the eloquence of men's and women's formal wear, the music of Cole Porter and the Gershwins, the visionary architectural designs of Hugh Ferriss, and the illustrative work of artists like Leyendecker, Parrish, and Booth. The retro-futuristic massive flying machines of *Things to Come* and the first Dick Tracy serial became some of my favorite model effects work of any era. And I consider Milton Caniff's pre-World War Two *Terry and the Pirates* the greatest adventure comic strip ever.

So when Captain Ron gave me the opportunity to write a Ravenwood novel set in 1930s Hollywood, you could say I'd been preparing for it for forty years! But I dug deeper into the background research for the story at hand, so that when Ravenwood steps into a hotel or eating establishment or on a movie set, it is, as much as possible, described as it existed in period—with the occasional dramatic license.

And here is where I drop in the disclaimer that all characters in *Ravenwood: Return of the Dugpa* are either fictional or used fictitiously. I would also like to thank Angela Bacon Reid, Roman Leary, Arthur Congleton, and Michael Howell for their invaluable suggestions during the preparing of the manuscript.

I especially would like to thank Bret Blevins, former comic book artist for both Marvel and D.C. and now an Emmy award winning storyboard artist in animation, who not only agreed to paint the cover when I asked but also graciously volunteered to draw the interior illustrations as well.

And, of course, a major thanks to Ron Fortier and Airship 27 for the opportunity to write the first Ravenwood novel in the character's almost seventy year existence!

# Artist

### BRET BLEVINS

I was born in 1960, found my way to pencil and paper shortly thereafter and haven't stopped drawing since. I started a professional career early, selling drawings of monsters and hot rods to my elementary school classmates for 25 cents, which in those days bought a comic book and a candy bar. I began submitting samples to comic book publishers at the age of 13, and illustrated a book for one of my junior high school teachers at the age of 14, for which I received the astonishing sum of one hundred (1974) dollars. In high school I did political cartoons for the local legal newspaper, for $5.00 each, which I spent on books and art supplies---and an occasional root beer float. After seven years of pestering various editors, Marvel sent me a trial script at the age of 20-- soon after I lucked into pencilling an adaptation of the *Dark Crystal* film and I've been illustrating stories for print or film ever since.

After ten years at Marvel working on most of their characters at one time or another, I spent a few years at DC drawing Batman, then essentially left comic books to create animation storyboards for Warner Bros. on *Batman, Superman, Batman Beyond, Justice League, Legion of Superheroes, Batman Brave and Bold, Tarzan* and *Atlantis* for Disney, *X-men* for Film Roman, *Ben 10* and a few other shows for Cartoon Network. Along the way I've illustrated a graphic novel of Redwall for Penguin books, created all kinds of artwork for various publishing, film and advertising projects, filled dozens of sketchbooks and painted hundreds of easel pictures in watercolor, gouache, casein and oil, taught art classes, conducted a few workshops, shown and sold my work in art galleries and written many how-to articles for *Draw!* magazine. I spend most of my waking hours drawing or painting and that probably won't ever change as long as I can hold a pencil or brush. That about sums me up!

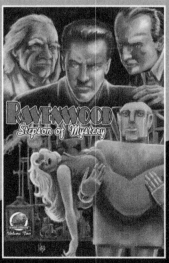

Printed in Great Britain
by Amazon

44259500R00099